W9-AWL-245

THE RED BADGE
OF COURAGE

broadview editions
series editor: L.W. Conolly

Pencil sketch of Stephen Crane by Gwen Nagel.

THE RED BADGE
OF COURAGE:
AN EPISODE OF THE
AMERICAN CIVIL WAR

Stephen Crane

edited by James Nagel

broadview editions

© 2015 James Nagel

All rights reserved. The use of any part of this publication reproduced, transmitted in any form or by any means, electronic, mechanical, photocopying, recording, or otherwise, or stored in a retrieval system, without prior written consent of the publisher—or in the case of photocopying, a licence from Access Copyright (Canadian Copyright Licensing Agency), One Yonge Street, Suite 1900, Toronto, Ontario M5E 1E5—is an infringement of the copyright law.

Library and Archives Canada Cataloguing in Publication

Crane, Stephen, 1871-1900, author
    The red badge of courage : an episode of the American Civil War
/ Stephen Crane ; edited by James Nagel.

(Broadview editions)
Includes bibliographical references
ISBN 978-1-55481-127-4 (pbk.)

    1. Chancellorsville, Battle of, Chancellorsville, Va., 1863—Fiction.
2. Virginia—History—Civil War, 1861-1865—Fiction. 3. Historical
Fiction. I. Nagel, James, editor II. Title. III. Series: Broadview editions

PS1449.C85R3 2015   813'.4   C2014-907271-6

Broadview Editions
The Broadview Editions series represents the ever-changing canon of literature in English by bringing together texts long regarded as classics with valuable lesser-known works.

Advisory editor for this volume: Michel Pharand

Broadview Press is an independent, international publishing house, incorporated in 1985.

We welcome comments and suggestions regarding any aspect of our publications—please feel free to contact us at the addresses below or at broadview@broadviewpress.com.

North America
PO Box 1243, Peterborough, Ontario K9J 7H5, Canada
555 Riverwalk Parkway, Tonawanda, NY 14150, USA
Tel: (705) 743-8990; Fax: (705) 743-8353
email: customerservice@broadviewpress.com

UK, Europe, Central Asia, Middle East, Africa, India, and Southeast Asia
Eurospan Group, 3 Henrietta St., London WC2E 8LU, United Kingdom
Tel: 44 (0) 1767 604972; Fax: 44 (0) 1767 601640
email: eurospan@turpin-distribution.com

Australia and New Zealand
Footprint Books
1/6a Prosperity Parade, Warriewood, NSW 2102, Australia
Tel: + 61 2 9997 3973; Fax: + 61 2 9997 3185
email: info@footprint.com.au

www.broadviewpress.com

Broadview Press acknowledges the financial support of the Government of Canada through the Canada Book Fund for our publishing activities.

Typesetting and assembly: True to Type Inc., Claremont, Canada.

PRINTED IN CANADA

For Alfred Bendixen

Contents

Acknowledgements

Scholarly endeavors are inherently collaborative, each new generation building upon the work done by predecessors and by current colleagues. Stephen Crane studies is such a field, with early scholars recording biographical and bibliographical information that paved the way for more specialized approaches to the journalism, poetry, and fiction of this remarkable writer who died at the astonishingly early age of twenty-eight.

It is a pleasure, therefore, to express my gratitude to my colleagues in the Stephen Crane Society who have, collectively, sustained and enriched serious engagement with this important author from the end of the nineteenth century. Among those who have provided the most direct influence on my work are Donald Pizer, Matthew J. Bruccoli, James B. Colvert, Paul Sorrentino, Stanley Werthcim, and Edwin Cady. My graduate students at the University of Georgia provided enormous stimulation and enthusiasm, and I am forever grateful to them, especially to Katherine Barrow, Bradley Bazzle, Nicole Camastra, Jon Dawson, and Steven Florczyk. My wife, Gwen, is a constant source of encouragement, support, and candid evaluation, and my life is enriched by her companionship.

My editor at Broadview, Marjorie Mather, was unfailingly helpful and courteous, and it was a pleasure to work with her. I am indebted to the University of Georgia for my appointment as the first Eidson Distinguished Professor of American Literature and to Dartmouth College for my position as a visiting scholar, which facilitated my research in Baker Library. My colleagues in the American Literature Association have provided a collegial atmosphere, intellectual stimulation, and enduring fellowship. In recognition of his outstanding leadership of that organization for the last twenty-five years, I dedicate this volume to Alfred Bendixen.

Introduction

The most momentous event in the history of the United States was the Civil War, fought between 1861 and 1865, and the most important novel covering that devastating conflict has been widely regarded to be Stephen Crane's *The Red Badge of Courage*. It has been celebrated internationally for its vivid portrait of both the physical action of battle and for the psychological realism of the protagonist's internal struggle to control his fear, regulate his fantasies, and live up to the heroism he had earlier imagined. Somewhat in the background of the book itself are astonishing biographical details: the author was only twenty-three when his famous novel appeared, and he had never seen military action in any form. Despite the precise descriptions of the scenes of battle in his fiction, he was not born until six years after the war had ended, a fact that stunned the European reviewers who had proudly proclaimed that only someone who had actually lived through these events could possibly have presented them so vividly.

The Red Badge of Courage and the War Novel

As a war novel, *The Red Badge* was startlingly anomalous. It features as a protagonist a young private who does not understand the battle, knows nothing of its strategy, and who grapples with confusion and misunderstandings throughout the events. The action begins in the middle of a battle and ends before that conflict is over, leaving uncertain which side was the victor. The precise battle itself is never mentioned, although in a later short story, "The Veteran" (1896; see Appendix E), an older Henry Fleming explains to his grandson that it was the Battle of Chancellorsville, his first engagement and the one in which he was so frightened that he ran away from the fighting. The initial title that Crane had given his novel, "Private Fleming: His Various Battles," seems an apt indication of the multiple psychological struggles that young Fleming engages in the three days covered in the action, since the physical confrontations are the least of his problems. His most important fight is with himself, and the resolution of that internal conflict is the climax of the plot. Even though he is not an heroic figure but a run of the mill private struggling to perform adequately, the implication is that his thoughts and feelings are important, a point that was not lost on what had until recently been a nation of yeoman farmers and village dwellers. Henry is ordinary, and that is the best thing about him.

No one had ever read a novel quite like *The Red Badge of Courage*. The great European writers had covered military engagements in brilliant fashion, and the most celebrated account of military conflict was Leo Tolstoy's *War and Peace* (1869), although even his earlier *Sevastopol Sketches* (1855) dealt with epic events and aristocratic characters.[1] As was typically expected in war fiction, *Sevastopol* was based on Tolstoy's personal experiences in the Crimea. Often regarded as the greatest such novel in any language, *War and Peace* is an epic set on a gigantic stage. It involves nearly 600 characters, many of them drawn from important historical figures, and it takes place in impressive locations, including the headquarters of Napoleon and the formal court of Alexander I of Russia. The battle scenes are set in genuine locations as well, including the celebrated engagements at Austerlitz and Borodino. The principal characters are drawn from five aristocratic families, and the gentlemen, as would be expected, serve among the highest officers of the army, while the women back home entertain royalty in their salons. The romantic intrigues of the major characters are intertwined with their heroics on the battlefront, and infidelity, bravery, nobility, and events of enormous consequence are at the forefront. The sweep of the plot covers the French invasion of Russia in 1812 during the Napoleonic Wars, and in the background is the reign of Catherine the Great, Alexander I, and Napoleon. Nothing could be quite so grand.

Crane's portrait of an American war is of a totally different sort. The protagonist is an ordinary young man who dropped out of high school to enlist in the Union army. He has no outstanding military skills and carries the lowest rank in his regiment, that of private.[2] In an epic, the future of an entire civilization hangs on the survival of the protagonist and the victory of his cause. In *The Red Badge*, it does not matter much to the war effort whether Henry Fleming lives or dies. The traditional hero exhibits transcendent courage, and his bravery is an inspiration to the men under his command. Henry runs in his first battle; his only wound, his ironic badge of courage, is caused by being hit in the head by one of his own men; his ultimate victory over his fear is

---

1 For an excellent discussion of European influences on Crane's fiction, see Lars Ahnebrink, *The Beginnings of Naturalism in American Fiction, 1891-1902* (Uppsala: American Institute of the University of Uppsala, 1950).

2 For a discussion of possible sources for the novel, see Stanley Wertheim, "*The Red Badge of Courage* and Personal Narratives of the Civil War," *American Literary Realism* 6 (1973): 61-65.

not in being a grand hero but in simply becoming one with his fellows, in doing his basic duty. The battle he is engaged in is not crucial to the outcome of the war as a whole, and, in historical fact, his side, the union army, lost the confrontation at Chancellorsville.[1] Indeed, the defeat was somewhat ignominious in that General Joseph Hooker's Army of the Potomac was twice the size of General Robert E. Lee's Confederate Army of Northern Virginia. In a stunning maneuver, Lee divided his men and attacked a larger force from two directions, ultimately driving the North back across the Rapidan River in early May of 1863, giving the North yet another thrashing in a string of such encounters. The most significant loss for the Southern side was the death of Stonewall Jackson, who was shot by his own men as he rode through heavy cover on his way back to his headquarters.

The novel does not cover these concluding events. In fact, it ends before the battle is decided, at a moment when the North has seized the initiative. It is significant in literary history, however, that virtually all of the standards of the traditional, heroic novel have been contravened, and what emerges is a new look at war, one based on a common soldier facing normative anxiety about how he will behave in dangerous circumstances. The genius of the novel is that Crane took the thoughts and emotions of an ordinary young private and made them into one of the great novels in American literature.[2]

Stephen Crane's Life

It would seem almost impossible that Crane should have been able to write such a book when he did. He was only twenty-three when his most famous novel was published, and he was so broke that he had to borrow money from Hamlin Garland to pay the typist for the manuscript.[3] Born in 1871 in Newark, New Jersey, Crane was the youngest of fourteen children in a religious house-

---

1   For a discussion of the Battle of Chancellorsville, see Harold R. Hungerford, "'That Was Chancellorsville': The Factual Framework of *The Red Badge of Courage*," *American Literature* 34 (1963): 520-31.

2   For a contrasting reading of Crane's work, see John Fagg, *On the Cusp: Stephen Crane, George Bellows, and Modernism* (Tuscaloosa: U of Alabama P, 2009).

3   For an extensive discussion of the background of the novel, see J.C. Levenson, "Introduction" to *The Red Badge of Courage*, vol. 2 of *The Works of Stephen Crane*, ed. Fredson Bowers (Charlottesville: UP of Virginia, 1975), xiii-xcii.

hold in which the reading of scripture was mandatory and novels were suspect. His father, the Reverend Jonathan Townley Crane, was a Methodist minister, and his mother, Mary Helen Peck Crane, the daughter of one, and the language and imagery of Christianity were everywhere in the household. Crane seems to have rejected almost all of the beliefs his parents endorsed. In fact, he grew up to scoff at religious traditions, to smoke, drink, use opium, and cavort with women of ill repute. He was not a particularly good student in school, and he twice was invited to leave college, first by Lafayette College in Pennsylvania, where he studied mining engineering, and then by Syracuse University, where he played baseball and joined the Delta Upsilon fraternity. He did not return for his sophomore year. There is little in his early life, in other words, to suggest genius or even special ability except for his proclivity for writing. Authorship was a skill he inherited from both sides of the family, one exhibited in both of his parents and in a brother who was a successful journalist.

Crane's father, who wrote for religious magazines and published several books on spiritual matters, died when Stephen was only eight, and his mother had to support the family. The older children were out on their own by this time, but the younger ones were under her care. She moved the family to Asbury Park, New Jersey, a Methodist stronghold, and she wrote for religious magazines and for newspapers, including *The New York Tribune*, where her son Townley was on the staff. Stephen seems to have taken naturally to the pen, writing his first short story, "Uncle Jake and the Bell-Handle," when he was only fourteen. During his brief interlude at Syracuse University, he published a heavily ironic story, "The King's Favor," in the *Syracuse University Herald*. When he left school after his freshman year, he began writing sophisticated journalism for New York newspapers, covering literary speeches, sports, and social events, and he remained basically a journalist his entire life.[1] He was only twenty-one when he wrote *Maggie: A Girl of the Streets*, often considered the first important Naturalistic novel in American literature. This book, with its frank depiction of poverty in the Bowery, displays violence, ignorance, cruelty, and self-deception in an urban Irish family. Its central focus is on an innocent young girl who is seduced, abandoned, and ultimately driven to prostitution to support herself, an outcome rather too strong for the New York publishers, to say

1 For an excellent discussion of Crane as a journalist, see Michael Robertson, *Stephen Crane, Journalism, and the Making of Modern American Literature* (New York: Columbia UP, 1997).

nothing of her suicide at the end of the novel. So Crane paid to have it printed under the pseudonym Johnston Smith. It did not sell well, but it did impress both Hamlin Garland and William Dean Howells, the most important literary figure of the late nineteenth century, and their encouragement inspired Crane to move on to other projects. This was the humble context in which Crane began his most important work. Still impoverished, living in the old Art Students League with a number of struggling painters, he wrote the first draft of *The Red Badge of Courage*, a novel that changed his life and the course of American literature.

The remaining five years of Crane's life were filled with adventure and life outside of the United States. Returning to his roots in journalism, he covered wars in both Cuba and Greece, and his articles were carried in major newspapers. In Florida, on his way to cover American shipments of supplies to the revolutionaries in Cuba, he met Cora Taylor, the daughter of a Boston artist, who owned a famous house of assignation in Jacksonville, and they lived together as husband and wife until Crane's death in 1900. They could not marry because Cora was unable to get a divorce from her second husband, a British military man serving in India. They both wrote war dispatches on the battles between Turkey and Greece, she publishing under the name "Imogene Carter," which established her as the first American female war correspondent. When that brief conflict ended, they moved to England together and lived there until Crane contracted tuberculosis, a condition that rapidly progressed. Since his British treatments were ineffective, Cora took him to Germany in 1900 to find respite in the warm springs at Badenweiler, and he died on June 5. Cora had his body shipped back to the United States, and he is buried in Hillside, New Jersey.

The Manuscript Revisions

What is known about this period in the development of the novel is that in April of 1894, Crane took the manuscript of *The Red Badge of Courage* to Hamlin Garland, who read it and made suggestions for revision. Crane seems to have held a deep respect for the writer of *Main-Travelled Roads* (1891), who had become an important figure in New York. The two men met in the summer of 1891 when Garland had lectured on Howells and Realism at Avon-by-the-Sea, a resort.[1] Both baseball players, he and Crane

---

1 See Stephen Crane, "Howell's Discussed at Avon-by-the-Sea," *New York Tribune* (18 August 1891): 5.

played catch together and talked about American literature. They saw one another again in 1892 and many times beginning in March of 1893, when Crane moved into the city.[1] Garland read the draft and made a number of important suggestions, nearly all of which were followed before the novel was published. For example, in the text that Garland read, the characters were known from the beginning by their full names, granting the narrator full knowledge of them. Garland suggested removing the names and calling them by their most outstanding character trait, something that could be observed by someone on the scene, thus humanizing the point of view. In response, Crane removed the names of the characters from the opening and substituted the epithets by which they are now known. Henry Fleming became "the youth," Jim Conklin the "tall soldier," and Wilson the "loud soldier." Since initially both Fleming and Wilson were described as young or youthful, he changed the adjectives for Wilson to emphasize his loudness. Only Henry remained noticeably young.

Crane also followed Garland's suggestions in recasting the use of regional language. In the manuscript, all of the characters spoke in heavy dialect, a device consistent with the Local Color movement still in vogue in America. Garland, who had used the vernacular himself in his most famous book, objected, saying that his friend had overdone it. Crane then changed the manuscript so that Henry now, for the most part, speaks standard English, but he left a good bit of dialect in the speech of Wilson and Conklin.[2] As a result, Fleming became a normative identity, a more universal figure with whom it was easy to identify, while his two closest friends remain regional characters from upstate New York.

Perhaps the most significant alteration Crane made to his manuscript, however, was the deletion of what had been the original Chapter 12, a section entirely devoid of action but one in which Henry reflects on his separation from his regiment, the difficulties of rejoining it, and the death of Jim Conklin. The record of correspondence between Crane and his publisher, Appleton &

---

1 For information about the friendship between Garland and Crane during this period, see Hamlin Garland, "Stephen Crane as I Knew Him," *Yale Review* 3 (1914): 505.

2 For a detailed discussion of the composition and revision of the manuscript, see Fredson Bowers, "The Text: History and Analysis," *The Red Badge of Courage: An Episode of the American Civil War*, vol. 2 of *The University of Virginia Edition of The Works of Stephen Crane* (Charlottesville: UP of Virginia, 1975), 183-252.

Company, is incomplete on this point, but the author seems to have either made the change himself or agreed to having his editor delete the original chapter himself.

In a spirited essay entitled "*The Red Badge of Courage* Nobody Knows," Henry Binder advanced a suggestion by Hershel Parker[1] that the deleted Chapter 12, along with several other cuts from the manuscript, be restored in order to produce a text closer to Crane's original intentions. The effect of doing so, Binder maintained, was to make the novel consistently ironic, a text in which Henry Fleming does not mature or grow.[2] Binder conceded that there was no evidence that an editor had made the deletion and that the alterations were made by Crane himself, but he insisted that the Appleton editor Ripley Hitchcock forced the author to do so. Nearly everything deleted consisted of interior monologues in which Henry attempts to blame various cosmic forces for his desertion.

Binder's argument falters on several basic points. For one thing, there is no documentary evidence that Hitchcock insisted on the deletions, nor is it likely that Crane would have made them if it so altered his basic plan for the novel. Nor does Binder have a firm foundation for his argument by basing it on his sense of Crane's "intentions," psychological motivations that are not available to Binder and about which he can only guess. Furthermore, the patterns of imagery that move from persistent suggestions that Henry is a mere "babe" and a "youth" in the first half of the novel to the concluding images of him as a "man" whose soul has changed support the interpretation that Henry has grown, has matured enough to at least take responsibility for his own behavior. Were he, at the end, still attempting to rationalize his running away, to expiate his sense of guilt by blaming mysterious powers for his desertion, he would hardly qualify as a "man." Those readers who have rejected the idea that Henry grows would seem to be insensitive to the thematic implications of imagery. Whether Hitchcock suggested such things or not, Crane might easily have realized that Henry's progressive maturation, particularly after his epiphany in Chapter 18, required that he now take the blame upon himself, as he does in the final chapter.

---

1 Hershel Parker's comments were originally presented in a speech at the Modern Literature Association meeting in 1977. The best record of his position is in *Flawed Texts and Verbal Icons: Literary Authority in American Fiction* (Evanston: Northwestern UP, 1984), 147-97.

2 Henry Binder, "*The Red Badge of Courage* Nobody Knows," *Studies in the Novel* 10 (1978): 9-47.

There could also have been another motivation for the deletion. Crane often imbedded a firm structural design in his fiction. His earlier novel, *Maggie*, for example, divides in half, the first part establishing the motivation for her decision to lose her virginity to Pete, the second group of chapters delineating the consequences of her doing so. She ultimately commits suicide. Similarly, in a long story, "The Monster," Crane broke the action exactly in half, the first part leading up to a fire in which Henry Johnson's face is burned when he rescues a young boy from the blaze, the second section showing the consequences of Henry's disfigured scars, as his face is made horrible and he, and the Trescott family who care for him, become outcasts of the community. *The Red Badge of Courage* is similarly a precisely-structured work of fiction, with four sections of six chapters each, a symmetrical design the original manuscript lacked.[1] In any event, the novel was published in New York in 1895 with the original Chapter 12 deleted. When it appeared in the English edition a year later, Crane made no attempt to have any of the deleted material restored.

An Analysis of *The Red Badge of Courage*

It is not only in subject that *The Red Badge* succeeds as a novel. What is most impressive about it, in fact, is the relationship between its art and its surprising subject, a common soldier caught in the midst of an incomplete battle. It has both thematic coherence and aesthetic congruence. The basic idea at the center of the depiction of Henry's three days in war is supported by the way in which it is told, the imagery expressing the quality of his mind,[2] the organization of the whole into four balanced sections

---

1 For a more extensive investigation of this controversy, see Hershel Parker, "The New Scholarship," *Studies in American Fiction* 9 (1981): 181-97. Parker advocates the restoration of the deleted material. However, Donald Pizer strenuously objects in "*The Red Badge of Courage*: Text, Theme, and Form," *South Atlantic Quarterly* 84 (1985): 302-13. Also of interest is James Colvert's "Crane, Hitchcock, and the Binder Edition of *The Red Badge of Courage*," in *Critical Essays on Stephen Crane's* The Red Badge of Courage, ed. Donald Pizer (Boston: G.K. Hall, 1990), 238-63. Colvert also advocates reading the Appleton text as it was originally published.

2 For an excellent early discussion of the imagistic pattern of the novel, see James Trammel Cox, "The Imagery of *The Red Badge of Courage*," *Modern Fiction Studies* 5 (1959): 209-19.

each six chapters long, and the psychological realism that holds everything together. In essence, Crane's novel fit the austere standard Edgar Allan Poe set for the unity of the short story earlier in "The Philosophy of Composition" in 1846, in which he argued that every word in a poem should be carefully chosen to contribute to a unified effect. Such short stories as "The Cask of Amontillado" demonstrated how this rigorous standard could be applied to fiction, although Poe's stories set a mark achieved by very few works.

Much of the success of the novel as a work of art derives from its narrative method, the manner of the telling of it. The central strategy is restriction. As Orm Øverland has observed, except for the very opening and the conclusion, where the point of view draws back to a larger vantage point, the action is continually described as Henry could see it.[1] No larger perspective is available, nor is any greater understanding of the battle or its strategy. The immediacy is a product of the recording of the sensory data received by Henry's mind, information that is there mingled at times with fantasy, memory, and projection. The narration is thus much more about the concept of perception and understanding than it is about the Civil War itself.[2]

Although perception can involve many of the senses, sounds and feelings as well as visual information, the emphasis throughout is on what Henry can see. Often his sight is restricted, sometimes by darkness, by the smoke from guns and artillery pieces, by distance, the branches of trees, and the hills that hide the opposing forces. In the early part of the novel, he has trouble seeing and comprehending much of anything. In the climax, in Chapter 18, when he experiences an epiphany that brings new insight to him, the narrator says that "new eyes were given to him," and with them he can perceive that he is insignificant. The stress on vision is thus metaphorical, taking on elements of understanding as well as perceiving. In this sense, the novel is a form of *Bildungsroman* in which Henry Fleming grows from a child who lives in a world of dreams and heroic fantasy to a more mature young man who can see things realistically. After that

---

1 See Orm Øverland, "The Impressionism of Stephen Crane: A Study in Style and Technique," *Americana Norvegica: Norwegian Contributions to American Studies*, I, ed. Sigmund Skard and Henry H. Waser (Philadelphia: U of Pennsylvania P, 1966), 241-54.

2 For a discussion of the point of view and Impressionism, see James Nagel, "Stephen Crane and the Narrative Methods of Impressionism," *Studies in the Novel* 10 (1978): 76-85.

point, he does not see any more dragons or monsters threatening to devour him but only Southern soldiers who are very much like himself.[1]

This internal growth is conveyed not by direct assertion by the narrator but by the patterns of imagery that reveal how Henry perceives the world at any given moment. In the first six chapters, which conclude when he runs from battle, he is described in terms of his youth; indeed, he is portrayed as a "babe." These images convey not only his chronological youth but his inexperience in war, his innocence and lack of knowledge of the world. He is late of the seminary, the guiding arm of his mother, the counsel of the church. When he thinks of the enemy it is in terms of pagan gods, monsters that devour children, the supernatural iconography of the Old Testament. Alone in his tent, he has visions of a "thousand-tongued fear," and when he gazes through the smoke of the battlefield the next day, he thinks he sees "redoubtable dragons" and "red and green monsters." In the face of such enemies, he is afraid before he actually sees an enemy soldier, for he could not be expected to compete with such gigantic opponents.

What is often missed in discussions of the novel is how artfully the parts of it fit together. The central psychological mood of the first six chapters, from the opening to his desertion under fire, is one of fear, his struggle to control his terror of being killed in the conflict. To deal with this overpowering emotion, he secludes himself in his tent and thinks about the upcoming engagement. He has no experience in warfare, but he seems to have read about it in school, since he is afraid of a "Greek-like struggle" in which armies move in a "Homeric" fashion. In short, he has read *The Iliad,* and all he knows about war comes from that experience. Civil War soldiers did not carry shields, but Homer's Greeks did in their siege of Troy, so Henry is disappointed in his parting from his mother because she had said "nothing whatever about returning with his shield or on it."

Henry's conflicts do not have epic stature of those faced by Homer's major characters; in fact, his most important initial struggle is within himself, in his attempt to "mathematically prove to himself that he would not run from a battle." That is the "question" that dominates the opening chapter, and to answer it

---

1   For a contrasting interpretation, one that regards the novel as Naturalistic, see Donald Pizer, "Late Nineteenth-Century American Naturalism," *Bucknell Review* 13 (1965): 1-18.

he must gain self-knowledge, "information of himself." As the time of actual engagement draws near, his problem becomes more acute, his fear more exaggerated. As he looks across the river in the morning, the campfires of the enemy seem to him to be "the orbs of a row of dragons" and the moving army "huge crawling reptiles," images that express his continuing fear rather than the reality before him. The descriptions of Henry himself suggest an infant "just born of the earth." He thinks of the war as a "blood-swollen god," recalling perhaps the Ammonite deity Moloch, who devoured children. The worship of him by the Canaanites and the Phoenicians involved child sacrifice, a practice condemned in Christian tradition in *Deuteronomy* and the *Book of Leviticus*. Henry's religious training apparently led him to the study of the *Old Testament*.

The dominant theme of the first six chapters is fear, and it is supported by images that project Henry's distortions of sensory experiences to cause them to suggest monsters and blood-swollen gods. In the second six chapters, 7-12, the predominant themes are those of guilt and humiliation, and Henry's quest is to justify his fleeing in the face of the enemy. The imagistic patterns suggest hatred of himself and a desire for death, the only means of escape from the self-contempt that overwhelms him. He quickly learns that his earlier assumptions had been inaccurate, that his regiment had held the line, that his running was unnecessary. He feels he has been wronged, that he had done the "sagacious" thing in fleeing, that he had acted on the basis of superior knowledge. These rationalizations do not sustain him, however, and he soon feels waves of shame: "His mind heard howls of derision." To prove to himself that he was justified in running, he throws a pine cone at a squirrel, which scampers up a tree, and he tries to convince himself that his instinct for preservation had been part of Nature.

Wandering pointlessly behind the lines, he comes on a procession of wounded men, and he falls in with them until a tattered man asks him where he was wounded, and Henry flees in shame. When he later rejoins the wounded, he discovers his old friend from home, Jim Conklin, who has been transformed by his severe injury. He swears to take good care of him, but as they limp along the former tall soldier suddenly stiffens and falls dead. Henry Fleming shakes his fist at the sky and says "Hell," and the narrator injects an image to end the chapter: "The red sun was pasted in the sky like a wafer." That line is perhaps the most famous simile in American literature.

That image has elicited a great deal of controversy, most of it inspired by the contention of Robert W. Stallman that the wafer is a symbol that is part of a Christian allegory of redemption for Henry Fleming. He argues that Jim Conklin "is intended to represent Jesus Christ" and that "Crane intended to suggest here the sacrificial death celebrated in communion." Hence the wafer becomes the body of Christ that brings about Henry's spiritual redemption. Jim Conklin, J.C., is the savior, and his sacrifice saves Henry Fleming, who then sheds his fear and shame and goes on to serve well in the front lines of battle.[1] For a decade after World War II, scholars were obsessed with Christ imagery, and virtually every important work of literature was interpreted as a Christian allegory. Stallman gave the effort a muscular effort in this analysis of *The Red Badge*, but it is one that is not finally convincing.

For one thing, there are many kinds of literal wafers associated with Henry's situation: the wafers that held back the powder and the ball in the cannons, the red wax wafers used to seal envelopes in this era before glue became common, and the sun as a wafer just above the horizon that Monet painted in *Impression, Sunrise* and Rudyard Kipling described in his novel *The Light That Failed* (1891). Furthermore, there is little indication that Henry is redeemed in any sense by Conklin's death: he continues to feel ashamed of his running and humiliation among the men who have actually been wounded. The red wafer would seem to express his feelings, his sense of rage that his friend is dead, his resentment that fate has been so cruel.[2]

As further evidence that Henry has not been redeemed by Conklin's death, in the very next chapter Fleming reaches the low-point of his psychological decline. As he looks at another tattered soldier wandering behind the lines, his shame overwhelms him: "He now thought that he wished he was dead." Rather than fantasizing about heroism, "he thought of the magnificent pathos of his dead body." He is filled with self-hatred. Even worse, he begins to wish for the defeat of his own regiment, as if their

---

1   Robert W. Stallman, "Introduction" to *The Red Badge of Courage* by Stephen Crane (New York: Modern Library, 1951), v-xxxiii.

2   For more detailed commentary on the wafer image, see Jean G. Marlowe, "Crane's Wafer Image: Reference to an Artillery Primer?" *American Literature* 43 (1972): 645-47; Scott C. Osborn, "Stephen Crane's Imagery: 'Pasted Like a Wafer,'" *American Literature* 23 (1951): 362; and Edward Stone, "The Many Suns of *The Red Badge of Courage*," *American Literature* 29 (1957): 325.

deaths and wounding would justify his desertion. He would return to his regiment if only he could, but he has no rifle, no wound, and no excuse for the time he has been away. Then, in the confusion of another rush to move troops to the front lines, he grabs another Union soldier by the arm, and the man swings his rifle, inflicting a gash on Henry's head. Another man guides him back to the front lines, where his head wound quickly explains his separation from the unit, and he rejoins his regiment without further explanation. Thus, he became separated in Chapter 6 and reunited in Chapter 12, the very center of the novel. The second half will prove to be equally symmetrical.

If the first six chapters were dominated by fear, and the second six by guilt and shame, the third section deals with Henry's quest to understand himself and his place in the world. Initially he is concerned about being questioned about his absence from his regiment for four hours, but his wound explains things sufficiently. He lies by saying he was shot in the head, and that explanation is accepted. Wilson takes care of him, offering him his blankets, and Henry is able to sleep. In fact, Wilson, the loud soldier from the first six chapters, is loud no longer but exhibits a "fine reliance" with "inward confidence" born of new realizations. Henry can see that his friend "had now climbed a peak of wisdom from which he could perceive himself as a very wee thing," and his newborn humility has softened him, made him a better person.

Wilson has had an epiphany, a sudden transformative insight, and he has changed as a human being. In this respect, he functions as a *Doppelgänger*, a psychological double for Henry, who will later undergo a similar experience. In Chapter 17, the Southern forces attack, but Henry holds his position, performs well, and earns the praise of his lieutenant. The climax of the novel comes in the next chapter, however, for it is there that Henry has his own epiphany, one that mirrors what has happened to Wilson. As the two young men are sent to get water for the men, they overhear some officers discussing the impending engagement, and his regiment is described as a lot of "mule-drivers," men worthless in the fighting. Furthermore, it is clear that they will be assigned to a dangerous position and that not many of them will survive. At that instant, Henry feels he has grown, that "new eyes were given to him. And the most startling thing was to learn suddenly that he was very insignificant." That humble realization brings about a new maturity for Henry, one described in images of vision. He must confront the fact that his mother had been right when she said he was not "special" but simply one fellow among a whole bunch of others. The thought is humiliating, but it is also realistic, liberating, and transformative, and it allows him to become a man.

That subject is what dominates the final six chapters, the dramatic growth in his maturity expressed in images of vision stressing that Henry now sees with "new eyes."[1] The narrator describes the new awareness: "It seemed to the youth that he saw everything. Each blade of the green grass was bold and clear." If his actual visual acuity has been improved, his metaphoric view of himself has also changed, and he accepts himself as part of his regiment. He carries the flag into the next battle, and when the South attacks, his regiment holds the line and forces them to retreat. Far from being described as a "babe" in the early chapters of the novel, Henry has now become a man, as have the rest of the regiment: "They gazed about them with looks of uplifted pride, feeling new trust in the grim, always-confident weapons in their hands. And they were men."

Those are the thematic values of the conclusion of the novel, Henry's growth to see himself as one with the other fellows, and his realization that he is no more significant than they. This humble idea allows him to accept normal risks and to do his duty. He carries the flag well, at the front of the line, and he and Wilson are praised for bravery. In the next engagement, Wilson captures the Confederate flag from a Southern flag-bearer, and Henry and Wilson congratulate each other.

The final chapter serves as a recapitulation of the entire novel. Henry has grown, has come to terms with himself and his place in the regiment, and he performs well. As he looks back over the last three days, he feels guilt at his desertion, but he knows that he has faced death without fear and that he has become a man. As the narrator asserts, "at last he was enabled to more closely comprehend himself and circumstance." He even seems to understand how he acted in the past: "His eyes seemed to open to some new ways. He found that he could look back upon the brass and bombast of his earlier gospels and see them truly." Indeed, "his soul changed," and he feels self-assurance and a sense of peace. The final image, which Crane added to the conclusion of the manuscript, expresses this optimistic psychological

---

1 For an extended discussion of the imagery of vision and its relation to the Impressionist movement, see James Nagel, *Stephen Crane and Literary Impressionism* (University Park: Pennsylvania State UP, 1980).

growth: "Over the river a golden ray of sun came through the hosts of leaden rain clouds."[1]

Critical Approaches to the Novel: A Brief Commentary

Part of the appeal of *The Red Badge of Courage* is simply its subject, the experience of a common soldier in the most momentous and destructive event ever to occur on American soil, the Civil War. That Henry Fleming grows over a few days seems plausible in the heightened drama of activity of military conflict, in which psychological transformations might very well be accelerated. The only three characters who are given any depth at all are Henry, who is seen largely in terms of internal thoughts and feelings, as well as Jim Conklin and Wilson, who are described from the outside. The surrounding soldiers of the regiment, the officers on horses shouting commands to the men, and the wounded men behind the lines are all drawn realistically, in some detail, and in accord with the reports and photographs that appeared in popular magazines.

The European reviewers who assumed that Crane had actually lived through events similar to those depicted in *The Red Badge* were not as foolish as it might seem. No one had previously rendered fiction with such sharp sensory details who had not been a witness to the scene, nor had anyone traced the psychological fluctuations of a youth in battle in a manner that seemed so believable to a post-war audience. When the truth about the age of the author became widely known, he seemed a genius of invention who could draw his readers into a scene so that they could see and hear the action. This was precisely the Impressionistic aesthetic that Joseph Conrad was advocating in his essays and speeches,[2] and his new American friend Stephen Crane was his premier practitioner.

This fact has not been lost on students of literary history, although Crane's most famous novel has elicited a wide spectrum of approaches. He talked a good deal about his work as being essentially Impressionistic, and wrote about it on several occasions, and his contemporaries also spoke of him in that way. In

---

1   For the best collection of diverse readings of the novel, see Donald Pizer, ed., *Critical Essays on Stephen Crane's* The Red Badge of Courage (Boston: G.K. Hall, 1990). Pizer's introduction alone is a valuable overview of the critical controversies that began after World War II.

2   The best articulation of Joseph Conrad's Impressionistic aesthetic is in his "Introduction" to *The Nigger of the "Narcissus"* (1897).

modern criticism, a host of scholars have continued to approach *The Red Badge* in those terms, including Orm Øverland, who early on gave a detailed look at the artistic aspects of Impressionism in Crane's work.[1] The Italian scholar Sergio Perosa broadened the discussion by comparing Impressionistic aesthetics to those of Naturalism in Crane's fiction, especially with regard to *The Red Badge*.[2] Rodney O. Rogers added to the investigation of Impressionism in Crane's work by considering it in association with conceptions of reality, finding what is real to be ephemeral and evanescent.[3] James Nagel gave Impressionism the most substantial consideration in his book *Stephen Crane and Literary Impressionism*, discussing not only *The Red Badge* in these terms but the entire body of Crane's fiction.[4]

Among the other major approaches to the novel that have been given serious consideration, R.W. Stallman's interpretation of the wafer image as a reference to Christian communion and the novel as a study of spiritual redemption had a significant influence for many years. In "*The Red Badge of Courage* as Myth and Symbol," John E. Hart argued that Henry is reborn at the center of the novel, consistent with Stallman's basic thesis.[5] Daniel Hoffman, in what is primarily a study of Crane's poetry, also discussed *The Red Badge* as a redemption novel.[6] But many scholars came to reject this religious approach in favor of interpretive strategies derived from scientific and philosophical developments in the nineteenth century.

For example, Charles C. Walcutt's contention that *The Red Badge* is essentially Naturalistic held sway for decades beginning in the 1950s. From his point of view, the violence of war and the savage bravery it demands were an apt expression of the aggression inherent in the human psyche reaching back to animal

---

1 Orm Øverland, "The Impressionism of Stephen Crane: A Study in Style and Technique," *Americana Norvegica* 1 (1966): 239-85.

2 Sergio Perosa, "Naturalism and Impressionism in Stephen Crane's Fiction," in *Stephen Crane: A Collection of Critical Essays*, ed. Maurice Bassan (Englewood Cliffs: Prentice Hall, 1967), 80-94.

3 Rodney O. Rogers, "Stephen Crane and Impressionism," *Nineteenth-Century Fiction* 24 (1969): 292-304.

4 James Nagel, *Stephen Crane and Literary Impressionism* (University Park: Pennsylvania State UP, 1980).

5 John E. Hart, "*The Red Badge of Courage* as Myth and Symbol," *University of Kansas City Review*, 19 (1953): 249-56.

6 Daniel Hoffman, *The Poetry of Stephen Crane* (New York: Columbia UP, 1957).

ancestors.[1] From this perspective, the war was the result of Deterministic forces at play in society and took place independent of the moral agency of any of the individuals involved.[2] In Naturalism, personal decisions, the exercise of will, have no effect on the outcome of events, nor do individuals carry any moral responsibility for their actions. They are driven by forces beyond their control, powers hostile to the well-being of the human population, and life is inevitably tragic. Donald Gibson essentially endorsed this view of the novel in his *The Fiction of Stephen Crane* in 1968, although his emphasis is on Darwinism and pessimistic Determinism, dominant concerns at the end of the nineteenth century.[3] A multitude of scholars have contributed articles and book chapters advancing this view of Crane's work, the most convincing of which have dealt not with *The Red Badge* but with *Maggie: A Girl of the Streets, George's Mother*, and the tales of the Bowery.

Yet another stance in a reading of the novel stresses the mythic background of tales of war and the use of symbols to convey important elements of the central ideas. John E. Hart has argued, for example, that Henry's story follows the traditional pattern for a mythic hero of separation, initiation, and return. In the course of these events, he is filled with wonder at the supernatural as he encounters the overwhelming power of war, and by confronting them he becomes an archetypal "hero," able to commune with his fellows and lead them to greater glory.[4] Chester A. Wolford did a spirited study of Crane's use of myth and the epic tradition, finding these the keys to his best works.[5] Harry B. Henderson also reached to the past for his explanation of the novel, not to its mythic heritage but for its portrayal of history. He points out that any direct indication of the ultimate meaning of the Civil War is entirely absent in Crane's novel, but the idea that it is a signifi-

---

1 William B. Dillingham argues that Henry himself reverts to being an animal. See "Insensibility in *The Red Badge of Courage*," *College English* 25 (1963): 194-98.

2 For one Naturalistic interpretation of the novel, please see Charles C. Walcutt, *American Literary Naturalism: A Divided Stream* (Minneapolis: U of Minnesota P, 1956), 66-82.

3 Donald Gibson, *The Fiction of Stephen Crane* (Carbondale: Southern Illinois UP, 1968).

4 For one such reading, see John E. Hart, "*The Red Badge of Courage* as Myth and Symbol," *University of Kansas City Review* 19 (1953): 249-56.

5 Chester A. Wolford, *The Anger of Stephen Crane: Fiction and the Epic Tradition* (Lincoln: U of Nebraska P, 1983).

cant event is implicit throughout. Henry has only the most tawdry conception of time, and that keeps *The Red Badge* from being regarded as a great historical novel, although it is representative of those works that place a protagonist in the midst of a violent action he is powerless to control.[1]

The Red Badge of Courage is sufficiently complex to provide a rich construct of details that can be interpreted in a wide spectrum of approaches, each with some textual data that can be used for support. What remains evident after a century of reactions to the novel is that the substance of it continues to intrigue readers for a wide variety of reasons. Some simply regard it as an entertaining account of action in the Civil War, while others largely ignore the military details and concentrate on Henry Fleming's psychological state and his growth toward maturity. Many scholars have studied the aesthetic of the novel, its style, imagery, structure, and unifying theme, and from this perspective *The Red Badge* is among the foremost works of American fiction. Other scholars, looking at it from the perspective of the sweep of literary history, have placed it among the great European novels that preceded it for its realistic presentation of the sensory details of warfare. What remains clear, in the final analysis, is that interest in Crane's novel was not only sustained but grew steadily throughout the twentieth century, and that energy has accelerated in the early years of the twenty-first. Whatever the approach, whatever the context in which it is placed, *The Red Badge of Courage* has secured a permanent place among the most important novels in the history of American literature.

---

1 Harry B. Henderson, "*The Red Badge of Courage:* The Search for Historical Identity," in *Versions of the Past: The Historical Imagination in American Fiction* (New York: Oxford UP, 1974), 219-31.

Stephen Crane: A Brief Chronology

1871   Stephen Crane is born on 1 November in Newark, New Jersey, the fourteenth child of the Reverend Jonathan Townley Crane, a Methodist minister, and Mary Helen Peck Crane, the daughter of a clergyman. Rev. Crane is an active lecturer on moral and temperance issues and the author of several books on religious concerns. Crane's mother is also active socially and becomes president of the Woman's Christian Temperance Union.

1878   The family moves to Port Jervis, New York, where the Rev. Crane becomes the pastor of Drew Church. Stephen begins attending public school.

1880   Rev. Crane dies of a heart ailment. Crane's mother writes for Methodist magazines and other publications, including *The New York Tribune*, to help support the family.

1883   Mrs. Crane moves the family to Asbury Park, New Jersey, where Stephen enrolls in the public school.

1885   Stephen Crane writes his earliest known short story, "Uncle Jake and the Bell-Handle." He enrolls at Pennington Seminary.

1888   Crane enrolls at Claverack College and Hudson River Institute in Claverack, New York, where he receives military training. That summer he works for his brother Townley's news agency.

1890   Crane enters Lafayette College in Pennsylvania, majoring in mining engineering. He is asked to leave at the end of the fall semester.

1891   Crane uses family connections (his mother's ancestors had founded the university) to gain entrance to Syracuse University, where he joins the Delta Upsilon fraternity and plays on the baseball team. He also publishes a story, "The King's Favor," in the *Syracuse University Herald*. He leaves school in the spring. He begins work as a journalist, covering Hamlin Garland's speech on William Dean Howells, and the two men become friends. Mrs. Crane dies in December.

1892   Crane writes for a number of New York newspapers, including the *Herald* and the *Press*. He submits his first novel, *Maggie: A Girl of the Streets*, to a publisher, but it is rejected. His sketches of Sullivan County, Pennsylvania, are issued by *The New York Tribune*, and he publishes the first of his stories of the Bowery, "The Broken-Down Van."

1893   Crane borrows the money to publish *Maggie* under the name Johnston Smith. The novel does not sell well but he receives encouragement from Garland and Howells. Crane writes *The Red Badge of Courage*.

1894   *The Red Badge* appears in the *Philadelphia Press* and in other newspapers.

1895   Appleton and Company publishes the hardbound edition of *The Red Badge*, which sells well. Crane continues work as a journalist and travels to Nebraska to cover a severe drought, where he is interviewed by Willa Cather, then a student at the University of Nebraska. He continues his journey, going south to Texas and Mexico.

1896   The British edition of *The Red Badge* is published to strong reviews. Crane publishes his volume of poetry, *The Black Riders and Other Lines*, and a novel, *George's Mother*, set in the same tenement as *Maggie*. He appears in court in defense of a prostitute, Dora Clark, and becomes unpopular with the New York department of police. He publishes a volume of short stories of the Civil War, *The Little Regiment*, and a revised edition of *Maggie*. He goes to Jacksonville, Florida, late in the year to board a filibustering ship bound for Cuba. He meets Cora Taylor, who owns a house of prostitution called Hotel de Dream. She is married to her second husband, Captain Stewart, an English military man. Crane sails for Cuba on New Year's Eve.

1897   Crane's ship, *The Commodore*, sinks off the coast of Florida, and he performs heroic duty in getting passengers into lifeboats. Finally, he and four other men get into a ten-foot dinghy and strike out for shore. They spend the night in the small boat and capsize in the breakers as they approach land. One man is drowned but the other three are rescued and taken to safety, Cranc among them. Crane publishes an account of the incident entitled "Stephen Crane's Own Story." Later he writes "The Open Boat" about the adventure, one of the most famous stories in English. He and Cora go to England on their way to cover the war in Greece.

1898   Crane sails to Cuba to cover the Spanish-American War
        as a journalist. Crane publishes many of his best short
        stories, including "The Blue Hotel," "The Monster,"
        and "The Bride Comes to Yellow Sky."

1899   Crane is back in England living with Cora (who is
        introduced as his wife) in a castle called Brede Place in
        Sussex. Publishes *War Is Kind*, a volume of verse, and
        The Monster and Other Stories.

1900   Crane contracts tuberculosis and is taken to Baden-
        weiler, Germany, for treatment, where he dies at age
        twenty-eight. Henry James helps Cora raise money to
        send Crane's body back to the United States. Cora
        returns to Jacksonville and opens a new house of assig-
        nation.

1910   Cora, having married and divorced for the third time,
        dies and is buried under the name Cora E. Crane.

A Note on the Text

The text of *The Red Badge of Courage* reprinted here is that of the first edition published in New York by D. Appleton and Company in 1895. Crane's original manuscript has been published, so that a study of his original version of the novel is possible: see *The Red Badge of Courage: A Facsimile of the Manuscript,* ed. Fredson Bowers (Washington, DC: NCR/Microcard Edition, 1972).

Unfortunately, the typescript of the novel, on which Crane's editor would have made suggestions and alterations, has not been found. It is therefore impossible to know for certain which changes from the manuscript were made by the author and which by the publisher. The manuscript is inconsistent in the handling of punctuation and other details, as is the Appleton edition, and no better version is available. Numerous newspapers published an abridged version of the novel in 1894, but Crane did not participate in making any of the substantial deletions. In the 1890s, newspapers were notorious for cutting novels to fit the available space, without regard to the artistic integrity or meaning of the novel. In 1896 an edition of the novel was published in England, but it essentially followed the Appleton text in all but the British spelling of a few words. Since Crane did not participate in making any of the alterations, this version has not been regarded as having editorial authority. A more detailed discussion of the publication history of the novel is given in the introduction of this volume.

Had the typescript of the novel been found, it would have clarified numerous issues about the quest for a reliable text. As the situation stands, the author's final intentions on various details cannot be verified, a point crucially important in that the Appleton text varies from the manuscript in many matters. In that Crane does not appear to have made any attempt to restore those passages to his original draft, I have followed the Appleton text throughout and inserted footnotes where I thought a change of meaning needed clarification. For example, it makes a difference whether Henry thinks he sees "fiends" or "friends." My textual comments are minimal, however, to offer the experience of reading the same novel that Appleton published in 1895.

THE RED BADGE OF COURAGE

AN EPISODE OF THE AMERICAN CIVIL WAR

Chapter I

THE cold passed reluctantly from the earth, and the retiring fogs revealed an army stretched out on the hills, resting. As the landscape changed from brown to green, the army awakened, and began to tremble with eagerness at the noise of rumors. It cast its eyes upon the roads, which were growing from long troughs of liquid mud to proper thoroughfares. A river, amber-tinted in the shadow of its banks, purled at the army's feet; and at night, when the stream had become of a sorrowful blackness, one could see across it the red, eye-like gleam of hostile campfires set in the low brows of distant hills.

Once a certain tall soldier developed virtues and went resolutely to wash a shirt. He came flying back from a brook waving his garment bannerlike.[1] He was swelled with a tale he had heard from a reliable friend, who had heard it from a truthful cavalryman, who had heard it from his trustworthy brother, one of the orderlies at division headquarters. He adopted the important air of a herald in red and gold.

"We're goin' t' move t' morrah—sure," he said pompously to a group in the company street. "We're goin' 'way up the river, cut across, an' come around in behint 'em."

To his attentive audience he drew a loud and elaborate plan of a very brilliant campaign. When he had finished, the blue-clothed men scattered into small arguing groups between the rows of squat brown huts. A negro teamster who had been dancing upon a cracker box with the hilarious encouragement of twoscore soldiers was deserted. He sat mournfully down. Smoke drifted lazily from a multitude of quaint chimneys.

"It's a lie! that's all it is—a thunderin' lie!" said another private loudly. His smooth face was flushed, and his hands were thrust sulkily into his trousers' pockets. He took the matter as an affront to him. "I don't believe the derned old army's ever going to move. We're set. I've got ready to move eight times in the last two weeks, and we ain't moved yet."

The tall soldier felt called upon to defend the truth of a rumor he himself had introduced. He and the loud one came near to fighting over it.

---

1 Crane was inconsistent in his handling of punctuation and often omitted the hyphen in words such as "eye-like" and "banner-like." The Appleton edition of 1895 did not add them, and that text serves as the basis for this Broadview edition.

A corporal began to swear before the assemblage. He had just put a costly board floor in his house, he said. During the early spring he had refrained from adding extensively to the comfort of his environment because he had felt that the army might start on the march at any moment. Of late, however, he had been impressed that they were in a sort of eternal camp.

Many of the men engaged in a spirited debate. One outlined in a peculiarly lucid manner all the plans of the commanding general. He was opposed by men who advocated that there were other plans of campaign. They clamored at each other, numbers making futile bids for the popular attention. Meanwhile, the soldier who had fetched the rumor bustled about with much importance. He was continually assailed by questions.

"What's up, Jim?"

"Th' army's goin' t' move."

"Ah, what yeh talkin' about? How yeh know it is?"

"Well, yeh kin b'lieve me er not, jest as yeh like. I don't care a hang."

There was much food for thought in the manner in which he replied. He came near to convincing them by disdaining to produce proofs. They grew excited over it.

There was a youthful private who listened with eager ears to the words of the tall soldier and to the varied comments of his comrades. After receiving a fill of discussions concerning marches and attacks, he went to his hut and crawled through an intricate hole that served it as a door. He wished to be alone with some new thoughts that had lately come to him.

He lay down on a wide bunk that stretched across the end of the room. In the other end, cracker boxes were made to serve as furniture. They were grouped about the fireplace. A picture from an illustrated weekly was upon the log walls, and three rifles were paralleled on pegs. Equipments hung on handy projections, and some tin dishes lay upon a small pile of firewood. A folded tent was serving as a roof. The sunlight, without, beating upon it, made it glow a light yellow shade. A small window shot an oblique square of whiter light upon the cluttered floor. The smoke from the fire at times neglected the clay chimney and wreathed into the room, and this flimsy chimney of clay and sticks made endless threats to set ablaze the whole establishment.

The youth was in a little trance of astonishment. So they were at last going to fight. On the morrow, perhaps, there would be a battle, and he would be in it. For a time he was obliged to labor to make himself believe. He could not accept with assurance an omen that he was about to mingle in one of those great affairs of the earth.

He had, of course, dreamed of battles all his life—of vague and bloody conflicts that had thrilled him with their sweep and fire. In visions he had seen himself in many struggles. He had imagined peoples secure in the shadow of his eagle-eyed prowess. But awake he had regarded battles as crimson blotches on the pages of the past. He had put them as things of the bygone with his thought-images of heavy crowns and high castles. There was a portion of the world's history which he had regarded as the time of wars, but it, he thought, had been long gone over the horizon and had disappeared forever.

From his home his youthful eyes had looked upon the war in his own country with distrust. It must be some sort of a play affair. He had long despaired of witnessing a Greeklike struggle.[1] Such would be no more, he had said. Men were better, or more timid. Secular and religious education had effaced the throat grappling instinct, or else firm finance held in check the passions.

He had burned several times to enlist. Tales of great movements shook the land. They might not be distinctly Homeric, but there seemed to be much glory in them. He had read of marches, sieges, conflicts, and he had longed to see it all. His busy mind had drawn for him large pictures extravagant in color, lurid with breathless deeds.

But his mother had discouraged him. She had affected to look with some contempt upon the quality of his war ardor and patriotism. She could calmly seat herself and with no apparent difficulty give him many hundreds of reasons why he was of vastly more importance on the farm than on the field of battle. She had had certain ways of expression that told him that her statements on the subject came from a deep conviction. Moreover, on her side, was his belief that her ethical motive in the argument was impregnable.

At last, however, he had made firm rebellion against this yellow light thrown upon the color of his ambitions. The newspapers, the gossip of the village, his own picturings had aroused him to an uncheckable degree. They were in truth fighting finely down there. Almost every day the newspapers printed accounts of a decisive victory.

---

1   That Henry thinks of war as "a Greeklike struggle" suggests his youth and innocence. He knows nothing of actual combat except for what he has read in school, apparently Homer's *The Iliad*.

One night, as he lay in bed, the winds had carried to him the clangoring of the church bell as some enthusiast jerked the rope frantically to tell the twisted news of a great battle. This voice of the people rejoicing in the night had made him shiver in a prolonged ecstasy of excitement. Later, he had gone down to his mother's room and had spoken thus: "Ma, I'm going to enlist."

"Henry, don't you be a fool," his mother had replied. She had then covered her face with the quilt. There was an end to the matter for that night.

Nevertheless, the next morning he had gone to a town that was near his mother's farm and had enlisted in a company that was forming there. When he had returned home his mother was milking the brindle cow.[1] Four others stood waiting. "Ma, I've enlisted," he had said to her diffidently. There was a short silence. "The Lord's will be done, Henry," she had finally replied, and had then continued to milk the brindle cow.

When he had stood in the doorway with his soldier's clothes on his back, and with the light of excitement and expectancy in his eyes almost defeating the glow of regret for the home bonds, he had seen two tears leaving their trails on his mother's scarred cheeks.

Still, she had disappointed him by saying nothing whatever about returning with his shield or on it.[2] He had privately primed himself for a beautiful scene. He had prepared certain sentences which he thought could be used with touching effect. But her words destroyed his plans. She had doggedly peeled potatoes and addressed him as follows: "You watch out, Henry, an' take good care of yerself in this here fighting business—you watch out, an' take good care of yerself. Don't go a-thinkin' you can lick the hull rebel army at the start, because yeh can't. Yer jest one little feller amongst a hull lot of others, and yeh've got to keep quiet an' do what they tell yeh. I know how you are, Henry.

"I've knet yeh eight pair of socks, Henry, and I've put in all yer best shirts, because I want my boy to be jest as warm and comf'able as anybody in the army. Whenever they get holes in 'em, I want yeh to send 'em right-away back to me, so's I kin dern 'em.

"An' allus be careful an' choose yer comp'ny. There's lots of bad men in the army, Henry. The army makes 'em wild, and they like nothing better than the job of leading off a young feller like you, as ain't never been away from home much and has allus had

---

1 One with dark stripes on a tan or light brown body of color.
2 She does not see his service in classical heroic terms.

a mother, an' a-learning 'em to drink and swear. Keep clear of them folks, Henry. I don't want yeh to ever do anything, Henry, that yeh would be 'shamed to let me know about. Jest think as if I was a-watchin' yeh. If yes keep that in yer mind allus, I guess yeh'll come out about right.

"Yes must allus remember yer father, too, child, an' remember he never drunk a drop of licker in his life, and seldom swore a cross oath.

"I don't know what else to tell yeh, Henry, excepting that yeh must never do no shirking, child, on my account. If so be a time comes when yeh have to be kilt or do a mean thing, why, Henry, don't think of anything 'cept what's right, because there's many a woman has to bear up 'ginst sech things these times, and the Lord 'll take keer of us all.

"Don't forgit about the socks and the shirts, child; and I've put a cup of blackberry jam with yer bundle, because I know yeh like it above all things. Good by, Henry. Watch out, and be a good boy."

He had, of course, been impatient under the ordeal of this speech. It had not been quite what he expected, and he had borne it with an air of irritation. He departed feeling vague relief.

Still, when he had looked back from the gate, he had seen his mother kneeling among the potato parings. Her brown face, upraised, was stained with tears, and her spare form was quivering. He bowed his head and went on, feeling suddenly ashamed of his purposes.

From his home he had gone to the seminary[1] to bid adieu to many schoolmates. They had thronged about him with wonder and admiration. He had felt the gulf now between them and had swelled with calm pride. He and some of his fellows who had donned blue were quite overwhelmed with privileges for all of one afternoon, and it had been a very delicious thing. They had strutted.

A certain light-haired girl had made vivacious fun at his martial spirit, but there was another and darker girl whom he had gazed at steadfastly, and he thought she grew demure and sad at [the] sight of his blue and brass. As he had walked down the path between the rows of oaks, he had turned his head and detected her at a window watching his departure. As he perceived her, she had immediately begun to stare up through the high tree branches at the sky. He had seen a good deal of flurry and haste

---

1 Henry's high school, not an institution for religious training.

in her movement as she changed her attitude. He often thought of it.

On the way to Washington his spirit had soared. The regiment was fed and caressed at station after station until the youth had believed that he must be a hero. There was a lavish expenditure of bread and cold meats, coffee, and pickles and cheese. As he basked in the smiles of the girls and was patted and complimented by the old men, he had felt growing within him the strength to do mighty deeds of arms.

After complicated journeyings with many pauses, there had come months of monotonous life in a camp. He had had the belief that real war was a series of death struggles with small time in between for sleep and meals; but since his regiment had come to the field the army had done little but sit still and try to keep warm.

He was brought then gradually back to his old ideas. Greek-like struggles would be no more. Men were better, or more timid. Secular and religious education had effaced the throat-grappling instinct, or else firm finance held in check the passions.

He had grown to regard himself merely as a part of a vast blue demonstration. His province was to look out, as far as he could, for his personal comfort. For recreation he could twiddle his thumbs and speculate on the thoughts which must agitate the minds of the generals. Also, he was drilled and drilled and reviewed, and drilled and drilled and reviewed.

The only foes he had seen were some pickets along the river bank. They were a sun-tanned, philosophical lot, who sometimes shot reflectively at the blue pickets. When reproached for this afterward, they usually expressed sorrow, and swore by their gods that the guns had exploded without their permission. The youth, on guard duty one night, conversed across the stream with one of them. He was a slightly ragged man, who spat skillfully between his shoes and possessed a great fund of bland and infantile assurance. The youth liked him personally.

"Yank," the other had informed him, "yer a right dum good feller." This sentiment, floating to him upon the still air, had made him temporarily regret war.

Various veterans had told him tales. Some talked of gray, bewhiskered hordes who were advancing with relentless curses and chewing tobacco with unspeakable valor; tremendous bodies of fierce soldiery who were sweeping along like the Huns.[1] Others

---

1 An eastern European people who, under their leader Attila, conquered enormous territory with their fierce fighting.

spoke of tattered and eternally hungry men who fired despondent powders. "They'll charge through hell's fire an' brimstone t' git a holt on a haversack, an' sech stomachs ain't a-lastin' long," he was told. From the stories, the youth imagined the red, live bones sticking out through slits in the faded uniforms.

Still, he could not put a whole faith in veterans' tales, for recruits were their prey. They talked much of smoke, fire, and blood, but he could not tell how much might be lies. They persistently yelled "Fresh fish!" at him, and were in no wise to be trusted.

However, he perceived now that it did not greatly matter what kind of soldiers he was going to fight, so long as they fought, which fact no one disputed. There was a more serious problem. He lay in his bunk pondering upon it. He tried to mathematically prove to himself that he would not run from a battle.

Previously he had never felt obliged to wrestle too seriously with this question. In his life he had taken certain things for granted, never challenging his belief in ultimate success, and bothering little about means and roads. But here he was confronted with a thing of moment. It had suddenly appeared to him that perhaps in a battle he might run. He was forced to admit that as far as war was concerned he knew nothing of himself.

A sufficient time before he would have allowed the problem to kick its heels at the outer portals of his mind, but now he felt compelled to give serious attention to it.

A little panic-fear grew in his mind. As his imagination went forward to a fight, he saw hideous possibilities. He contemplated the lurking menaces of the future, and failed in an effort to see himself standing stoutly in the midst of them. He recalled his visions of broken-bladed glory, but in the shadow of the impending tumult he suspected them to be impossible pictures.

He sprang from the bunk and began to pace nervously to and fro. "Good Lord, what's th' matter with me?" he said aloud.

He felt that in this crisis his laws of life were useless. Whatever he had learned of himself was here of no avail. He was an unknown quantity. He saw that he would again be obliged to experiment as he had in early youth. He must accumulate information of himself, and meanwhile he resolved to remain close upon his guard lest those qualities of which he knew nothing should everlastingly disgrace him. "Good Lord!" he repeated in dismay.

After a time the tall soldier slid dexterously through the hole. The loud private followed. They were wrangling.

"That's all right," said the tall soldier as he entered. He waved his hand expressively. "You can believe me or not, jest as you like. All you got to do is to sit down and wait as quiet as you can. Then pretty soon you'll find out I was right."

His comrade grunted stubbornly. For a moment he seemed to be searching for a formidable reply. Finally he said: "Well, you don't know everything in the world, do you?"

"Didn't say I knew everything in the world," retorted the other sharply. He began to stow various articles snugly into his knapsack.

The youth, pausing in his nervous walk, looked down at the busy figure. "Going to be a battle, sure, is there, Jim?" he asked.

"Of course there is," replied the tall soldier. "Of course there is. You jest wait 'til to-morrow, and you'll see one of the biggest battles ever was. You jest wait."

"Thunder!" said the youth.

"Oh, you'll see fighting this time, my boy, what'll be regular out-and-out fighting," added the tall soldier, with the air of a man who is about to exhibit a battle for the benefit of his friends.

"Huh!" said the loud one from a corner.

"Well," remarked the youth, "like as not this story'll turn out jest like them others did."

"Not much it won't," replied the tall soldier, exasperated. "Not much it won't. Didn't the cavalry all start this morning?" He glared about him. No one denied his statement. "The cavalry started this morning," he continued. "They say there ain't hardly any cavalry left in camp. They're going to Richmond, or some place, while we fight all the Johnnies.[1] It's some dodge like that. The regiment's got orders, too. A feller what seen 'em go to headquarters told me a little while ago. And they're raising blazes all over camp—anybody can see that."

"Shucks!" said the loud one.

The youth remained silent for a time. At last he spoke to the tall soldier. "Jim!"

"What?"

"How do you think the reg'ment 'll do?"

"Oh, they'll fight all right, I guess, after they once get into it," said the other with cold judgment. He made a fine use of the third person. "There's been heaps of fun poked at 'em because they're new, of course, and all that; but they'll fight all right, I guess."

---

1   Confederate soldiers were often referred to by the Union troops as "Johnny Rebs."

"Think any of the boys 'll run?" persisted the youth.

"Oh, there may be a few of 'em run, but there's them kind in every regiment, 'specially when they first goes under fire," said the other in a tolerant way. "Of course it might happen that the hull kit-and-boodle might start and run, if some big fighting came first off, and then again they might stay and fight like fun. But you can't bet on nothing. Of course they ain't never been under fire yet, and it ain't likely they'll lick the hull rebel army all-to-oncet the first time; but I think they'll fight better than some, if worse than others. That's the way I figger. They call the reg'-ment 'Fresh fish' and everything; but the boys come of good stock, and most of 'em 'll fight like sin after they oncet git shoot-in'," he added, with a mighty emphasis on the last four words.

"Oh, you think you know—" began the loud soldier with scorn.

The other turned savagely upon him. They had a rapid alter-cation, in which they fastened upon each other various strange epithets.

The youth at last interrupted them. "Did you ever think you might run yourself, Jim?" he asked. On concluding the sentence he laughed as if he had meant to aim a joke. The loud soldier also giggled.

The tall private waved his hand. "Well," said he profoundly, "I've thought it might get too hot for Jim Conklin in some of them scrimmages, and if a whole lot of boys started and run, why, I s'pose I'd start and run. And if I once started to run, I'd run like the devil, and no mistake. But if everybody was a-standing and a-fighting, why, I'd stand and fight. Be jiminey, I would. I'll bet on it."

"Huh!" said the loud one.

The youth of this tale felt gratitude for these words of his comrade. He had feared that all of the untried men possessed a great and correct confidence. He now was in a measure reas-sured.

Chapter II

THE next morning the youth discovered that his tall comrade had been the fast-flying messenger of a mistake. There was much scoffing at the latter by those who had yesterday been firm adherents of his views, and there was even a little sneering by men who had never believed the rumor. The tall one fought with a man from Chatfield Corners and beat him severely.

The youth felt, however, that his problem was in no wise lifted from him. There was, on the contrary, an irritating prolongation. The tale had created in him a great concern for himself. Now, with the newborn question in his mind, he was compelled to sink back into his old place as part of a blue demonstration.

For days he made ceaseless calculations, but they were all wondrously unsatisfactory. He found that he could establish nothing. He finally concluded that the only way to prove himself was to go into the blaze, and then figuratively to watch his legs to discover their merits and faults. He reluctantly admitted that he could not sit still and with a mental slate and pencil derive an answer. To gain it, he must have blaze, blood, and danger, even as a chemist requires this, that, and the other. So he fretted for an opportunity.

Meanwhile he continually tried to measure himself by his comrades. The tall soldier, for one, gave him some assurance. This man's serene unconcern dealt him a measure of confidence, for he had known him since childhood, and from his intimate knowledge he did not see how he could be capable of anything that was beyond him, the youth. Still, he thought that his comrade might be mistaken about himself. Or, on the other hand, he might be a man heretofore doomed to peace and obscurity, but, in reality, made to shine in war.

The youth would have liked to have discovered another who suspected himself. A sympathetic comparison of mental notes would have been a joy to him.

He occasionally tried to fathom a comrade with seductive sentences. He looked about to find men in the proper mood. All attempts failed to bring forth any statement which looked in any way like a confession to those doubts which he privately acknowledged in himself. He was afraid to make an open declaration of his concern, because he dreaded to place some unscrupulous confidant upon the high plane of the unconfessed from which elevation he could be derided.

In regard to his companions his mind wavered between two opinions, according to his mood. Sometimes he inclined to believing them all heroes. In fact, he usually admitted in secret the superior development of the higher qualities in others. He could conceive of men going very insignificantly about the world bearing a load of courage unseen, and although he had known many of his comrades through boyhood, he began to fear that his judgment of them had been blind. Then, in other moments, he flouted these theories and assured himself that his fellows were all privately wondering and quaking.

His emotions made him feel strange in the presence of men who talked excitedly of a prospective battle as of a drama they were about to witness, with nothing but eagerness and curiosity apparent in their faces. It was often that he suspected them to be liars.

He did not pass such thoughts without severe condemnation of himself. He dinned reproaches at times. He was convicted by himself of many shameful crimes against the gods of traditions.

In his great anxiety his heart was continually clamoring at what he considered the intolerable slowness of the generals. They seemed content to perch tranquilly on the river bank and leave him bowed down by the weight of a great problem. He wanted it settled forthwith. He could not long bear such a load, he said. Sometimes his anger at the commanders reached an acute stage, and he grumbled about the camp like a veteran.

One morning, however, he found himself in the ranks of his prepared regiment. The men were whispering speculations and recounting the old rumors. In the gloom before the break of the day their uniforms glowed a deep purple hue. From across the river the red eyes were still peering. In the eastern sky there was a yellow patch like a rug laid for the feet of the coming sun; and against it, black and pattern like, loomed the gigantic figure of the colonel on a gigantic horse.

From off in the darkness came the trampling of feet. The youth could occasionally see dark shadows that moved like monsters. The regiment stood at rest for what seemed a long time. The youth grew impatient. It was unendurable the way these affairs were managed. He wondered how long they were to be kept waiting.

As he looked all about him and pondered upon the mystic gloom, he began to believe that at any moment the ominous distance might be aflare, and the rolling crashes of an engagement come to his ears. Staring once at the red eyes across the river, he conceived them to be growing larger, as the orbs of a row of dragons advancing. He turned toward the colonel and saw him lift his gigantic arm and calmly stroke his mustache.

At last he heard from along the road at the foot of the hill the clatter of a horse's galloping hoofs. It must be the coming of orders. He bent forward, scarce breathing. The exciting clickety-click, as it grew louder and louder, seemed to be beating upon his soul. Presently a horseman with jangling equipment drew rein before the colonel of the regiment. The two held a short, sharp-worded conversation. The men in the foremost ranks craned their necks.

As the horseman wheeled his animal and galloped away he turned to shout over his shoulder, "Don't forget that box of cigars!" The colonel mumbled in reply. The youth wondered what a box of cigars had to do with war.

A moment later the regiment went swinging off into the darkness. It was now like one of those moving monsters wending with many feet. The air was heavy, and cold with dew. A mass of wet grass, marched upon, rustled like silk.

There was an occasional flash and glimmer of steel from the backs of all these huge crawling reptiles. From the road came creakings and grumblings as some surly guns were dragged away.

The men stumbled along still muttering speculations. There was a subdued debate. Once a man fell down, and as he reached for his rifle a comrade, unseeing, trod upon his hand. He of the injured fingers swore bitterly and aloud. A low, tittering laugh went among his fellows.

Presently they passed into a roadway and marched forward with easy strides. A dark regiment moved before them, and from behind also came the tinkle of equipments on the bodies of marching men.

The rushing yellow of the developing day went on behind their backs. When the sunrays at last struck full and mellowingly upon the earth, the youth saw that the landscape was streaked with two long, thin, black columns which disappeared on the brow of a hill in front and rearward vanished in a wood. They were like two serpents crawling from the cavern of the night.

The river was not in view. The tall soldier burst into praises of what he thought to be his powers of perception.

Some of the tall one's companions cried with emphasis that they, too, had evolved the same thing, and they congratulated themselves upon it. But there were others who said that the tall one's plan was not the true one at all. They persisted with other theories. There was a vigorous discussion.

The youth took no part in them. As he walked along in careless line he was engaged with his own eternal debate. He could not hinder himself from dwelling upon it. He was despondent and sullen, and threw shifting glances about him. He looked ahead, often expecting to hear from the advance the rattle of firing.

But the long serpents crawled slowly from hill to hill without bluster of smoke. A dun-colored cloud of dust floated away to the right. The sky overhead was of a fairy blue.

The youth studied the faces of his companions, ever on the watch to detect kindred emotions. He suffered disappointment. Some ardor of the air which was causing the veteran commands to move with glee—almost with song—had infected the new regiment. The men began to speak of victory as of a thing they knew. Also, the tall soldier received his vindication. They were certainly going to come around in behind the enemy. They expressed commiseration for that part of the army which had been left upon the river bank, felicitating themselves upon being a part of a blasting host.

The youth, considering himself as separated from the others, was saddened by the blithe and merry speeches that went from rank to rank. The company wags all made their best endeavors. The regiment tramped to the tune of laughter.

The blatant soldier often convulsed whole files by his biting sarcasms aimed at the tall one.

And it was not long before all the men seemed to forget their mission. Whole brigades grinned in unison, and regiments laughed.

A rather fat soldier attempted to pilfer a horse from a dooryard. He planned to load his knap sack upon it. He was escaping with his prize when a young girl rushed from the house and grabbed the animal's mane. There followed a wrangle. The young girl, with pink cheeks and shining eyes, stood like a dauntless statue.

The observant regiment, standing at rest in the roadway, whooped at once, and entered whole-souled upon the side of the maiden. The men became so engrossed in this affair that they entirely ceased to remember their own large war. They jeered the piratical private, and called attention to various defects in his personal appearance; and they were wildly enthusiastic in support of the young girl.

To her, from some distance, came bold advice. "Hit him with a stick."

There were crows and catcalls showered upon him when he retreated without the horse. The regiment rejoiced at his downfall. Loud and vociferous congratulations were showered upon the maiden, who stood panting and regarding the troops with defiance.

At nightfall the column broke into regimental pieces, and the fragments went into the fields to camp. Tents sprang up like strange plants. Camp fires, like red, peculiar blossoms, dotted the night.

The youth kept from intercourse with his companions as much as circumstances would allow him. In the evening he wandered a few paces into the gloom. From this little distance the many fires, with the black forms of men passing to and fro before the crimson rays, made weird and satanic effects.

He lay down in the grass. The blades pressed tenderly against his cheek. The moon had been lighted and was hung in a treetop. The liquid stillness of the night enveloping him made him feel vast pity for himself. There was a caress in the soft winds; and the whole mood of the darkness, he thought, was one of sympathy for himself in his distress.

He wished, without reserve, that he was at home again making the endless rounds from the house to the barn, from the barn to the fields, from the fields to the barn, from the barn to the house. He remembered he had often cursed the brindle cow and her mates, and had sometimes flung milking stools. But, from his present point of view, there was a halo of happiness about each of their heads, and he would have sacrificed all the brass buttons on the continent to have been enabled to return to them. He told himself that he was not formed for a soldier. And he mused seriously upon the radical differences between himself and those men who were dodging imp-like around the fires.

As he mused thus he heard the rustle of grass, and, upon turning his head, discovered the loud soldier. He called out, "Oh, Wilson!"

The latter approached and looked down. "Why, hello, Henry; is it you? What you doing here?"

"Oh, thinking," said the youth.

The other sat down and carefully lighted his pipe. "You're getting blue, my boy. You're looking thundering peeked. What the dickens is wrong with you?"

"Oh, nothing," said the youth.

The loud soldier launched then into the subject of the anticipated fight. "Oh, we've got 'em now!" As he spoke his boyish face was wreathed in a gleeful smile, and his voice had an exultant ring. "We've got 'em now. At last, by the eternal thunders, we'll lick 'em good!"

"If the truth was known," he added, more soberly, "*they've* licked *us* about every clip up to now; but this time—this time—we'll lick 'em good!"

"I thought you was objecting to this march a little while ago," said the youth coldly.

"Oh, it wasn't that," explained the other. "I don't mind marching, if there's going to be fighting at the end of it. What I hate is this getting moved here and moved there, with no good coming of it, as far as I can see, excepting sore feet and damned short rations."

"Well, Jim Conklin says we'll get a plenty of fighting this time."

"He's right for once, I guess, though I can't see how it come. This time we're in for a big battle, and we've got the best end of it, certain sure. Gee rod! how we will thump 'em!"

He arose and began to pace to and fro excitedly. The thrill of his enthusiasm made him walk with an elastic step. He was sprightly, vigorous, fiery in his belief in success. He looked into the future with clear, proud eye, and he swore with the air of an old soldier.

The youth watched him for a moment in silence. When he finally spoke his voice was as bitter as dregs. "Oh, you're going to do great things, I s'pose!"

The loud soldier blew a thoughtful cloud of smoke from his pipe. "Oh, I don't know," he remarked with dignity; "I don't know. I s'pose I'll do as well as the rest. I'm going to try like thunder." He evidently complimented himself upon the modesty of this statement.

"How do you know you won't run when the time comes?" asked the youth.

"Run?" said the loud one; "run?—of course not!" He laughed.

"Well," continued the youth, "lots of good a-'nough men have thought they was going to do great things before the fight, but when the time come they skedaddled."

"Oh, that's all true, I s'pose," replied the other; "but I'm not going to skedaddle. The man that bets on my running will lose his money, that's all." He nodded confidently.

"Oh, shucks!" said the youth. "You ain't the bravest man in the world, are you?"

"No, I ain't," exclaimed the loud soldier indignantly; "and I didn't say I was the bravest man in the world, neither. I said I was going to do my share of fighting—that's what I said. And I am, too. Who are you, anyhow. You talk as if you thought you was Napoleon Bonaparte." He glared at the youth for a moment, and then strode away.

The youth called in a savage voice after his comrade: "Well, you needn't git mad about it!" But the other continued on his way and made no reply.

He felt alone in space when his injured comrade had disappeared. His failure to discover any mite of resemblance in their view points made him more miserable than before. No one seemed to be wrestling with such a terrific personal problem. He was a mental outcast.

He went slowly to his tent and stretched himself on a blanket by the side of the snoring tall soldier. In the darkness he saw visions of a thousand-tongued fear that would babble at his back and cause him to flee, while others were going coolly about their country's business. He admitted that he would not be able to cope with this monster. He felt that every nerve in his body would be an ear to hear the voices, while other men would remain stolid and deaf.

And as he sweated with the pain of these thoughts, he could hear low, serene sentences. "I'll bid five." "Make it six." "Seven." "Seven goes."

He stared at the red, shivering reflection of a fire on the white wall of his tent until, exhausted and ill from the monotony of his suffering, he fell asleep.

Chapter III

WHEN another night came the columns, changed to purple streaks, filed across two pontoon bridges. A glaring fire wine-tinted the waters of the river. Its rays, shining upon the moving masses of troops, brought forth here and there sudden gleams of silver or gold. Upon the other shore a dark and mysterious range of hills was curved against the sky. The insect voices of the night sang solemnly.

After this crossing the youth assured himself that at any moment they might be suddenly and fearfully assaulted from the caves of the lowering woods. He kept his eyes watchfully upon the darkness.

But his regiment went unmolested to a camping place, and its soldiers slept the brave sleep of wearied men. In the morning they were routed out with early energy and hustled along a narrow road that led deep into the forest.

It was during this rapid march that the regiment lost many of the marks of a new command.

The men had begun to count the miles upon their fingers, and they grew tired. "Sore feet an' damned short rations, that's all," said the loud soldier. There was perspiration and grumblings. After a time they began to shed their knapsacks. Some tossed them unconcernedly down; others hid them carefully, asserting their plans to return for them at some convenient time. Men extricated themselves from thick shirts. Presently few carried anything but their necessary clothing, blankets, haversacks, canteens, and arms and ammunition. "You can now eat and shoot," said the tall soldier to the youth. "That's all you want to do."

There was sudden change from the ponderous infantry of theory to the light and speedy infantry of practice. The regiment, relieved of a burden, received a new impetus. But there was much loss of valuable knapsacks, and, on the whole, very good shirts.

But the regiment was not yet veteranlike in appearance. Veteran regiments in the army were likely to be very small aggregations of men. Once, when the command had first come to the field, some perambulating veterans, noting the length of their column, had accosted them thus: "Hey, fellers, what brigade is that?" And when the men had replied that they formed a regiment and not a brigade,[1] the older soldiers had laughed, and said, "O Gawd!"

---

1 A regiment is made up of as many as a thousand men. A brigade consists of two or more regiments. Henry's unit is so large for *(continued)*

Also, there was too great a similarity in the hats. The hats of a regiment should properly represent the history of headgear for a period of years. And, moreover, there were no letters of faded gold speaking from the colors. They were new and beautiful, and the color bearer habitually oiled the pole.

Presently the army again sat down to think. The odor of the peaceful pines was in the men's nostrils. The sound of monotonous axe blows rang through the forest, and the insects, nodding upon their perches, crooned like old women. The youth returned to his theory of a blue demonstration.

One gray dawn, however, he was kicked in the leg by the tall soldier, and then, before he was entirely awake, he found himself running down a wood road in the midst of men who were panting from the first effects of speed. His canteen banged rhythmically upon his thigh, and his haversack bobbed softly. His musket bounced a trifle from his shoulder at each stride and made his cap feel uncertain upon his head.

He could hear the men whisper jerky sentences: "Say—what's all this—about?" "What th' thunder—we—skedaddlin' this way fer?" "Billie—keep off m' feet. Yeh run—like a cow." And the loud soldier's shrill voice could be heard: "What th' devil they in sich a hurry for?"

The youth thought the damp fog of early morning moved from the rush of a great body of troops. From the distance came a sudden spatter of firing.

He was bewildered. As he ran with his comrades he strenuously tried to think, but all he knew was that if he fell down those coming behind would tread upon him. All his faculties seemed to be needed to guide him over and past obstructions. He felt carried along by a mob.

The sun spread disclosing rays, and, one by one, regiments burst into view like armed men just born of the earth. The youth perceived that the time had come. He was about to be measured. For a moment he felt in the face of his great trial like a babe, and the flesh over his heart seemed very thin. He seized time to look about him calculatingly.

But he instantly saw that it would be impossible for him to escape from the regiment. It inclosed him. And there were iron laws of tradition and law on four sides. He was in a moving box.

---

a regiment that it is clear to the other soldiers that they have not seen action and have not lost many men.

As he perceived this fact it occurred to him that he had never wished to come to the war. He had not enlisted of his free will. He had been dragged by the merciless government. And now they were taking him out to be slaughtered.

The regiment slid down a bank and wallowed across a little stream. The mournful current moved slowly on, and from the water, shaded black, some white bubble eyes looked at the men.

As they climbed the hill on the farther side artillery began to boom. Here the youth forgot many things as he felt a sudden impulse of curiosity. He scrambled up the bank with a speed that could not be exceeded by a bloodthirsty man.

He expected a battle scene.

There were some little fields girted and squeezed by a forest. Spread over the grass and in among the tree trunks, he could see knots and waving lines of skirmishers who were running hither and thither and firing at the landscape. A dark battle line lay upon a sunstruck clearing that gleamed orange color. A flag fluttered.

Other regiments floundered up the bank. The brigade was formed in line of battle, and after a pause started slowly through the woods in the rear of the receding skirmishers, who were continually melting into the scene to appear again farther on. They were always busy as bees, deeply absorbed in their little combats.

The youth tried to observe everything. He did not use care to avoid trees and branches, and his forgotten feet were constantly knocking against stones or getting entangled in briers. He was aware that these battalions with their commotions were woven red and startling into the gentle fabric of softened greens and browns. It looked to be a wrong place for a battle field.

The skirmishers in advance fascinated him. Their shots into thickets and at distant and prominent trees spoke to him of tragedies—hidden, mysterious, solemn.

Once the line encountered the body of a dead soldier. He lay upon his back staring at the sky. He was dressed in an awkward suit of yellowish brown.[1] The youth could see that the soles of his shoes had been worn to the thinness of writing paper, and from a great rent in one the dead foot projected piteously. And it was as if fate had betrayed the soldier. In death it exposed to his enemies that poverty which in life he had perhaps concealed from his friends.

The ranks opened covertly to avoid the corpse. The invulnerable dead man forced a way for himself. The youth looked keenly

---

1 The uniform of a Confederate soldier.

at the ashen face. The wind raised the tawny beard. It moved as if a hand were stroking it. He vaguely desired to walk around and around the body and stare; the impulse of the living to try to read in dead eyes the answer to the Question.

During the march the ardor which the youth had acquired when out of view of the field rapidly faded to nothing. His curiosity was quite easily satisfied. If an intense scene had caught him with its wild swing as he came to the top of the bank, he might have gone roaring on. This advance upon Nature was too calm. He had opportunity to reflect. He had time in which to wonder about himself and to attempt to probe his sensations.

Absurd ideas took hold upon him. He thought that he did not relish the landscape. It threatened him. A coldness swept over his back, and it is true that his trousers felt to him that they were no fit for his legs at all.

A house standing placidly in distant fields had to him an ominous look. The shadows of the woods were formidable. He was certain that in this vista there lurked fierce eyed hosts. The swift thought came to him that the generals did not know what they were about. It was all a trap. Suddenly those close forests would bristle with rifle barrels. Ironlike brigades would appear in the rear. They were all going to be sacrificed. The generals were stupids. The enemy would presently swallow the whole command. He glared about him, expecting to see the stealthy approach of his death.

He thought that he must break from the ranks and harangue his comrades. They must not all be killed like pigs; and he was sure it would come to pass unless they were informed of these dangers. The generals were idiots to send them marching into a regular pen. There was but one pair of eyes in the corps. He would step forth and make a speech. Shrill and passionate words came to his lips.

The line, broken into moving fragments by the ground, went calmly on through fields and woods. The youth looked at the men nearest him, and saw, for the most part, expressions of deep interest, as if they were investigating something that had fascinated them. One or two stepped with overvaliant airs as if they were already plunged into war. Others walked as upon thin ice. The greater part of the untested men appeared quiet and absorbed. They were going to look at war, the red animal—war, the blood-swollen god. And they were deeply engrossed in this march.

As he looked the youth gripped his outcry at his throat. He saw that even if the men were tottering with fear they would laugh at his warning. They would jeer him, and, if practicable, pelt him with missiles. Admitting that he might be wrong, a frenzied declamation of the kind would turn him into a worm.

He assumed, then, the demeanor of one who knows that he is doomed alone to unwritten responsibilities. He lagged, with tragic glances at the sky.

He was surprised presently by the young lieutenant of his company, who began heartily to beat him with a sword, calling out in a loud and insolent voice: "Come, young man, get up into ranks there. No skulking 'll do here." He mended his pace with suitable haste. And he hated the lieutenant, who had no appreciation of fine minds. He was a mere brute.

After a time the brigade was halted in the cathedral light of a forest. The busy skirmishers were still popping. Through the aisles of the wood could be seen the floating smoke from their rifles. Sometimes it went up in little balls, white and compact.

During this halt many men in the regiment began erecting tiny hills in front of them. They used stones, sticks, earth, and anything they thought might turn a bullet. Some built comparatively large ones, while others seemed content with little ones.

This procedure caused a discussion among the men. Some wished to fight like duelists, believing it to be correct to stand erect and be, from their feet to their foreheads, a mark. They said they scorned the devices of the cautious. But the others scoffed in reply, and pointed to the veterans on the flanks who were digging at the ground like terriers. In a short time there was quite a barricade along the regimental fronts. Directly, however, they were ordered to withdraw from that place.

This astounded the youth. He forgot his stewing over the advance movement. "Well, then, what did they march us out here for?" he demanded of the tall soldier. The latter with calm faith began a heavy explanation, although he had been compelled to leave a little protection of stones and dirt to which he had devoted much care and skill.

When the regiment was aligned in another position each man's regard for his safety caused another line of small intrenchments. They ate their noon meal behind a third one. They were moved from this one also. They were marched from place to place with apparent aimlessness.

The youth had been taught that a man became another thing in a battle. He saw his salvation in such a change. Hence this waiting was an ordeal to him. He was in a fever of impatience. He considered that there was denoted a lack of purpose on the part of the generals. He began to complain to the tall soldier. "I can't stand this much longer," he cried. "I don't see what good it does to make us wear out our legs for nothin'." He wished to return to camp, knowing that this affair was a blue demonstration; or else to go into a battle and discover that he had been a fool in his doubts, and was, in truth, a man of traditional courage. The strain of present circumstances he felt to be intolerable.

The philosophical tall soldier measured a sandwich of cracker and pork and swallowed it in a nonchalant manner. "Oh, I suppose we must go reconnoitering around the country jest to keep 'em from getting too close, or to develop 'em, or something."

"Huh!" said the loud soldier.

"Well," cried the youth, still fidgeting, "I'd rather do anything 'most than go tramping 'round the country all day doing no good to nobody and jest tiring ourselves out."

"So would I," said the loud soldier. "It ain't right. I tell you if anybody with any sense was a-runnin' this army it—"

"Oh, shut up!" roared the tall private. "You little fool. You little damn' cuss. You ain't had that there coat and them pants on for six months, and yet you talk as if—"

"Well, I wanta do some fighting anyway," interrupted the other. "I didn't come here to walk. I could 'ave walked to home— 'round an' 'round the barn, if I jest wanted to walk."

The tall one, red-faced, swallowed another sandwich as if taking poison in despair.

But gradually, as he chewed, his face became again quiet and contented. He could not rage in fierce argument in the presence of such sandwiches. During his meals he always wore an air of blissful contemplation of the food he had swallowed. His spirit seemed then to be communing with the viands.

He accepted new environment and circumstance with great coolness, eating from his haversack at every opportunity. On the march he went along with the stride of a hunter, objecting to neither gait nor distance. And he had not raised his voice when he had been ordered away from three little protective piles of earth and stone, each of which had been an engineering feat worthy of being made sacred to the name of his grandmother.

In the afternoon the regiment went out over the same ground it had taken in the morning. The landscape then ceased to threaten the youth. He had been close to it and become familiar with it.

When, however, they began to pass into a new region, his old fears of stupidity and incompetence reassailed him, but this time he doggedly let them babble. He was occupied with his problem, and in his desperation he concluded that the stupidity did not greatly matter.

Once he thought he had concluded that it would be better to get killed directly and end his troubles. Regarding death thus out of the corner of his eye, he conceived it to be nothing but rest, and he was filled with a momentary astonishment that he should have made an extraordinary commotion over the mere matter of getting killed. He would die; he would go to some place where he would be understood. It was useless to expect appreciation of his profound and fine senses from such men as the lieutenant. He must look to the grave for comprehension.

The skirmish fire increased to a long clattering sound. With it was mingled far-away cheering. A battery spoke.

Directly the youth would[1] see the skirmishers running. They were pursued by the sound of musketry fire. After a time the hot, dangerous flashes of the rifles were visible. Smoke clouds went slowly and insolently across the fields like observant phantoms. The din became crescendo, like the roar of an oncoming train.

A brigade ahead of them and on the right went into action with a rending roar. It was as if it had exploded. And thereafter it lay stretched in the distance behind a long gray wall, that one was obliged to look twice at to make sure that it was smoke.

The youth, forgetting his neat plan of getting killed, gazed spell bound. His eyes grew wide and busy with the action of the scene. His mouth was a little ways open.

Of a sudden he felt a heavy and sad hand laid upon his shoulder. Awakening from his trance of observation he turned and beheld the loud soldier.

"It's my first and last battle, old boy," said the latter, with intense gloom. He was quite pale and his girlish lip was trembling.

"Eh?" murmured the youth in great astonishment.

"It's my first and last battle, old boy," continued the loud soldier. "Something tells me—"

"What?"

"I'm a gone coon this first time and—and I w-want you to take these here things—to—my—folks." He ended in a quavering sob of pity for himself. He handed the youth a little packet done up in a yellow envelope.

"Why, what the devil—" began the youth again.

But the other gave him a glance as from the depths of a tomb, and raised his limp hand in a prophetic manner and turned away.

---

1 Crane's manuscript reads: could.

Chapter IV

THE brigade was halted in the fringe of a grove. The men crouched among the trees and pointed their restless guns out at the fields. They tried to look beyond the smoke.

Out of this haze they could see running men. Some shouted information and gestured as they hurried.

The men of the new regiment watched and listened eagerly, while their tongues ran on in gossip of the battle. They mouthed rumors that had flown like birds out of the unknown.

"They say Perry has been driven in with big loss."

"Yes, Carrott went t' th' hospital. He said he was sick. That smart lieutenant is commanding 'G' Company. Th' boys say they won't be under Carrott no more if they all have t' desert. They allus knew he was a—"

"Hannises' batt'ry is took."

"It ain't either. I saw Hannises' batt'ry off on th' left not more'n fifteen minutes ago."

"Well—"

"Th' general, he ses he is goin' t' take th' hull cammand of th' 304th when we go inteh action, an' then he ses we'll do sech fightin' as never another one reg'ment done."[1]

"They say we're catchin' it over on th' left. They say th' enemy driv' our line inteh a devil of a swamp an' took Hannises' batt'ry."

"No sech thing. Hannises' batt'ry was 'long here 'bout a minute ago."

"That young Hasbrouck, he makes a good off'cer. He ain't afraid 'a nothin'."

"I met one of th' 148th Maine boys an' he ses his brigade fit th' hull rebel army fer four hours over on th' turnpike road an' killed about five thousand of 'em. He ses one more sech fight as that an' th' war 'll be over."

"Bill wasn't scared either. No, sir! It wasn't that. Bill ain't a-gittin' scared easy. He was jest mad, that's what he was. When that feller trod on his hand, he up an' sed that he was willin' t' give his hand t' his country, but he be dumbed if he was goin' t' have every dumb bushwhacker in th' kentry walkin' 'round on it. Se[2] he went t' th' hospital disregardless of th' fight. Three fingers

---

1   The New York regiments had no 304th.
2   Crane's manuscript reads: So.

was crunched. Th' dern doctor wanted t' amputate 'm, an' Bill, he raised a heluva row, I hear. He's a funny feller."

The din in front swelled to a tremendous chorus. The youth and his fellows were frozen to silence. They could see a flag that tossed in the smoke angrily. Near it were the blurred and agitated forms of troops. There came a turbulent stream of men across the fields. A battery changing position at a frantic gallop scattered the stragglers right and left.

A shell screaming like a storm banshee[1] went over the huddled heads of the reserves. It landed in the grove, and exploding redly flung the brown earth. There was a little shower of pine needles.

Bullets began to whistle among the branches and nip at the trees. Twigs and leaves came sailing down. It was as if a thousand axes, wee and invisible, were being wielded. Many of the men were constantly dodging and ducking their heads.

The lieutenant of the youth's company was shot in the hand. He began to swear so wondrously that a nervous laugh went along the regimental line. The officer's profanity sounded conventional. It relieved the tightened senses of the new men. It was as if he had hit his fingers with a tack hammer at home.

He held the wounded member carefully away from his side so that the blood would not drip upon his trousers.

The captain of the company, tucking his sword under his arm, produced a handkerchief and began to bind with it the lieutenant's wound. And they disputed as to how the binding should be done.

The battle flag in the distance jerked about madly. It seemed to be struggling to free itself from an agony. The billowing smoke was filled with horizontal flashes.

Men running swiftly emerged from it. They grew in numbers until it was seen that the whole command was fleeing. The flag suddenly sank down as if dying. Its motion as it fell was a gesture of despair.

Wild yells came from behind the walls of smoke. A sketch in gray and red dissolved into a moblike body of men who galloped like wild horses.

The veteran regiments on the right and left of the 304th immediately began to jeer. With the passionate song of the bullets and the banshee shrieks of shells were mingled loud catcalls and bits of facetious advice concerning places of safety.

But the new regiment was breathless with horror. "Gawd! Saunders's got crushed!" whispered the man at the youth's

---

1 A spirit who warns of impending death.

elbow. They shrank back and crouched as if compelled to await a flood.

The youth shot a swift glance along the blue ranks of the regiment. The profiles were motionless, carven; and afterward he remembered that the color sergeant[1] was standing with his legs apart, as if he expected to be pushed to the ground.

The following throng went whirling around the flank. Here and there were officers carried along on the stream like exasperated chips. They were striking about them with their swords and with their left fists, punching every head they could reach. They cursed like highway-men.

A mounted officer displayed the furious anger of a spoiled child. He raged with his head, his arms, and his legs.

Another, the commander of the brigade, was galloping about bawling. His hat was gone and his clothes were awry. He resembled a man who has come from bed to go to a fire. The hoofs of his horse often threatened the heads of the running men, but they scampered with singular fortune. In this rush they were apparently all deaf and blind. They heeded not the largest and longest of the oaths that were thrown at them from all directions.

Frequently over this tumult could be heard the grim jokes of the critical veterans; but the retreating men apparently were not even conscious of the presence of an audience.

The battle reflection that shone for an instant in the faces on the mad current made the youth feel that forceful hands from heaven would not have been able to have held him in place if he could have got intelligent control of his legs.

There was an appalling imprint upon these faces. The struggle in the smoke had pictured an exaggeration of itself on the bleached cheeks and in the eyes wild with one desire.

The sight of this stampede exerted a floodlike force that seemed able to drag sticks and stones and men from the ground. They of the reserves had to hold on. They grew pale and firm, and red and quaking.

The youth achieved one little thought in the midst of this chaos. The composite monster which had caused the other troops to flee had not then appeared. He resolved to get a view of it, and then, he thought he might very likely run better than the best of them.

---

1 The color sergeant carried the regimental flag.

Chapter V

THERE were moments of waiting. The youth thought of the village street at home before the arrival of the circus parade on a day in the spring. He remembered how he had stood, a small, thrillful boy, prepared to follow the dingy lady upon the white horse, or the band in its faded chariot. He saw the yellow road, the lines of expectant people, and the sober houses. He particularly remembered an old fellow who used to sit upon a cracker box in front of the store and feign to despise such exhibitions. A thousand details of color and form surged in his mind. The old fellow upon the cracker box appeared in middle prominence.

Some one cried, "Here they come!" ——→ *perspective shift*

There was rustling and muttering among the men. They displayed a feverish desire to have every possible cartridge ready to their hands. The boxes were pulled around into various positions, and adjusted with great care. It was as if seven hundred new bonnets were being tried on.

The tall soldier, having prepared his rifle, produced a red handkerchief of some kind. He was engaged in knitting[1] it about his throat with exquisite attention to its position, when the cry was repeated up and down the line in a muffled roar of sound.

"Here they come! Here they come!" Gun locks clicked.

Across the smoke-infested fields came a brown swarm of running men who were giving shrill yells. They came on, stooping and swinging their rifles at all angles. A flag, tilted forward, sped near the front.

As he caught sight of them the youth was momentarily startled by a thought that perhaps his gun was not loaded. He stood trying to rally his faltering intellect so that he might recollect the moment when he had loaded, but he could not.

A hatless general pulled his dripping horse to a stand near the colonel of the 304th. He shook his fist in the other's face. "You 've got to hold 'em back!" he shouted, savagely; "you 've got to hold 'em back!"

In his agitation the colonel began to stammer. "A-all r-right, General, all right, by Gawd! We we'll do our—we-we'll d-d-do—do our best, General." The general made a passionate gesture and galloped away. The colonel, perchance to relieve his feelings, began to scold like a wet parrot. The youth, turning swiftly to

---

1 Crane's manuscript reads: knotting.

make sure that the rear was unmolested, saw the commander regarding his men in a highly regretful manner, as if he regretted above everything his association with them.

The man at the youth's elbow was mumbling, as if to himself: "Oh, we 're in for it now! oh, we 're in for it now!"

The captain of the company had been pacing excitedly to and fro in the rear. He coaxed in schoolmistress fashion, as to a congregation of boys with primers. His talk was an endless repetition. "Reserve your fire, boys—don't shoot till I tell you—save your fire—wait till they get close up—don't be damned fools—"

Perspiration streamed down the youth's face, which was soiled like that of a weeping urchin. He frequently, with a nervous movement, wiped his eyes with his coat sleeve. His mouth was still a little ways open.

He got the one glance at the foe-swarming field in front of him, and instantly ceased to debate the question of his piece being loaded. Before he was ready to begin—before he had announced to himself that he was about to fight—he threw the obedient, well-balanced rifle into position and fired a first wild shot. Directly he was working at his weapon like an automatic affair.

He suddenly lost concern for himself, and forgot to look at a menacing fate. He became not a man but a member. He felt that something of which he was a part—a regiment, an army, a cause, or a country—was in a crisis. He was welded into a common personality which was dominated by a single desire. For some moments he could not flee no more than a little finger can commit a revolution from a hand.

If he had thought the regiment was about to be annihilated perhaps he could have amputated himself from it. But its noise gave him assurance. The regiment was like a firework that, once ignited, proceeds superior to circumstances until its blazing vitality fades. It wheezed and banged with a mighty power. He pictured the ground before it as strewn with the discomfited.

There was a consciousness always of the presence of his comrades about him. He felt the subtle battle brotherhood more potent even than the cause for which they were fighting. It was a mysterious fraternity born of the smoke and danger of death.

He was at a task. He was like a carpenter who has made many boxes, making still another box, only there was furious haste in his movements. He, in his thought, was careering off in other places, even as the carpenter who as he works whistles and thinks of his friend or his enemy, his home or a saloon. And these jolted dreams were never perfect to him afterward, but remained a mass of blurred shapes.

Presently he began to feel the effects of the war atmosphere— a blistering sweat, a sensation that his eyeballs were about to crack like hot stones. A burning roar filled his ears.

Following this came a red rage. He developed the acute exasperation of a pestered animal, a well-meaning cow worried by dogs. He had a mad feeling against his rifle, which could only be used against one life at a time. He wished to rush forward and strangle with his fingers. He craved a power that would enable him to make a world-sweeping gesture and brush all back. His impotency appeared to him, and made his rage into that of a driven beast.

Buried in the smoke of many rifles his anger was directed not so much against the men whom he knew were rushing toward him as against the swirling battle phantoms which were choking him, stuffing their smoke robes down his parched throat. He fought frantically for respite for his senses, for air, as a babe being smothered attacks the deadly blankets.

There was a blare of heated rage mingled with a certain expression of intentness on all faces. Many of the men were making low-toned noises with their mouths, and these subdued cheers, snarls, imprecations, prayers, made a wild, barbaric song that went as an undercurrent of sound, strange and chantlike with the resounding chords of the war march. The man at the youth's elbow was babbling. In it there was something soft and tender like the monologue of a babe. The tall soldier was swearing in a loud voice. From his lips came a black procession of curious oaths. Of a sudden another broke out in a querulous way like a man who has mislaid his hat. "Well, why don't they support us? Why don't they send supports? Do they think—"

The youth in his battle sleep heard this as one who dozes hears.

There was a singular absence of heroic poses. The men bending and surging in their haste and rage were in every impossible attitude. The steel ramrods clanked and clanged with incessant din as the men pounded them furiously into the hot rifle barrels. The flaps of the cartridge boxes were all unfastened, and bobbed idiotically with each movement. The rifles, once loaded, were jerked to the shoulder and fired without apparent aim into the smoke or at one of the blurred and shifting forms which upon the field before the regiment had been growing larger and larger like puppets under a magician's hand.

The officers, at their intervals, rearward, neglected to stand in picturesque attitudes. They were bobbing to and fro roaring directions and encouragements. The dimensions of their howls were extraordinary. They expended their lungs with prodigal wills. And often they nearly stood upon their heads in their anxiety to observe the enemy on the other side of the tumbling smoke.

The lieutenant of the youth's company had encountered a soldier who had fled screaming at the first volley of his comrades. Behind the lines these two were acting a little isolated scene. The man was blubbering and staring with sheeplike eyes at the lieutenant, who had seized him by the collar and was pommeling[1] him. He drove him back into the ranks with many blows. The soldier went mechanically, dully, with his animal-like eyes upon the officer. Perhaps there was to him a divinity expressed in the voice of the other—stern, hard, with no reflection of fear in it. He tried to reload his gun, but his shaking hands prevented. The lieutenant was obliged to assist him.

The men dropped here and there like bundles. The captain of the youth's company had been killed in an early part of the action. His body lay stretched out in the position of a tired man resting, but upon his face there was an astonished and sorrowful look, as if he thought some friend had done him an ill turn. The babbling man was grazed by a shot that made the blood stream widely down his face. He clapped both hands to his head. "Oh!" he said, and ran. Another grunted suddenly as if he had been struck by a club in the stomach. He sat down and gazed ruefully. In his eyes there was mute, indefinite reproach. Farther up the line a man, standing behind a tree, had had his knee joint splintered by a ball. Immediately he had dropped his rifle and gripped the tree with both arms. And there he remained, clinging desperately and crying for assistance that he might withdraw his hold upon the tree.

At last an exultant yell went along the quivering line. The firing dwindled from an uproar to a last vindictive popping. As the smoke slowly eddied away, the youth saw that the charge had been repulsed. The enemy were scattered into reluctant groups. He saw a man climb to the top of the fence, straddle the rail, and fire a parting shot. The waves had receded, leaving bits of dark *débris* upon the ground.

Some in the regiment began to whoop frenziedly. Many were silent. Apparently they were trying to contemplate themselves.

---

1   Crane most likely meant pummeling.

After the fever had left his veins, the youth thought that at last he was going to suffocate. He became aware of the foul atmosphere in which he had been struggling. He was grimy and dripping like a laborer in a foundry. He grasped his canteen and took a long swallow of the warmed water.

A sentence with variations went up and down the line. "Well, we 've helt 'em back. We 've helt 'em back; derned if we haven't." The men said it blissfully, leering at each other with dirty smiles.

The youth turned to look behind him and off to the right and off to the left. He experienced the joy of a man who at last finds leisure in which to look about him.

Under foot there were a few ghastly forms motionless. They lay twisted in fantastic contortions. Arms were bent and heads were turned in incredible ways. It seemed that the dead men must have fallen from some great height to get into such positions. They looked to be dumped out upon the ground from the sky.

From a position in the rear of the grove a battery was throwing shells over it. The flash of the guns startled the youth at first. He thought they were aimed directly at him. Through the trees he watched the black figures of the gunners as they worked swiftly and intently. Their labor seemed a complicated thing. He wondered how they could remember its formula in the midst of confusion.

The guns squatted in a row like savage chiefs. They argued with abrupt violence. It was a grim pow-wow. Their busy servants ran hither and thither.

A small procession of wounded men were going drearily toward the rear. It was a flow of blood from the torn body of the brigade.

To the right and to the left were the dark lines of other troops. Far in front he thought he could see lighter masses protruding in points from the forest. They were suggestive of unnumbered thousands.

Once he saw a tiny battery go dashing along the line of the horizon. The tiny riders were beating the tiny horses.

From a sloping hill came the sound of cheerings and clashes. Smoke welled slowly through the leaves.

Batteries were speaking with thunderous oratorical effort. Here and there were flags, the red in the stripes dominating. They splashed bits of warm color upon the dark lines of troops.

The youth felt the old thrill at the sight of the emblem. They were like beautiful birds strangely undaunted in a storm.

As he listened to the din from the hillside, to a deep pulsating thunder that came from afar to the left, and to the lesser clamors which came from many directions, it occurred to him that they were fighting, too, over there, and over there, and over there. Heretofore he had supposed that all the battle was directly under his nose.

As he gazed around him the youth felt a flash of astonishment at the blue, pure sky and the sun gleamings on the trees and fields. It was surprising that Nature had gone tranquilly on with her golden process in the midst of so much devilment.

Chapter VI

THE youth awakened slowly. He came gradually back to a position from which he could regard himself. For moments he had been scrutinizing his person in a dazed way as if he had never before seen himself. Then he picked up his cap from the ground. He wriggled in his jacket to make a more comfortable fit, and kneeling replaced his shoe. He thoughtfully mopped his reeking features.

So it was all over at last! The supreme trial had been passed. The red, formidable difficulties of war had been vanquished.

He went into an ecstasy of self-satisfaction. He had the most delightful sensations of his life. Standing as if apart from himself, he viewed that last scene. He perceived that the man who had fought thus was magnificent.

He felt that he was a fine fellow. He saw himself even with those ideals which he had considered as far beyond him. He smiled in deep gratification.

Upon his fellows he beamed tenderness and good will. "Gee! ain't it hot, hey?" he said affably to a man who was polishing his streaming face with his coat sleeves.

"You bet!" said the other, grinning sociably. "I never seen sech dumb hotness." He sprawled out luxuriously on the ground. "Gee, yes! An' I hope we don't have no more fightin' till a week from Monday."

There were some handshakings and deep speeches with men whose features were familiar, but with whom the youth now felt the bonds of tied hearts. He helped a cursing comrade to bind up a wound of the shin.

But, of a sudden, cries of amazement broke out along the ranks of the new regiment. "Here they come ag'in! Here they come ag'in!" The man who had sprawled upon the ground started up and said, "Gosh!"

The youth turned quick eyes upon the field. He discerned forms begin to swell in masses out of a distant wood. He again saw the tilted flag speeding forward.

The shells, which had ceased to trouble the regiment for a time, came swirling again, and exploded in the grass or among the leaves of the trees. They looked to be strange war flowers bursting into fierce bloom.

The men groaned. The luster faded from their eyes. Their smudged countenances now expressed a profound dejection.

They moved their stiffened bodies slowly, and watched in sullen mood the frantic approach of the enemy. The slaves toiling in the temple of this god began to feel rebellion at his harsh tasks.

They fretted and complained each to each. "Oh, say, this is too much of a good thing! Why can't somebody send us supports?"

"We ain't never goin' to stand this second banging. I didn't come here to fight the hull damn' rebel army."

There was one who raised a doleful cry. "I wish Bill Smithers had trod on my hand, insteader me treddin' on his'n." The sore joints of the regiment creaked as it painfully floundered into position to repulse.

The youth stared. Surely, he thought, this impossible thing was not about to happen. He waited as if he expected the enemy to suddenly stop, apologize, and retire bowing. It was all a mistake.

But the firing began somewhere on the regimental line and ripped along in both directions. The level sheets of flame developed great clouds of smoke that tumbled and tossed in the mild wind near the ground for a moment, and then rolled through the ranks as through a gate. The clouds were tinged an earthlike yellow in the sunrays and in the shadow were a sorry blue. The flag was sometimes eaten and lost in this mass of vapor, but more often it projected, sun-touched, resplendent.

Into the youth's eyes there came a look that one can see in the orbs of a jaded horse. His neck was quivering with nervous weakness and the muscles of his arms felt numb and bloodless. His hands, too, seemed large and awkward as if he was wearing invisible mittens. And there was a great uncertainty about his knee joints.

The words that comrades had uttered previous to the firing began to recur to him. "Oh, say, this is too much of a good thing! What do they take us for—why don't they send supports? I didn't come here to fight the hull damned rebel army."

He began to exaggerate the endurance, the skill, and the valor of those who were coming. Himself reeling from exhaustion, he was astonished beyond measure at such persistency. They must be machines of steel. It was very gloomy struggling against such affairs, wound up perhaps to fight until sundown.

He slowly lifted his rifle and catching a glimpse of the thick-spread field he blazed at a cantering cluster. He stopped then and began to peer as best he could through the smoke. He caught changing views of the ground covered with men who were all running like pursued imps, and yelling.

To the youth it was an onslaught of redoubtable dragons. He became like the man who lost his legs at the approach of the red and green monster. He waited in a sort of a horrified, listening attitude. He seemed to shut his eyes and wait to be gobbled.

A man near him who up to this time had been working feverishly at his rifle suddenly stopped and ran with howls. A lad whose face had borne an expression of exalted courage, the majesty of he who dares give his life, was, at an instant, smitten abject. He blanched like one who has come to the edge of a cliff at midnight and is suddenly made aware. There was a revelation. He, too, threw down his gun and fled. There was no shame in his face. He ran like a rabbit.

Others began to scamper away through the smoke. The youth turned his head, shaken from his trance by this movement as if the regiment was leaving him behind. He saw the few fleeting forms.

He yelled then with fright and swung about. For a moment, in the great clamor, he was like a proverbial chicken. He lost the direction of safety. Destruction threatened him from all points.

Directly he began to speed toward the rear in great leaps. His rifle and cap were gone. His unbuttoned coat bulged in the wind. The flap of his cartridge box bobbed wildly, and his canteen, by its slender cord, swung out behind. On his face was all the horror of those things which he imagined.

The lieutenant sprang forward bawling. The youth saw his features wrathfully red, and saw him make a dab with his sword. His one thought of the incident was that the lieutenant was a peculiar creature to feel interested in such matters upon this occasion.

He ran like a blind man. Two or three times he fell down. Once he knocked his shoulder so heavily against a tree that he went headlong.

Since he had turned his back upon the fight his fears had been wondrously magnified. Death about to thrust him between the shoulder blades was far more dreadful than death about to smite him between the eyes. When he thought of it later, he conceived the impression that it is better to view the appalling than to be merely within hearing. The noises of the battle were like stones; he believed himself liable to be crushed.

As he ran he mingled with others. He dimly saw men on his right and on his left, and he heard footsteps behind him. He thought that all the regiment was fleeing, pursued by these ominous crashes.

In his flight the sound of these following footsteps gave him his one meager relief. He felt vaguely that death must make a first choice of the men who were nearest; the initial morsels for the dragons would be then those who were following him. So he displayed the zeal of an insane sprinter in his purpose to keep them in the rear. There was a race.

As he, leading, went across a little field, he found himself in a region of shells. They hurtled over his head with long wild screams. As he listened he imagined them to have rows of cruel teeth that grinned at him. Once one lit before him and the livid lightning of the explosion effectually barred the way in his chosen direction. He groveled on the ground and then springing up went careering off through some bushes.

He experienced a thrill of amazement when he came within view of a battery in action. The men there seemed to be in conventional moods, altogether unaware of the impending annihilation. The battery was disputing with a distant antagonist and the gunners were wrapped in admiration of their shooting. They were continually bending in coaxing postures over the guns. They seemed to be patting them on the back and encouraging them with words. The guns, stolid and undaunted, spoke with dogged valor.

The precise gunners were coolly enthusiastic. They lifted their eyes every chance to the smoke wreathed hillock from whence the hostile battery addressed them. The youth pitied them as he ran. Methodical idiots! Machine-like fools! The refined joy of planting shells in the midst of the other battery's formation would appear a little thing when the infantry came swooping out of the woods.

The face of a youthful rider, who was jerking his frantic horse with an abandon of temper he might display in a placid barnyard, was impressed deeply upon his mind. He knew that he looked upon a man who would presently be dead.

Too, he felt a pity for the guns, standing, six good comrades, in a bold row.

He saw a brigade going to the relief of its pestered fellows. He scrambled upon a wee hill and watched it sweeping finely, keeping formation in difficult places. The blue of the line was crusted with steel color, and the brilliant flags projected. Officers were shouting.

This sight also filled him with wonder. The brigade was hurrying briskly to be gulped into the infernal mouths of the war god. What manner of men were they, anyhow? Ah, it was some wondrous breed! Or else they didn't comprehend—the fools.

A furious order caused commotion in the artillery. An officer on a bounding horse made maniacal motions with his arms. The teams went swinging up from the rear, the guns were whirled about, and the battery scampered away. The cannon with their noses poked slantingly at the ground grunted and grumbled like stout men, brave but with objections to hurry.

The youth went on, moderating his pace since he had left the place of noises.

Later he came upon a general of division seated upon a horse that pricked its ears in an interested way at the battle. There was a great gleaming of yellow and patent leather about the saddle and bridle. The quiet man astride looked mouse-colored upon such a splendid charger.

A jingling staff was galloping hither and thither. Sometimes the general was surrounded by horsemen and at other times he was quite alone. He looked to be much harassed. He had the appearance of a business man whose market is swinging up and down.

The youth went slinking around this spot. He went as near as he dared trying to overhear words. Perhaps the general, unable to comprehend chaos, might call upon him for information. And he could tell him. He knew all concerning it. Of a surety the force was in a fix, and any fool could see that if they did not retreat while they had opportunity—why—

He felt that he would like to thrash the general, or at least approach and tell him in plain words exactly what he thought him to be. It was criminal to stay calmly in one spot and make no effort to stay destruction. He loitered in a fever of eagerness for the division commander to apply to him.

As he warily moved about, he heard the general call out irritably: "Tompkins, go over an' see Taylor, an' tell him not t' be in such an all all-fired hurry; tell him t' halt his brigade in th' edge of th' woods; tell him t' detach a reg'ment—say I think th' center 'll break if we don't help it out some; tell him t' hurry up."

A slim youth on a fine chestnut horse caught these swift words from the mouth of his superior. He made his horse bound into a gallop almost from a walk in his haste to go upon his mission. There was a cloud of dust.

A moment later the youth saw the general bounce excitedly in his saddle.

"Yes, by heavens, they have!" The officer leaned forward. His face was aflame with excitement. "Yes, by heavens, they 've held 'im! They 've held 'im!"

He began to blithely roar at his staff: "We 'll wallop 'im now. We 'll wallop 'im now. We 've got 'em sure." He turned suddenly upon an aid:[1] "Here—you—Jones—quick—ride after Tompkins—see Taylor—tell him t' go in—everlastingly—like blazes—anything."

As another officer sped his horse after the first messenger, the general beamed upon the earth like a sun. In his eyes was a desire to chant a paean.[2] He kept repeating, "They 've held 'em, by heavens!"

His excitement made his horse plunge, and he merrily kicked and swore at it. He held a little carnival of joy on horseback.

---

1 Crane's manuscript reads: aide.
2 A joyous song of praise.

Chapter VII

THE youth cringed as if discovered in a crime. By heavens, they had won after all! The imbecile line had remained and become victors. He could hear cheering.

He lifted himself upon his toes and looked in the direction of the fight. A yellow fog lay wallowing on the treetops. From beneath it came the clatter of musketry. Hoarse cries told of an advance.

He turned away amazed and angry. He felt that he had been wronged.

He had fled, he told himself, because annihilation approached. He had done a good part in saving himself, who was a little piece of the army. He had considered the time, he said, to be one in which it was the duty of every little piece to rescue itself if possible. Later the officers could fit the little pieces together again, and make a battle front. If none of the little pieces were wise enough to save themselves from the flurry of death at such a time, why, then, where would be the army? It was all plain that he had proceeded according to very correct and commendable rules. His actions had been sagacious things. They had been full of strategy. They were the work of a master's legs.

Thoughts of his comrades came to him. The brittle blue line had withstood the blows and won. He grew bitter over it. It seemed that the blind ignorance and stupidity of those little pieces had betrayed him. He had been overturned and crushed by their lack of sense in holding the position, when intelligent deliberation would have convinced them that it was impossible. He, the enlightened man who looks afar in the dark, had fled because of his superior perceptions and knowledge. He felt a great anger against his comrades. He knew it could be proved that they had been fools.

He wondered what they would remark when later he appeared in camp. His mind heard howls of derision. Their density would not enable them to understand his sharper point of view.

He began to pity himself acutely. He was ill used. He was trodden beneath the feet of an iron injustice. He had proceeded with wisdom and from the most righteous motives under heaven's blue only to be frustrated by hateful circumstances.

A dull, animal-like rebellion against his fellows, war in the abstract, and fate grew within him. He shambled along with bowed head, his brain in a tumult of agony and despair. When he looked loweringly up, quivering at each sound, his eyes had the expression of those of a criminal who thinks his guilt and his punishment great, and knows that he can find no words.

He went from the fields into a thick woods, as if resolved to bury himself. He wished to get out of hearing of the crackling shots which were to him like voices.

The ground was cluttered with vines and bushes, and the trees grew close and spread out like bouquets. He was obliged to force his way with much noise. The creepers, catching against his legs, cried out harshly as their sprays were torn from the barks of trees. The swishing saplings tried to make known his presence to the world. He could not conciliate the forest. As he made his way, it was always calling out protestations. When he separated embraces of trees and vines the disturbed foliages waved their arms and turned their face leaves toward him. He dreaded lest these noisy motions and cries should bring men to look at him. So he went far, seeking dark and intricate places.

After a time the sound of musketry grew faint and the cannon boomed in the distance. The sun, suddenly apparent, blazed among the trees. The insects were making rhythmical noises. They seemed to be grinding their teeth in unison. A woodpecker stuck his impudent head around the side of a tree. A bird flew on lighthearted wing.

Off was the rumble of death. It seemed now that Nature had no ears.

This landscape gave him assurance. A fair field holding life. It was the religion of peace. It would die if its timid eyes were compelled to see blood. He conceived Nature to be a woman with a deep aversion to tragedy.

He threw a pine cone at a jovial squirrel, and he ran with chattering fear. High in a treetop he stopped, and, poking his head cautiously from behind a branch, looked down with an air of trepidation.

The youth felt triumphant at this exhibition. There was the law, he said. Nature had given him a sign. The squirrel, immediately upon recognizing danger, had taken to his legs without ado. He did not stand stolidly baring his furry belly to the missile, and die with an upward glance at the sympathetic heavens. On the contrary, he had fled as fast as his legs could carry him; and he was but an ordinary squirrel, too—doubtless no philosopher of his race. The youth wended, feeling that Nature was of his mind. She re-enforced his argument with proofs that lived where the sun shone.

Once he found himself almost into a swamp. He was obliged to walk upon bog tufts and watch his feet to keep from the oily mire. Pausing at one time to look about him he saw, out at some black water, a small animal pounce in and emerge directly with a gleaming fish.

The youth went again into the deep thickets. The brushed branches made a noise that drowned the sounds of cannon. He walked on, going from obscurity into promises of a greater obscurity.

At length he reached a place where the high, arching boughs made a chapel. He softly pushed the green doors aside and entered. Pine needles were a gentle brown carpet. There was a religious half light.

Near the threshold he stopped, horror-stricken at the sight of a thing.

He was being looked at by a dead man who was seated with his back against a columnlike tree. The corpse was dressed in a uniform that once had been blue, but was now faded to a melancholy shade of green. The eyes, staring at the youth, had changed to the dull hue to be seen on the side of a dead fish. The mouth was open. Its red had changed to an appalling yellow. Over the gray skin of the face ran little ants. One was trundling some sort of a bundle along the upper lip.

The youth gave a shriek as he confronted the thing. He was for moments turned to stone before it. He remained staring into the liquid looking eyes. The dead man and the living man exchanged a long look. Then the youth cautiously put one hand behind him and brought it against a tree. Leaning upon this he retreated, step by step, with his face still toward the thing. He feared that if he turned his back the body might spring up and stealthily pursue him.

The branches, pushing against him, threatened to throw him over upon it. His unguided feet, too, caught aggravatingly in brambles; and with it all he received a subtle suggestion to touch the corpse. As he thought of his hand upon it he shuddered profoundly.

At last he burst the bonds which had fastened him to the spot and fled, unheeding the underbrush. He was pursued by a sight of the black ants swarming greedily upon the gray face and venturing horribly near to the eyes.

After a time he paused, and, breathless and panting, listened. He imagined some strange voice would come from the dead throat and squawk after him in horrible menaces.

The trees about the portal of the chapel moved soughingly in a soft wind. A sad silence was upon the little guarding edifice.

Chapter VIII

THE trees began softly to sing a hymn of twilight. The sun sank until slanted bronze rays struck the forest. There was a lull in the noises of insects as if they had bowed their beaks and were making a devotional pause. There was silence save for the chanted chorus of the trees.

Then, upon this stillness, there suddenly broke a tremendous clangor of sounds. A crimson roar came from the distance.

The youth stopped. He was transfixed by this terrific medley of all noises. It was as if worlds were being rended. There was the ripping sound of musketry and the breaking crash of the artillery.

His mind flew in all directions. He conceived the two armies to be at each other panther fashion. He listened for a time. Then he began to run in the direction of the battle. He saw that it was an ironical thing for him to be running thus toward that which he had been at such pains to avoid. But he said, in substance, to himself that if the earth and the moon were about to clash, many persons would doubtless plan to get upon the roofs to witness the collision.

As he ran, he became aware that the forest had stopped its music, as if at last becoming capable of hearing the foreign sounds. The trees hushed and stood motionless. Everything seemed to be listening to the crackle and clatter and earshaking thunder. The chorus pealed over the still earth.

It suddenly occurred to the youth that the fight in which he had been was, after all, but perfunctory popping. In the hearing of this present din he was doubtful if he had seen real battle scenes. This uproar explained a celestial battle; it was tumbling hordes a-struggle in the air.

Reflecting, he saw a sort of a humor in the point of view of himself and his fellows during the late encounter. They had taken themselves and the enemy very seriously and had imagined that they were deciding the war. Individuals must have supposed that they were cutting the letters of their names deep into everlasting tablets of brass, or enshrining their reputations forever in the hearts of their countrymen, while, as to fact, the affair would appear in printed reports under a meek and immaterial title. But he saw that it was good, else, he said, in battle every one would surely run save forlorn hopes and their ilk.

He went rapidly on. He wished to come to the edge of the forest that he might peer out.

As he hastened, there passed through his mind pictures of stupendous conflicts. His accumulated thought upon such subjects was used to form scenes. The noise was as the voice of an eloquent being, describing.

Sometimes the brambles formed chains and tried to hold him back. Trees, confronting him, stretched out their arms and forbade him to pass. After its previous hostility this new resistance of the forest filled him with a fine bitterness. It seemed that Nature could not be quite ready to kill him.

But he obstinately took roundabout ways, and presently he was where he could see long gray walls of vapor where lay battle lines. The voices of cannon shook him. The musketry sounded in long irregular surges that played havoc with his ears. He stood regardant for a moment. His eyes had an awestruck expression. He gawked in the direction of the fight.

Presently he proceeded again on his forward way. The battle was like the grinding of an immense and terrible machine to him. Its complexities and powers, its grim processes, fascinated him. He must go close and see it produce corpses.

He came to a fence and clambered over it. On the far side, the ground was littered with clothes and guns. A newspaper, folded up, lay in the dirt. A dead soldier was stretched with his face hidden in his arm. Farther off there was a group of four or five corpses keeping mournful company. A hot sun had blazed upon the spot.

In this place the youth felt that he was an invader. This forgotten part of the battle ground was owned by the dead men, and he hurried, in the vague apprehension that one of the swollen forms would rise and tell him to begone.

He came finally to a road from which he could see in the distance dark and agitated bodies of troops, smoke-fringed. In the lane was a blood-stained crowd streaming to the rear. The wounded men were cursing, groaning, and wailing. In the air, always, was a mighty swell of sound that it seemed could sway the earth. With the courageous words of the artillery and the spiteful sentences of the musketry mingled red cheers. And from this region of noises came the steady current of the maimed.

One of the wounded men had a shoeful of blood. He hopped like a schoolboy in a game. He was laughing hysterically.

One was swearing that he had been shot in the arm through the commanding general's mismanagement of the army. One was marching with an air imitative of some sublime drum major. Upon his features was an unholy mixture of merriment and

agony. As he marched he sang a bit of doggerel in a high and quavering voice:

> "Sing a song 'a vic'try,
>> A pocketful 'a bullets,
> Five an' twenty dead men
>> Baked in a—pie."

Parts of the procession limped and staggered to this tune.

Another had the gray seal of death already upon his face. His
lips were curled in hard lines and his teeth were clinched. His
hands were bloody from where he had pressed them upon his
wound. He seemed to be awaiting the moment when he should
pitch headlong. He stalked like the specter of a soldier, his eyes
burning with the power of a stare into the unknown.

There were some who proceeded sullenly, full of anger at their
wounds, and ready to turn upon anything as an obscure cause.

An officer was carried along by two privates. He was peevish.
"Don't joggle so, Johnson, yeh fool," he cried. "Think m' leg is
made of iron? If yeh can't carry me decent, put me down an' let
some one else do it."

He bellowed at the tottering crowd who blocked the quick
march of his bearers. "Say, make way there, can't yeh? Make way,
dickens take it all."

They sulkily parted and went to the roadsides. As he was
carried past they made pert remarks to him. When he raged in
reply and threatened them, they told him to be damned.

The shoulder of one of the tramping bearers knocked heavily
against the spectral soldier who was staring into the unknown.

The youth joined this crowd and marched along with it. The
torn bodies expressed the awful machinery in which the men had
been entangled.

Orderlies and couriers occasionally broke through the throng
in the roadway, scattering wounded men right and left, galloping
on followed by howls. The melancholy march was continually disturbed by the messengers, and sometimes by bustling batteries
that came swinging and thumping down upon them, the officers
shouting orders to clear the way.

There was a tattered man, fouled with dust, blood and powder
stain from hair to shoes, who trudged quietly at the youth's side.
He was listening with eagerness and much humility to the lurid
descriptions of a bearded sergeant. His lean features wore an
expression of awe and admiration. He was like a listener in a
country store to wondrous tales told among the sugar barrels. He

eyed the story-teller with unspeakable wonder. His mouth was agape in yokel fashion.

The sergeant, taking note of this, gave pause to his elaborate history while he administered a sardonic comment. "Be keerful, honey, you 'll be a-ketchin' flies," he said.

The tattered man shrank back abashed.

After a time he began to sidle near to the youth, and in a different way try to make him a friend. His voice was gentle as a girl's voice and his eyes were pleading. The youth saw with surprise that the soldier had two wounds, one in the head, bound with a blood-soaked rag, and the other in the arm, making that member dangle like a broken bough.

After they had walked together for some time the tattered man mustered sufficient courage to speak. "Was pretty good fight, wa'n't it?" he timidly said. The youth, deep in thought, glanced up at the bloody and grim figure with its lamblike eyes. "What?"

"Was pretty good fight, wa'n't it?"

"Yes," said the youth shortly. He quickened his pace.

But the other hobbled industriously after him. There was an air of apology in his manner, but he evidently thought that he needed only to talk for a time, and the youth would perceive that he was a good fellow.

"Was pretty good fight, wa'n't it?" he began in a small voice, and then he achieved the fortitude to continue. "Dern me if I ever see fellers fight so. Laws, how they did fight! I knowed th' boys 'd like[1] when they onct got square at it. Th' boys ain't had no fair chanct up t' now, but this time they showed what they was. I knowed it 'd turn out this way. Yeh can't lick them boys. No, sir! They're fighters, they be."

He breathed a deep breath of humble admiration. He had looked at the youth for encouragement several times. He received none, but gradually he seemed to get absorbed in his subject.

"I was talkin' 'cross pickets with a boy from Georgie, onct, an' that boy, he ses, 'Your fellers 'll all run like hell when they onct hearn a gun,' he ses. 'Mebbe they will,' I ses, 'but I don't b'lieve none of it,' I ses; 'an' b'jiminey,' I ses back t' 'um, 'mebbe your fellers 'll all run like hell when they onct hearn a gun,' I ses. He larfed. Well, they didn't run t' day, did they, hey? No, sir! They fit, an' fit, an' fit."

---

1 Crane's manuscript reads: lick.

His homely face was suffused with a light of love for the army which was to him all things beautiful and powerful.

After a time he turned to the youth. "Where yeh hit, ol' boy?" he asked in a brotherly tone.

The youth felt instant panic at this question, although at first its full import was not borne in upon him.

"What?" he asked.

"Where yeh hit?" repeated the tattered man.

"Why," began the youth, "I—I—that is—why—I—"

He turned away suddenly and slid through the crowd. His brow was heavily flushed, and his fingers were picking nervously at one of his buttons. He bent his head and fastened his eyes studiously upon the button as if it were a little problem.

The tattered man looked after him in astonishment.

Chapter IX

THE youth fell back in the procession until the tattered soldier was not in sight. Then he started to walk on with the others.

But he was amid wounds. The mob of men was bleeding. Because of the tattered soldier's question he now felt that his shame could be viewed. He was continually casting sidelong glances to see if the men were contemplating the letters of guilt he felt burned into his brow.

At times he regarded the wounded soldiers in an envious way. He conceived persons with torn bodies to be peculiarly happy. He wished that he, too, had a wound, a red badge of courage.

The spectral soldier was at his side like a stalking reproach. The man's eyes were still fixed in a stare into the unknown. His gray, appalling face had attracted attention in the crowd, and men, slowing to his dreary pace, were walking with him. They were discussing his plight, questioning him and giving him advice. In a dogged way he repelled them, signing to them to go on and leave him alone. The shadows of his face were deepening and his tight lips seemed holding in check the moan of great despair. There could be seen a certain stiffness in the movements of his body, as if he were taking infinite care not to arouse the passion of his wounds. As he went on, he seemed always looking for a place, like one who goes to choose a grave.

Something in the gesture of the man as he waved the bloody and pitying soldiers away made the youth start as if bitten. He yelled in horror. Tottering forward he laid a quivering hand upon the man's arm. As the latter slowly turned his waxlike features toward him, the youth screamed:

"Gawd! Jim Conklin!"

The tall soldier made a little commonplace smile. "Hello, Henry," he said.

The youth swayed on his legs and glared strangely. He stuttered and stammered. "Oh, Jim—oh, Jim—oh, Jim—"

The tall soldier held out his gory hand. There was a curious red and black combination of new blood and old blood upon it. "Where yeh been, Henry?" he asked. He continued in a monotonous voice, "I thought mebbe yeh got keeled over. There 's been thunder t' pay t' day. I was worryin' about it a good deal."

The youth still lamented. "Oh, Jim—oh, Jim—oh, Jim—"

"Yeh know," said the tall soldier, "I was out there." He made a careful gesture. "An', Lord, what a circus! An', b'jiminey, I got shot—I got shot. Yes, b'jiminey, I got shot." He reiterated this fact in a bewildered way, as if he did not know how it came about.

The youth put forth anxious arms to assist him, but the tall soldier went firmly on as if propelled. Since the youth's arrival as a guardian for his friend, the other wounded men had ceased to display much interest. They occupied themselves again in dragging their own tragedies toward the rear.

Suddenly, as the two friends marched on, the tall soldier seemed to be overcome by a terror. His face turned to a semblance of gray paste. He clutched the youth's arm and looked all about him, as if dreading to be overheard. Then he began to speak in a shaking whisper:

"I tell yeh what I'm 'fraid of, Henry—I 'll tell yeh what I 'm 'fraid of. I 'm 'fraid I 'll fall down—an' then yeh know—them damned artillery wagons—they like as not 'll run over me. That 's what I 'm 'fraid of—"

The youth cried out to him hysterically: "I 'll take care of yeh, Jim! I'll take care of yeh! I swear t' Gawd I will!"

"Sure—will yeh, Henry?" the tall soldier beseeched.

"Yes—yes—I tell yeh—I'll take care of yeh, Jim!" protested the youth. He could not speak accurately because of the gulpings in his throat.

But the tall soldier continued to beg in a lowly way. He now hung babelike to the youth's arm. His eyes rolled in the wildness of his terror. "I was allus a good friend t' yeh, wa'n't I, Henry? I 've allus been a pretty good feller, ain't I? An' it ain't much t' ask, is it? Jest t' pull me along outer th' road? I 'd do it fer you, Wouldn't I, Henry?"

He paused in piteous anxiety to await his friend's reply.

The youth had reached an anguish where the sobs scorched him. He strove to express his loyalty, but he could only make fantastic gestures.

However, the tall soldier seemed suddenly to forget all those fears. He became again the grim, stalking specter of a soldier. He went stonily forward. The youth wished his friend to lean upon him, but the other always shook his head and strangely protested. "No—no—no—leave me be—leave me be—"

His look was fixed again upon the unknown. He moved with mysterious purpose, and all of the youth's offers he brushed aside. "No—no—leave me be—leave me be—"

The youth had to follow.

Presently the latter heard a voice talking softly near his shoulders. Turning he saw that it belonged to the tattered soldier. "Ye 'd better take 'im outa th' road, pardner. There 's a batt'ry comin' helitywhoop down th' road an' he 'll git runned over. He 's a goner anyhow in about five minutes—yeh kin see that. Ye 'd better take 'im outa th' road. Where th' blazes does he git his stren'th from?"

"Lord knows!" cried the youth. He was shaking his hands helplessly.

He ran forward presently and grasped the tall soldier by the arm. "Jim! Jim!" he coaxed, "come with me."

The tall soldier weakly tried to wrench himself free. "Huh," he said vacantly. He stared at the youth for a moment. At last he spoke as if dimly comprehending. "Oh! Inteh th' fields? Oh!"

He started blindly through the grass.

The youth turned once to look at the lashing riders and jouncing guns of the battery. He was startled from this view by a shrill outcry from the tattered man.

"Gawd! He's runnin'!"

Turning his head swiftly, the youth saw his friend running in a staggering and stumbling way toward a little clump of bushes. His heart seemed to wrench itself almost free from his body at this sight. He made a noise of pain. He and the tattered man began a pursuit. There was a singular race.

When he overtook the tall soldier he began to plead with all the words he could find. "Jim—Jim—what are you doing—what makes you do this way—you 'll hurt yerself."

The same purpose was in the tall soldier's face. He protested in a dulled way, keeping his eyes fastened on the mystic place of his intentions. "No—no—don't tech me—leave me be—leave me be—"

The youth, aghast and filled with wonder at the tall soldier, began quaveringly to question him. "Where yeh goin', Jim? What you thinking about? Where you going? Tell me, won't you, Jim?"

The tall soldier faced about as upon relentless pursuers. In his eyes there was a great appeal. "Leave me be, can't yeh? Leave me be fer a minnit."

The youth recoiled. "Why, Jim," he said, in a dazed way, "what's the matter with you?"

The tall soldier turned and, lurching dangerously, went on. The youth and the tattered soldier followed, sneaking as if whipped, feeling unable to face the stricken man if he should again confront them. They began to have thoughts of a solemn ceremony. There was something rite like in these movements of the doomed soldier. And there was a resemblance in him to a devotee of a mad religion, blood sucking, muscle wrenching, bone crushing. They were awed and afraid. They hung back lest he have at command a dreadful weapon.

At last, they saw him stop and stand motionless. Hastening up, they perceived that his face wore an expression telling that he had at last found the place for which he had struggled. His spare figure was erect; his bloody hands were quietly at his side. He was waiting with patience for something that he had come to meet. He was at the rendezvous. They paused and stood, expectant.

There was a silence.

Finally, the chest of the doomed soldier began to heave with a strained motion. It increased in violence until it was as if an animal was within and was kicking and tumbling furiously to be free.

This spectacle of gradual strangulation made the youth writhe, and once as his friend rolled his eyes, he saw something in them that made him sink wailing to the ground. He raised his voice in a last supreme call.

"Jim—Jim—Jim—"

The tall soldier opened his lips and spoke. He made a gesture. "Leave me be—don't tech me—leave me be—"

There was another silence while he waited.

Suddenly, his form stiffened and straightened. Then it was shaken by a prolonged ague. He stared into space. To the two watchers there was a curious and profound dignity in the firm lines of his awful face.

He was invaded by a creeping strangeness that slowly enveloped him. For a moment the tremor of his legs caused him to dance a sort of hideous hornpipe. His arms beat wildly about his head in expression of implike enthusiasm.

His tall figure stretched itself to its full height. There was a slight rending sound. Then it began to swing forward, slow and straight, in the manner of a falling tree. A swift muscular contortion made the left shoulder strike the ground first.

The body seemed to bounce a little way from the earth. "God!" said the tattered soldier.

The youth had watched, spellbound, this ceremony at the place of meeting. His face had been twisted into an expression of every agony he had imagined for his friend.

He now sprang to his feet and, going closer, gazed upon the pastelike face. The mouth was open and the teeth showed in a laugh.

As the flap of the blue jacket fell away from the body, he could see that the side looked as if it had been chewed by wolves.

The youth turned, with sudden, livid rage, toward the battle-field. He shook his fist. He seemed about to deliver a philippic.[1]

"Hell—"

The red sun was pasted in the sky like a wafer.

---

1   A bitter speech of denunciation. The term derives from orations by Demosthenes, an Athenian orator (4th century BCE), against Philip, King of Macedon. The word is thus an eponym and should be capitalized.

Chapter X

THE tattered man stood musing.

"Well, he was reg'lar jim-dandy fer nerve, wa'n't he," said he finally in a little awestruck voice. "A reg'lar jim-dandy." He thoughtfully poked one of the docile hands with his foot. "I wonner where he got 'is stren'th from? I never seen a man do like that before. It was a funny thing. Well, he was a reg'lar jim-dandy."

The youth desired to screech out his grief. He was stabbed, but his tongue lay dead in the tomb of his mouth. He threw himself again upon the ground and began to brood.

The tattered man stood musing.

"Look-a-here, pardner," he said, after a time. He regarded the corpse as he spoke. "He 's up an' gone, ain't 'e, an' we might as well begin t' look out fer ol' number one. This here thing is all over. He 's up an' gone, ain't 'e? An' he 's all right here. Nobody won't bother 'im. An' I must say I ain't enjoying any great health m'self these days."

The youth, awakened by the tattered soldier's tone, looked quickly up. He saw that he was swinging uncertainly on his legs and that his face had turned to a shade of blue.

"Good Lord!" he cried, "you ain't goin' t'—not you, too."

The tattered man waved his hand. "Nary die," he said. "All I want is some pea soup an' a good bed. Some pea soup," he repeated dreamfully.

The youth arose from the ground. "I wonder where he came from. I left him over there." He pointed. "And now I find 'im here. And he was coming from over there, too." He indicated a new direction. They both turned toward the body as if to ask of it a question.

"Well," at length spoke the tattered man, "there ain't no use in our stayin' here an' tryin' t' ask him anything."

The youth nodded an assent wearily. They both turned to gaze for a moment at the corpse.

The youth murmured something.

"Well, he was a jim-dandy, wa'n't 'e?" said the tattered man as if in response.

They turned their backs upon it and started away. For a time they stole softly, treading with their toes. It remained laughing there in the grass.

"I'm commencin' t' feel pretty bad," said the tattered man, suddenly breaking one of his little silences. "I'm commencin' t' feel pretty damn' bad."

The youth groaned. "O Lord!" He wondered if he was to be the tortured witness of another grim encounter.

But his companion waved his hand reassuringly. "Oh, I'm not goin' t' die yit! There too much dependin' on me fer me t' die yit. No, sir! Nary die! I *can't!* Ye'd oughta see th' swad a' chil'ren I've got, an' all like that."

The youth glancing at his companion could see by the shadow of a smile that he was making some kind of fun.

As they plodded on the tattered soldier continued to talk. "Besides, if I died, I wouldn't die th' way that feller did. That was th' funniest thing. I'd jest flop down, I would. I never seen a feller die th' way that feller did.

"Yeh know Tom Jamison, he lives next door t' me up home. He's a nice feller, he is, an' we was allus good friends. Smart, too. Smart as a steel trap. Well, when we was a-fightin' this afternoon, all-of-a-sudden he begin t' rip up an' cuss an' beller at me. 'Yer shot, yeh blamed infernal!'—he swear horrible—he ses t' me. I put up m' hand t' m' head an' when I looked at m' fingers, I seen, sure 'nough, I was shot. I give a holler an' begin t' run, but b'fore I could git away another one hit me in th' arm an' whirl' me clean 'round. I got skeared when they was all a shootin' b'hind me an' I run t' beat all, but I cotch it pretty bad. I've an idee I'd a' been fightin' yit, if t'was n't fer Tom Jamison."

Then he made a calm announcement: "There's two of 'em— little ones—but they 're beginnin' t' have fun with me now. I don't b'lieve I kin walk much furder."

They went slowly on in silence. "Yeh look pretty peek-ed yerself," said the tattered man at last. "I bet yeh 've got a worser one than yeh think. Ye'd better take keer of yer hurt. It don't do t' let sech things go. It might be inside mostly, an' them plays thunder. Where is it located?" But he continued his harangue without waiting for a reply. "I see 'a feller git hit plum in th' head when my reg'ment was a standin' at ease onct. An' everybody yelled out to 'im: Hurt, John? Are yeh hurt much? 'No,' ses he. He looked kinder surprised, an' he went on tellin' 'em how he felt. He sed he didn't feel nothin'. But, by dad, th' first thing that feller knowed he was dead. Yes, he was dead—stone dead. So, yeh wanta watch out. Yeh might have some queer kind 'a hurt yerself. Yeh can't never tell. Where is your'n located?"

The youth had been wriggling since the introduction of this topic. He now gave a cry of exasperation and made a furious motion with his hand. "Oh, don't bother me!" he said. He was enraged against the tattered man, and could have strangled him.

His companions seemed ever to play intolerable parts. They were ever upraising the ghost of shame on the stick of their curiosity. He turned toward the tattered man as one at bay. "Now, don't bother me," he repeated with desperate menace.

"Well, Lord knows I don't wanta bother anybody," said the other. There was a little accent of despair in his voice as he replied, "Lord knows I 've gota 'nough m' own t' tend to."

The youth, who had been holding a bitter debate with himself and casting glances of hatred and contempt at the tattered man, here spoke in a hard voice. "Good by," he said.

The tattered man looked at him in gaping amazement. "Why—why, pardner, where yeh goin'?" he asked unsteadily. The youth looking at him, could see that he, too, like that other one, was beginning to act dumb and animal-like. His thoughts seemed to be floundering about in his head. "Now—now—look—a—here, you Tom Jamison—now—I won't have this—this here won't do. Where—where yeh goin'?"

The youth pointed vaguely. "Over there," he replied.

"Well, now look—a—here—now," said the tattered man, rambling on in idiot fashion. His head was hanging forward and his words were slurred. "This thing won't do, now, Tom Jamison. It won't do. I know yeh, yeh pig-headed devil. Yeh wanta go trompin' off with a bad hurt. It ain't right—now—Tom Jamison—it ain't. Yeh wanta leave me take keer of yeh, Tom Jamison. It ain't—right—it ain't—fer yeh t' go—trompin' off—with a bad hurt—it ain't—ain't—ain't right—it ain't."

In reply the youth climbed a fence and started away. He could hear the tattered man bleating plaintively.

Once he faced about angrily. "What?"

"Look—a—here, now, Tom Jamison—now—it ain't—"

The youth went on. Turning at a distance he saw the tattered man wandering about helplessly in the field.

He now thought that he wished he was dead. He believed that he envied those men whose bodies lay strewn over the grass of the fields and on the fallen leaves of the forest.

The simple questions of the tattered man had been knife thrusts to him. They asserted a society that probes pitilessly at secrets until all is apparent. His late companion's chance persistency made him feel that he could not keep his crime concealed in his bosom. It was sure to be brought plain by one of those arrows which cloud the air and are constantly pricking, discovering, proclaiming those things which are willed to be forever hidden. He admitted that he could not defend himself against this agency. It was not within the power of vigilance.

Chapter XI

HE became aware that the furnace roar of the battle was growing louder. Great brown clouds had floated to the still heights of air before him. The noise, too, was approaching. The woods filtered men and the fields became dotted.

As he rounded a hillock, he perceived that the roadway was now a crying mass of wagons, teams, and men. From the heaving tangle issued exhortations, commands, imprecations. Fear was sweeping it all along. The cracking whips bit and horses plunged and tugged. The white-topped wagons strained and stumbled in their exertions like fat sheep.

The youth felt comforted in a measure by this sight. They were all retreating. Perhaps, then, he was not so bad after all. He seated himself and watched the terror-stricken wagons. They fled like soft, ungainly animals. All the roarers and lashers served to help him to magnify the dangers and horrors of the engagement that he might try to prove to himself that the thing with which men could charge him was in truth a symmetrical act. There was an amount of pleasure to him in watching the wild march of this vindication.

Presently the calm head of a forward-going column of infantry appeared in the road. It came swiftly on. Avoiding the obstructions gave it the sinuous movement of a serpent. The men at the head butted mules with their musket stocks. They prodded teamsters indifferent to all howls. The men forced their way through parts of the dense mass by strength. The blunt head of the column pushed. The raving teamsters swore many strange oaths.

The commands to make way had the ring of a great importance in them. The men were going forward to the heart of the din. They were to confront the eager rush of the enemy. They felt the pride of their onward movement when the remainder of the army seemed trying to dribble down this road. They tumbled teams about with a fine feeling that it was no matter so long as their column got to the front in time. This importance made their faces grave and stern. And the backs of the officers were very rigid.

As the youth looked at them the black weight of his woe returned to him. He felt that he was regarding a procession of chosen beings. The separation was as great to him as if they had marched with weapons of flame and banners of sunlight. He could never be like them. He could have wept in his longings.

He searched about in his mind for an adequate malediction for the indefinite cause, the thing upon which men turn the words of final blame. It—whatever it was—was responsible for him, he said. There lay the fault.

The haste of the column to reach the battle seemed to the forlorn young man to be something much finer than stout fighting. Heroes, he thought, could find excuses in that long seething lane. They could retire with perfect self respect and make excuses to the stars.

He wondered what those men had eaten that they could be in such haste to force their way to grim chances of death. As he watched his envy grew until he thought that he wished to change lives with one of them. He would have liked to have used a tremendous force, he said, throw off himself and become a better. Swift pictures of himself, apart, yet in himself, came to him—a blue desperate figure leading lurid charges with one knee forward and a broken blade high—a blue, determined figure standing before a crimson and steel assault, getting calmly killed on a high place before the eyes of all. He thought of the magnificent pathos of his dead body.

These thoughts uplifted him. He felt the quiver of war desire. In his ears, he heard the ring of victory. He knew the frenzy of a rapid successful charge. The music of the trampling feet, the sharp voices, the clanking arms of the column near him made him soar on the red wings of war. For a few moments he was sublime.

He thought that he was about to start for the front. Indeed, he saw a picture of himself, dust-stained, haggard, panting, flying to the front at the proper moment to seize and throttle the dark, leering witch of calamity.

Then the difficulties of the thing began to drag at him. He hesitated, balancing awkwardly on one foot.

He had no rifle; he could not fight with his hands, said he resentfully to his plan. Well, rifles could be had for the picking. They were extraordinarily profuse.

Also, he continued, it would be a miracle if he found his regiment. Well, he could fight with any regiment.

He started forward slowly. He stepped as if he expected to tread upon some explosive thing. Doubts and he were struggling.

He would truly be a worm if any of his comrades should see him returning thus, the marks of his flight upon him. There was a reply that the intent fighters did not care for what happened rearward saving that no hostile bayonets appeared there. In the battle-blur his face would, in a way be hidden, like the face of a cowled man.

But then he said that his tireless fate would bring forth, when the strife lulled for a moment, a man to ask of him an explanation. In imagination he felt the scrutiny of his companions as he painfully labored through some lies.

Eventually, his courage expended itself upon these objections. The debates drained him of his fire.

He was not cast down by this defeat of his plan, for, upon studying the affair carefully, he could not but admit that the objections were very formidable.

Furthermore, various ailments had begun to cry out. In their presence he could not persist in flying high with the wings of war; they rendered it almost impossible for him to see himself in a heroic light. He tumbled headlong.

He discovered that he had a scorching thirst. His face was so dry and grimy that he thought he could feel his skin crackle. Each bone of his body had an ache in it, and seemingly threatened to break with each movement. His feet were like two sores. Also, his body was calling for food. It was more powerful than a direct hunger. There was a dull, weight-like feeling in his stomach, and, when he tried to walk, his head swayed and he tottered. He could not see with distinctness. Small patches of green mist floated before his vision.

While he had been tossed by many emotions, he had not been aware of ailments. Now they beset him and made clamor. As he was at last compelled to pay attention to them, his capacity for self-hate was multiplied. In despair, he declared that he was not like those others. He now conceded it to be impossible that he should ever become a hero. He was a craven loon. Those pictures of glory were piteous things. He groaned from his heart and went staggering off.

A certain mothlike quality within him kept him in the vicinity of the battle. He had a great desire to see, and to get news. He wished to know who was winning.

He told himself that, despite his unprecedented suffering, he had never lost his greed for a victory, yet, he said, in a half apologetic manner to his conscience, he could not but know that a defeat for the army this time might mean many favorable things for him. The blows of the enemy would splinter regiments into fragments. Thus, many men of courage, he considered, would be obliged to desert the colors and scurry like chickens. He would appear as one of them. They would be sullen brothers in distress, and he could then easily believe he had not run any farther or faster than they. And if he himself could believe in his virtuous perfection, he conceived that there would be small trouble in convincing all others.

He said, as if in excuse for this hope, that previously the army had encountered great defeats and in a few months had shaken off all blood and tradition of them, emerging as bright and valiant as a new one; thrusting out of sight the memory of disaster, and appearing with the valor and confidence of unconquered legions. The shrilling voices of the people at home would pipe dismally for a time, but various generals were usually compelled to listen to these ditties. He of course felt no compunctions for proposing a general as a sacrifice. He could not tell who the chosen for the barbs might be, so he could center no direct sympathy upon him. The people were afar and he did not conceive public opinion to be accurate at long range. It was quite probable they would hit the wrong man who, after he had recovered from his amazement would perhaps spend the rest of his days in writing replies to the songs of his alleged failure. It would be very unfortunate, no doubt, but in this case a general was of no consequence to the youth.

In a defeat there would be a roundabout vindication of himself. He thought it would prove, in a manner, that he had fled early because of his superior powers of perception. A serious prophet upon predicting a flood should be the first man to climb a tree. This would demonstrate that he was indeed a seer.

A moral vindication was regarded by the youth as a very important thing. Without salve, he could not, he thought, wear the sore badge of his dishonor through life. With his heart continually assuring him that he was despicable, he could not exist without making it, through his actions, apparent to all men.

If the army had gone gloriously on he would be lost. If the din meant that now his army's flags were tilted forward he was a condemned wretch. He would be compelled to doom himself to isolation. If the men were advancing, their indifferent feet were trampling upon his chances for a successful life.

As these thoughts went rapidly through his mind, he turned upon them and tried to thrust them away. He denounced himself as a villain. He said that he was the most unutterably selfish man in existence. His mind pictured the soldiers who would place their defiant bodies before the spear of the yelling battle fiend, and as he saw their dripping corpses on an imagined field, he said that he was their murderer.

Again he thought that he wished he was dead. He believed that he envied a corpse. Thinking of the slain, he achieved a great contempt for some of them, as if they were guilty for thus becoming lifeless. They might have been killed by lucky chances, he said, before they had had opportunities to flee or before they had been really tested. Yet they would receive laurels from tradition. He cried out bitterly that their crowns were stolen and their robes of glorious memories were shams. However, he still said that it was a great pity he was not as they.

A defeat of the army had suggested itself to him as a means of escape from the consequences of his fall. He considered, now, however, that it was useless to think of such a possibility. His education had been that success for that mighty blue machine was certain; that it would make victories as a contrivance turns out buttons. He presently discarded all his speculations in the other direction. He returned to the creed of soldiers.

When he perceived again that it was not possible for the army to be defeated, he tried to bethink him of a fine tale which he could take back to his regiment, and with it turn the expected shafts of derision.

But, as he mortally feared these shafts, it became impossible for him to invent a tale he felt he could trust. He experimented with many schemes, but threw them aside one by one as flimsy. He was quick to see vulnerable places in them all.

Furthermore, he was much afraid that some arrow of scorn might lay him mentally low before he could raise his protecting tale.

He imagined the whole regiment saying: "Where's Henry Fleming? He run, didn't 'e? Oh, my!" He recalled various persons who would be quite sure to leave him no peace about it. They would doubtless question him with sneers, and laugh at his stammering hesitation. In the next engagement they would try to keep watch of him to discover when he would run.

Wherever he went in camp, he would encounter insolent and lingeringly cruel stares. As he imagined himself passing near a crowd of comrades, he could hear some one say, "There he goes!"

Then, as if the heads were moved by one muscle, all the faces were turned toward him with wide, derisive grins. He seemed to hear some one make a humorous remark in a low tone. At it the others all crowed and cackled. He was a slang phrase.

Chapter XII

THE column that had butted stoutly at the obstacles in the roadway was barely out of the youth's sight before he saw dark waves of men come sweeping out of the woods and down through the fields. He knew at once that the steel fibers had been washed from their hearts. They were bursting from their coats and their equipments as from entanglements. They charged down upon him like terrified buffaloes.

Behind them blue smoke curled and clouded above the tree-tops, and through the thickets he could sometimes see a distant pink glare. The voices of the cannon were clamoring in interminable chorus.

The youth was horrorstricken. He stared in agony and amazement. He forgot that he was engaged in combating the universe. He threw aside his mental pamphlets on the philosophy of the retreated and rules for the guidance of the damned.

The fight was lost. The dragons were coming with invincible strides. The army, helpless in the matted thickets and blinded by the overhanging night, was going to be swallowed. War, the red animal, war, the blood-swollen god, would have bloated fill.

Within him something bade to cry out. He had the impulse to make a rallying speech, to sing a battle hymn, but he could only get his tongue to call into the air: "Why—why—what—what 's th' matter?"

Soon he was in the midst of them. They were leaping and scampering all about him. Their blanched faces shone in the dusk. They seemed, for the most part, to be very burly men. The youth turned from one to another of them as they galloped along. His incoherent questions were lost. They were heedless of his appeals. They did not seem to see him.

They sometimes gabbled insanely. One huge man was asking of the sky: "Say, where de plank road? Where de plank road!" It was as if he had lost a child. He wept in his pain and dismay.

Presently, men were running hither and thither in all ways. The artillery booming, forward, rearward, and on the flanks made jumble of ideas of direction. Landmarks had vanished into the gathered gloom. The youth began to imagine that he had got into the center of the tremendous quarrel, and he could perceive no way out of it. From the mouths of the fleeing men came a thousand wild questions, but no one made answers.

The youth, after rushing about and throwing interrogations at the heedless bands of retreating infantry, finally clutched a man by the arm. They swung around face to face.

"Why—why—" stammered the youth struggling with his balking tongue.

The man screamed: "Let go me! Let go me!" His face was livid and his eyes were rolling uncontrolled. He was heaving and panting. He still grasped his rifle, perhaps having forgotten to release his hold upon it. He tugged frantically, and the youth being compelled to lean forward was dragged several paces.

"Let go me! Let go me!"

"Why—why—" stuttered the youth.

"Well, then!" bawled the man in a lurid rage. He adroitly and fiercely swung his rifle. It crushed upon the youth's head. The man ran on.

The youth's fingers had turned to paste upon the other's arm. The energy was smitten from his muscles. He saw the flaming wings of lightning flash before his vision. There was a deafening rumble of thunder within his head.

Suddenly his legs seemed to die. He sank writhing to the ground. He tried to arise. In his efforts against the numbing pain he was like a man wrestling with a creature of the air.

There was a sinister struggle.

Sometimes he would achieve a position half erect, battle with the air for a moment, and then fall again, grabbing at the grass. His face was of a clammy pallor. Deep groans were wrenched from him.

At last, with a twisting movement, he got upon his hands and knees, and from thence, like a babe trying to walk, to his feet. Pressing his hands to his temples he went lurching over the grass.

He fought an intense battle with his body. His dulled senses wished him to swoon and he opposed them stubbornly, his mind portraying unknown dangers and mutilations if he should fall upon the field. He went tall soldier fashion. He imagined secluded spots where he could fall and be unmolested. To search for one he strove against the tide of his pain.

Once he put his hand to the top of his head and timidly touched the wound. The scratching pain of the contact made him draw a long breath through his clinched teeth. His fingers were dabbled with blood. He regarded them with a fixed stare.

Around him he could hear the grumble of jolted cannon as the scurrying horses were lashed toward the front. Once, a young officer on a besplashed charger nearly ran him down. He turned and watched the mass of guns, men, and horses sweeping in a wide curve toward a gap in a fence. The officer was making excited motions with a gauntleted hand. The guns followed the teams with an air of unwillingness, of being dragged by the heels.

Some officers of the scattered infantry were cursing and railing like fishwives. Their scolding voices could be heard above the din. Into the unspeakable jumble in the roadway rode a squadron of cavalry. The faded yellow of their facings[1] shone bravely. There was a mighty altercation.

The artillery were assembling as if for a conference.

The blue haze of evening was upon the field. The lines of forest were long purple shadows. One cloud lay along the western sky partly smothering the red.

As the youth left the scene behind him, he heard the guns suddenly roar out. He imagined them shaking in black rage. They belched and howled like brass devils guarding a gate. The soft air was filled with the tremendous remonstrance. With it came the shattering peal of opposing infantry. Turning to look behind him, he could see sheets of orange light illumine the shadowy distance. There were subtle and sudden lightnings in the far air. At times he thought he could see heaving masses of men.

He hurried on in the dusk. The day had faded until he could barely distinguish place for his feet. The purple darkness was filled with men who lectured and jabbered. Sometimes he could see them gesticulating against the blue and somber sky. There seemed to be a great ruck[2] of men and munitions spread about in the forest and in the fields.

The little narrow roadway now lay lifeless. There were overturned wagons like sun-dried bowlders. The bed of the former torrent was choked with the bodies of horses and splintered parts of war machines.

It had come to pass that his wound pained him but little. He was afraid to move rapidly, however, for a dread of disturbing it. He held his head very still and took many precautions against stumbling. He was filled with anxiety, and his face was pinched and drawn in anticipation of the pain of any sudden mistake of his feet in the gloom.

His thoughts, as he walked, fixed intently upon his hurt. There was a cool, liquid feeling about it and he imagined blood moving

---

1 Brass decorations on a uniform, usually on the edges of the jacket.
2 A great deal of commotion, as in a scramble for the ball in rugby.

slowly down under his hair. His head seemed swollen to a size that made him think his neck to be inadequate.

The new silence of his wound made much worriment. The little blistering voices of pain that had called out from his scalp were, he thought, definite in their expression of danger. By them he believed that he could measure his plight. But when they remained ominously silent he became frightened and imagined terrible fingers that clutched into his brain.

Amid it he began to reflect upon various incidents and conditions of the past. He bethought him of certain meals his mother had cooked at home, in which those dishes of which he was particularly fond had occupied prominent positions. He saw the spread table. The pine walls of the kitchen were glowing in the warm light from the stove. Too, he remembered how he and his companions used to go from the schoolhouse to the bank of a shaded pool. He saw his clothes in disorderly array upon the grass of the bank. He felt the swash of the fragrant water upon his body. The leaves of the overhanging maple rustled with melody in the wind of youthful summer.

He was overcome presently by a dragging weariness. His head hung forward and his shoulders were stooped as if he were bearing a great bundle. His feet shuffled along the ground.

He held continuous arguments as to whether he should lie down and sleep at some near spot, or force himself on until he reached a certain haven. He often tried to dismiss the question, but his body persisted in rebellion and his senses nagged at him like pampered babies.

At last he heard a cheery voice near his shoulder: "Yeh seem t' be in a pretty bad way, boy?"

The youth did not look up, but he assented with thick tongue. "Uh!"

The owner of the cheery voice took him firmly by the arm. "Well," he said, with a round laugh, "I'm goin' your way. Th' hull gang is goin' your way. An' I guess I kin give yeh a lift." They began to walk like a drunken man and his friend.

As they went along, the man questioned the youth and assisted him with the replies like one manipulating the mind of a child. Sometimes he interjected anecdotes. "What reg'ment do yeh b'long teh? Eh? What's that? Th' 304th N' York? Why, what corps is that in? Oh, it is? Why, I thought they wasn't engaged t' day— they 're 'way over in th' center. Oh, they was, eh? Well, pretty nearly everybody got their share 'a fightin' t' day. By dad, I give myself up fer dead any number 'a times. There was shootin' here an' shootin' there, an' hollerin' here an' hollerin' there, in th' damn' darkness, until I couldn't tell t' save m' soul which side I was on. Sometimes I thought I was sure 'nough from Ohier, an' other times I could 'a swore I was from th' bitter end of Florida. It was th' most mixed up dern thing I ever see. An' these here hull woods is a reg'lar mess. It'll be a miracle if we find our reg'ments t' night. Pretty soon, though, we 'll meet a plenty of guards an' provost-guards,[1] an' one thing an' another. Ho! there they go with an off'cer, I guess. Look at his hand a draggin'. He 's got all th' war he wants, I bet. He won't be talkin' so big about his reputation an' all when they go t' sawin' off his leg. Poor feller! My brother 's got whiskers jest like that. How did yeh git 'way over here, anyhow? Your reg'ment is a long way from here, ain't it? Well, I guess we can find it. Yeh know there was a boy killed in my comp'ny t' day that I thought th' world an' all of. Jack was a nice feller. By ginger, it hurt like thunder t' see ol' Jack jest git knocked flat. We was a standin' purty peaceable fer a spell, 'though there was men runnin' ev'ry way all 'round us, an' while we was a standin' like that, 'long come a big fat feller. He began t' peck at Jack's elbow, an' he ses: 'Say, where 's th' road t' th' river?' An' Jack, he never paid no attention, an' th' feller kept on a peckin' at his elbow an' sayin': 'Say, where 's th' road t' th' river?' Jack was a lookin' ahead all th' time tryin' t' see th' Johnnies comin' through th' woods, an' he never paid no attention t' this big fat feller fer a long time, but at last he turned 'round an' he ses: 'Ah, go t' hell an' find th' road t' th' river!' An' jest then a shot slapped him bang on th' side th' head. He was a sergeant, too. Them was his last words. Thunder, I wish we was sure 'a findin' our reg'-ments t' night. It 's goin' t' be long huntin'. But I guess we kin do it."

In the search which followed, the man of the cheery voice seemed to the youth to possess a wand of a magic kind. He threaded the mazes of the tangled forest with a strange fortune. In encounters with guards and patrols he displayed the keenness of a detective and the valor of a gamin.[2] Obstacles fell before him and became of assistance. The youth, with his chin still on his breast, stood woodenly by while his companion beat ways and means out of sullen things.

The forest seemed a vast hive of men buzzing about in frantic circles, but the cheery man conducted the youth without mis-

---

1 Sentries on duty guarding supplies.
2 A street urchin, a ragamuffin (French).

takes, until at last he began to chuckle with glee and self satisfaction. "Ah, there yeh are! See that fire?"

The youth nodded stupidly.

"Well, there 's where your reg'ment is. An' now, good-by, ol' boy, good luck t' yeh."

A warm and strong hand clasped the youth's languid fingers for an instant, and then he heard a cheerful and audacious whistling as the man strode away. As he who had so befriended him was thus passing out of his life, it suddenly occurred to the youth that he had not once seen his face.

Chapter XIII

THE youth went slowly toward the fire indicated by his departed friend. As he reeled, he bethought him of the welcome his comrades would give him. He had a conviction that he would soon feel in his sore heart the barbed missiles of ridicule. He had no strength to invent a tale; he would be a soft target.

He made vague plans to go off into the deeper darkness and hide, but they were all destroyed by the voices of exhaustion and pain from his body. His ailments, clamoring, forced him to seek the place of food and rest, at whatever cost.

He swung unsteadily toward the fire. He could see the forms of men throwing black shadows in the red light, and as he went nearer it became known to him in some way that the ground was strewn with sleeping men.

Of a sudden he confronted a black and monstrous figure. A rifle barrel caught some glinting beams. "Halt! halt!" He was dismayed for a moment, but he presently thought that he recognized the nervous voice. As he stood tottering before the rifle barrel, he called out: "Why, hello, Wilson, you—you here?"

The rifle was lowered to a position of caution and the loud soldier came slowly forward. He peered into the youth's face. "That you, Henry?"

"Yes, it's—it's me."

"Well, well, ol' boy," said the other, "by ginger, I'm glad t' see yeh! I give yeh up fer a goner. I thought yeh was dead sure enough." There was husky emotion in his voice.

The youth found that now he could barely stand upon his feet. There was a sudden sinking of his forces. He thought he must hasten to produce his tale to protect him from the missiles already at the lips of his redoubtable comrades. So, staggering before the loud soldier, he began: "Yes, yes. I've—I've had an awful time. I've been all over. Way over on th' right. Ter'ble fightin' over there. I had an awful time. I got separated from th' reg'ment. Over on th' right, I got shot. In th' head. I never see sech fightin'. Awful time. I don't see how I could 'a got separated from th' reg'ment. I got shot, too."

His friend had stepped forward quickly. "What? Got shot? Why didn't yeh say so first? Poor ol' boy, we must—hol' on a minnit; what am I doin'. I'll call Simpson."

Another figure at that moment loomed in the gloom. They could see that it was the corporal. "Who yeh talkin' to, Wilson?" he demanded. His voice was anger toned. "Who yeh talkin' to? Yeh th' derndest sentinel—why—hello, Henry, you here? Why, I thought you was dead four hours ago! Great Jerusalem, they keep turnin' up every ten minutes or so! We thought we'd lost forty two men by straight count, but if they keep on a comin' this way, we'll git th' comp'ny all back by mornin' yit. Where was yeh?"

"Over on th' right. I got separated"—began the youth with considerable glibness.

But his friend had interrupted hastily. "Yes, an' he got shot in th' head an' he's in a fix, an' we must see t' him right away." He rested his rifle in the hollow of his left arm and his right around the youth's shoulder.

"Gee, it must hurt like thunder!" he said.

The youth leaned heavily upon his friend. "Yes, it hurts—hurts a good deal," he replied. There was a faltering in his voice.

"Oh," said the corporal. He linked his arm in the youth's and drew him forward. "Come on, Henry. I'll take keer 'a yeh."

As they went on together the loud private called out after them: "Put 'im t' sleep in my blanket, Simpson. An'—hol' on a minnit—here's my canteen. It's full 'a coffee. Look at his head by th' fire an' see how it looks. Maybe it's a pretty bad un. When I git relieved in a couple 'a minnits, I'll be over an' see t' him."

The youth's senses were so deadened that his friend's voice sounded from afar and he could scarcely feel the pressure of the corporal's arm. He submitted passively to the latter's directing strength. His head was in the old manner hanging forward upon his breast. His knees wobbled.

The corporal led him into the glare of the fire. "Now, Henry," he said, "let's have look at yer ol' head."

The youth sat down obediently and the corporal, laying aside his rifle, began to fumble in the bushy hair of his comrade. He was obliged to turn the other's head so that the full flush of the fire light would beam upon it. He puckered his mouth with a critical air. He drew back his lips and whistled through his teeth when his fingers came in contact with the splashed blood and the rare wound.

"Ah, here we are!" he said. He awkwardly made further investigations. "Jest as I thought," he added, presently. "Yeh've been grazed by a ball. It's raised a queer lump jest as if some feller had lammed yeh on th' head with a club. It stopped a-bleedin' long time ago. Th' most about it is that in th' mornin' yeh'll feel that a number ten hat wouldn't fit yeh. An' your head'll be all het up an' feel as dry as burnt pork. An' yeh may git a lot 'a other sicknesses, too, by mornin'. Yeh can't never tell. Still, I don't much think so. It's jest a damn' good belt on th' head, an' nothin' more. Now, you jest sit here an' don't move, while I go rout out th' relief. Then I'll send Wilson t' take keer 'a yeh."

The corporal went away. The youth remained on the ground like a parcel. He stared with a vacant look into the fire.

After a time he aroused, for some part, and the things about him began to take form. He saw that the ground in the deep shadows was cluttered with men, sprawling in every conceivable posture. Glancing narrowly into the more distant darkness, he caught occasional glimpses of visages that loomed pallid and ghostly, lit with a phosphorescent glow. These faces expressed in their lines the deep stupor of the tired soldiers. They made them appear like men drunk with wine. This bit of forest might have appeared to an ethereal wanderer as a scene of the result of some frightful debauch.

On the other side of the fire the youth observed an officer asleep, seated bolt upright, with his back against a tree. There was something perilous in his position. Badgered by dreams, perhaps, he swayed with little bounces and starts, like an old toddy-stricken grandfather in a chimney corner. Dust and stains were upon his face. His lower jaw hung down as if lacking strength to assume its normal position. He was the picture of an exhausted soldier after a feast of war.

He had evidently gone to sleep with his sword in his arms. These two had slumbered in an embrace, but the weapon had been allowed in time to fall unheeded to the ground. The brass-mounted hilt lay in contact with some parts of the fire.

Within the gleam of rose and orange light from the burning sticks were other soldiers, snoring and heaving, or lying deathlike in slumber. A few pairs of legs were stuck forth, rigid and straight. The shoes displayed the mud or dust of marches and bits of rounded trousers, protruding from the blankets, showed rents and tears from hurried pitchings through the dense brambles.

The fire crackled musically. From it swelled light smoke. Overhead the foliage moved softly. The leaves, with their faces turned toward the blaze, were colored shifting hues of silver, often edged with red. Far off to the right, through a window in the forest could be seen a handful of stars lying, like glittering pebbles, on the black level of the night.

Occasionally, in this low-arched hall, a soldier would arouse and turn his body to a new position, the experience of his sleep having taught him of uneven and objectionable places upon the ground under him. Or, perhaps, he would lift himself to a sitting posture, blink at the fire for an unintelligent moment, throw a swift glance at his prostrate companion, and then cuddle down again with a grunt of sleepy content.

The youth sat in a forlorn heap until his friend the loud young soldier came, swinging two canteens by their light strings. "Well, now, Henry, ol' boy," said the latter, "we'll have yeh fixed up in jest about a minnit."

He had the bustling ways of an amateur nurse. He fussed around the fire and stirred the sticks to brilliant exertions. He made his patient drink largely from the canteen that contained the coffee. It was to the youth a delicious draught. He tilted his head afar back and held the canteen long to his lips. The cool mixture went caressingly down his blistered throat. Having finished, he sighed with comfortable delight.

The loud young soldier watched his comrade with an air of satisfaction. He later produced an extensive handkerchief from his pocket. He folded it into a manner of bandage and soused water from the other canteen upon the middle of it. This crude arrangement he bound over the youth's head, tying the ends in a queer knot at the back of the neck.

"There," he said, moving off and surveying his deed, "yeh look like th' devil, but I bet yeh feel better."

The youth contemplated his friend with grateful eyes. Upon his aching and swelling head the cold cloth was like a tender woman's hand.

"Yeh don't holler ner say nothin'," remarked his friend approvingly. "I know I'm a blacksmith at takin' keer 'a sick folks, an' yeh never squeaked. Yer a good un, Henry. Most 'a men would a' been in th' hospital long ago. A shot in th' head ain't foolin' business."

The youth made no reply, but began to fumble with the buttons of his jacket.

"Well, come, now," continued his friend, "come on. I must put yeh t' bed an' see that yeh git a good night's rest."

The other got carefully erect, and the loud young soldier led him among the sleeping forms lying in groups and rows. Presently he stooped and picked up his blankets. He spread the rubber one upon the ground and placed the woolen one about the youth's shoulders.

"There now," he said, "lie down an' git some sleep."

The youth, with his manner of doglike obedience, got carefully down like a crone stooping. He stretched out with a murmur of relief and comfort. The ground felt like the softest couch.

But of a sudden he ejaculated: "Hol' on a minnit! Where you goin' t' sleep?"

His friend waved his hand impatiently. "Right down there by yeh."

"Well, but hol' on a minnit," continued the youth. "What yeh goin' t' sleep in? I've got your—"

The loud young soldier snarled: "Shet up an' go on t' sleep. Don't be makin' a damn' fool 'a yerself," he said severely.

After the reproof the youth said no more. An exquisite drowsiness had spread through him. The warm comfort of the blanket enveloped him and made a gentle languor. His head fell forward on his crooked arm and his weighted lids went softly down over his eyes. Hearing a splatter of musketry from the distance, he wondered indifferently if those men sometimes slept. He gave a long sigh, snuggled down into his blanket, and in a moment was like his comrades.

Chapter XIV

WHEN the youth awoke it seemed to him that he had been asleep for a thousand years, and he felt sure that he opened his eyes upon an unexpected world. Gray mists were slowly shifting before the first efforts of the sun rays. An impending splendor could be seen in the eastern sky. An icy dew had chilled his face, and immediately upon arousing he curled farther down into his blanket. He stared for a while at the leaves overhead, moving in a heraldic wind of the day.

The distance was splintering and blaring with the noise of fighting. There was in the sound an expression of a deadly persistency, as if it had not begun and was not to cease.

About him were the rows and groups of men that he had dimly seen the previous night. They were getting a last draught of sleep before the awakening. The gaunt, careworn features and dusty figures were made plain by this quaint light at the dawning, but it dressed the skin of the men in corpselike hues and made the tangled limbs appear pulseless and dead. The youth started up with a little cry when his eyes first swept over this motionless mass of men, thickspread upon the ground, pallid, and in strange postures. His disordered mind interpreted the hall of the forest as a charnel place.[1] He believed for an instant that he was in the house of the dead, and he did not dare to move lest these corpses start up, squalling and squawking. In a second, however, he achieved his proper mind. He swore a complicated oath at himself. He saw that this somber picture was not a fact of the present, but a mere prophecy.

He heard then the noise of a fire crackling briskly in the cold air, and, turning his head, he saw his friend pottering busily about a small blaze. A few other figures moved in the fog, and he heard the hard cracking of axe blows.

Suddenly there was a hollow rumble of drums. A distant bugle sang faintly. Similar sounds, varying in strength, came from near and far over the forest. The bugles called to each other like brazen gamecocks. The near thunder of the regimental drums rolled.

The body of men in the woods rustled. There was a general uplifting of heads. A murmuring of voices broke upon the air. In it there was much bass of grumbling oaths. Strange gods were addressed in condemnation of the early hours necessary to

---

1   A place for the deposit of dead bodies.

correct war. An officer's peremptory tenor rang out and quickened the stiffened movement of the men. The tangled limbs unraveled. The corpse-hued faces were hidden behind fists that twisted slowly in the eye sockets.

The youth sat up and gave vent to an enormous yawn. "Thunder!" he remarked petulantly. He rubbed his eyes, and then putting up his hand felt carefully of the bandage over his wound. His friend, perceiving him to be awake, came from the fire. "Well, Henry, ol' man, how do yeh feel this mornin'?" he demanded.

The youth yawned again. Then he puckered his mouth to a little pucker. His head, in truth, felt precisely like a melon, and there was an unpleasant sensation at his stomach.

"Oh, Lord, I feel pretty bad," he said.

"Thunder!" exclaimed the other. "I hoped ye'd feel all right this mornin'. Let's see th' bandage—I guess it's slipped." He began to tinker at the wound in rather a clumsy way until the youth exploded.

"Gosh dern it!" he said in sharp irritation; "you're the hangdest man I ever saw! You wear muffs on your hands. Why in good thunderation can't you be more easy? I'd rather you'd stand off an' throw guns at it. Now, go slow, an' don't act as if you was nailing down carpet."

He glared with insolent command at his friend, but the latter answered soothingly. "Well, well, come now, an' git some grub," he said. "Then, maybe, yeh'll feel better."

At the fireside the loud young soldier watched over his comrade's wants with tenderness and care. He was very busy marshaling the little black vagabonds of tin cups and pouring into them the streaming, iron colored mixture from a small and sooty tin pail. He had some fresh meat, which he roasted hurriedly upon a stick. He sat down then and contemplated the youth's appetite with glee.

The youth took note of a remarkable change in his comrade since those days of camp life upon the river bank. He seemed no more to be continually regarding the proportions of his personal prowess. He was not furious at small words that pricked his conceits. He was no more a loud young soldier. There was about him now a fine reliance. He showed a quiet belief in his purposes and his abilities. And this inward confidence evidently enabled him to be indifferent to little words of other men aimed at him.

The youth reflected. He had been used to regarding his comrade as a blatant child with an audacity grown from his inexperience, thoughtless, headstrong, jealous, and filled with a tinsel courage. A swaggering babe accustomed to strut in his own door-yard. The youth wondered where had been born these new eyes; when his comrade had made the great discovery that there were many men who would refuse to be subjected by him. Apparently, the other had now climbed a peak of wisdom from which he could perceive himself as a very wee thing. And the youth saw that ever after it would be easier to live in his friend's neighbor-hood.

His comrade balanced his ebony coffee cup on his knee. "Well, Henry," he said, "what d'yeh think th' chances are? D'yeh think we'll wallop 'em?"

The youth considered for a moment. "Day b'fore yesterday," he finally replied, with boldness, "you would 'a' bet you'd lick the hull kit-an'-boodle all by yourself."

His friend looked a trifle amazed. "Would I?" he asked. He pondered. "Well, perhaps I would," he decided at last. He stared humbly at the fire.

The youth was quite disconcerted at this surprising reception of his remarks. "Oh, no, you wouldn't either," he said, hastily trying to retrace.

But the other made a deprecating gesture. "Oh, yeh needn't mind, Henry," he said. "I believe I was a pretty big fool in those days." He spoke as after a lapse of years.

There was a little pause.

"All th' officers say we've got th' rebs in a pretty tight box," said the friend, clearing his throat in a commonplace way. "They all seem t' think we've got 'em jest where we want 'em."

"I don't know about that," the youth replied. "What I seen over on th' right makes me think it was th' other way about. From where I was, it looked as if we was gettin' a good poundin' yestir-day."

"D'yeh think so?" inquired the friend. "I thought we handled 'em pretty rough yestirday."

"Not a bit," said the youth. "Why, lord, man, you didn't see nothing of the fight. Why!" Then a sudden thought came to him. "Oh! Jim Conklin's dead."

His friend started. "What? Is he? Jim Conklin?"

The youth spoke slowly. "Yes. He's dead. Shot in th' side."

"Yeh don't say so. Jim Conklin. . . . poor cuss!"

All about them were other small fires surrounded by men with their little black utensils. From one of these near came sudden sharp voices in a row. It appeared that two light-footed soldiers had been teasing a huge, bearded man, causing him to spill coffee upon his blue knees. The man had gone into a rage and had sworn comprehensively. Stung by his language, his tormentors had immediately bristled at him with a great show of resenting unjust oaths. Possibly there was going to be a fight.

The friend arose and went over to them, making pacific motions with his arms. "Oh, here, now, boys, what's th' use?" he said. "We'll be at th' rebs in less'n an hour. What's th' good fightin' 'mong ourselves?"

One of the light-footed soldiers turned upon him red-faced and violent. "Yeh needn't come around here with yer preachin'. I s'pose yeh don't approve 'a fightin' since Charley Morgan licked yeh; but I don't see what business this here is 'a yours or anybody else."

"Well, it ain't," said the friend mildly. "Still I hate t' see—"

There was a tangled argument.

"Well, he—," said the two, indicating their opponent with accusative forefingers.

The huge soldier was quite purple with rage. He pointed at the two soldiers with his great hand, extended clawlike. "Well, they—"

But during this argumentative time the desire to deal blows seemed to pass, although they said much to each other. Finally the friend returned to his old seat. In a short while the three antagonists could be seen together in an amiable bunch.

"Jimmie Rogers ses I'll have t' fight him after th' battle t' day," announced the friend as he again seated himself. "He ses he don't allow no interferin' in his business. I hate t' see th' boys fightin' 'mong themselves."

The youth laughed. "Yer changed a good bit. Yeh ain't at all like yeh was. I remember when you an' that Irish feller—" He stopped and laughed again.

"No, I didn't use t' be that way," said his friend thoughtfully. "That's true 'nough."

"Well, I didn't mean—" began the youth.

The friend made another deprecatory gesture. "Oh, yeh needn't mind, Henry."

There was another little pause.

"Th' reg'ment lost over half th' men yesterday," remarked the friend eventually. "I thought a course they was all dead, but, laws, they kep' a-comin' back last night until it seems, after all, we didn't lose but a few. They'd been scattered all over, wanderin' around in th' woods, fightin' with other reg'ments, an' everything. Jest like you done."

"So?" said the youth.

Chapter XV

THE regiment was standing at order arms at the side of a lane, waiting for the command to march, when suddenly the youth remembered the little packet enwrapped in a faded yellow envelope which the loud young soldier with lugubrious words had intrusted to him. It made him start. He uttered an exclamation and turned toward his comrade.

"Wilson!"

"What?"

His friend, at his side in the ranks, was thoughtfully staring down the road. From some cause his expression was at that moment very meek. The youth, regarding him with sidelong glances, felt impelled to change his purpose. "Oh, nothing," he said.

His friend turned his head in some surprise, "Why, what was yeh goin' t' say?"

"Oh, nothing," repeated the youth.

He resolved not to deal the little blow. It was sufficient that the fact made him glad. It was not necessary to knock his friend on the head with the misguided packet.

He had been possessed of much fear of his friend, for he saw how easily questionings could make holes in his feelings. Lately, he had assured himself that the altered comrade would not tantalize him with a persistent curiosity, but he felt certain that during the first period of leisure his friend would ask him to relate his adventures of the previous day.

He now rejoiced in the possession of a small weapon with which he could prostrate his comrade at the first signs of a cross-examination. He was master. It would now be he who could laugh and shoot the shafts of derision.

The friend had, in a weak hour, spoken with sobs of his own death. He had delivered a melancholy oration previous to his funeral, and had doubtless in the packet of letters, presented various keepsakes to relatives. But he had not died, and thus he had delivered himself into the hands of the youth.

The latter felt immensely superior to his friend, but he inclined to condescension. He adopted toward him an air of patronizing good humor.

His self-pride was now entirely restored. In the shade of its flourishing growth he stood with braced and self-confident legs, and since nothing could now be discovered he did not shrink from an encounter with the eyes of judges, and allowed no thoughts of his own to keep him from an attitude of manfulness. He had performed his mistakes in the dark, so he was still a man.

Indeed, when he remembered his fortunes of yesterday, and looked at them from a distance he began to see something fine there. He had license to be pompous and veteranlike.

His panting agonies of the past he put out of his sight.

In the present, he declared to himself that it was only the doomed and the damned who roared with sincerity at circumstance. Few but they ever did it. A man with a full stomach and the respect of his fellows had no business to scold about anything that he might think to be wrong in the ways of the universe, or even with the ways of society. Let the unfortunates rail; the others may play marbles.

He did not give a great deal of thought to these battles that lay directly before him. It was not essential that he should plan his ways in regard to them. He had been taught that many obligations of a life were easily avoided. The lessons of yesterday had been that retribution was a laggard and blind. With these facts before him he did not deem it necessary that he should become feverish over the possibilities of the ensuing twenty-four hours. He could leave much to chance. Besides, a faith in himself had secretly blossomed. There was a little flower of confidence growing within him. He was now a man of experience. He had been out among the dragons, he said, and he assured himself that they were not so hideous as he had imagined them. Also, they were inaccurate; they did not sting with precision. A stout heart often defied, and defying, escaped.

And, furthermore, how could they kill him who was the chosen of gods and doomed to greatness?

He remembered how some of the men had run from the battle. As he recalled their terror-struck faces he felt a scorn for them. They had surely been more fleet and more wild than was absolutely necessary. They were weak mortals. As for himself, he had fled with discretion and dignity.

He was aroused from this reverie by his friend, who, having hitched about nervously and blinked at the trees for a time, suddenly coughed in an introductory way, and spoke.

"Fleming!"

"What?"

The friend put his hand up to his mouth and coughed again. He fidgeted in his jacket.

"Well," he gulped, at last, "I guess yeh might as well give me back them letters." Dark, prickling blood had flushed into his cheeks and brow.

"All right, Wilson," said the youth. He loosened two buttons of his coat, thrust in his hand, and brought forth the packet. As he extended it to his friend the latter's face was turned from him.

He had been slow in the act of producing the packet because during it he had been trying to invent a remarkable comment upon the affair. He could conjure nothing of sufficient point. He was compelled to allow his friend to escape unmolested with his packet. And for this he took unto himself considerable credit. It was a generous thing.

His friend at his side seemed suffering great shame. As he contemplated him, the youth felt his heart grow more strong and stout. He had never been compelled to blush in such manner for his acts; he was an individual of extraordinary virtues.

He reflected, with condescending pity: "Too bad! Too bad! The poor devil, it makes him feel tough!"

After this incident, and as he reviewed the battle pictures he had seen, he felt quite competent to return home and make the hearts of the people glow with stories of war. He could see himself in a room of warm tints telling tales to listeners. He could exhibit laurels. They were insignificant; still, in a district where laurels were infrequent, they might shine.

He saw his gaping audience picturing him as the central figure in blazing scenes. And he imagined the consternation and the ejaculations of his mother and the young lady at the seminary as they drank his recitals. Their vague feminine formula for beloved ones doing brave deeds on the field of battle without risk of life would be destroyed.

Chapter XVI

A SPUTTERING of musketry was always to be heard. Later, the cannon had entered the dispute. In the fog-filled air their voices made a thudding sound. The reverberations were continued. This part of the world led a strange, battleful existence.

The youth's regiment was marched to relieve a command that had lain long in some damp trenches. The men took positions behind a curving line of rifle pits that had been turned up, like a large furrow, along the line of woods. Before them was a level stretch, peopled with short, deformed stumps. From the woods beyond came the dull popping of the skirmishers and pickets, firing in the fog. From the right came the noise of a terrific fracas.

The men cuddled behind the small embankment and sat in easy attitudes awaiting their turn. Many had their backs to the firing. The youth's friend lay down, buried his face in his arms, and almost instantly, it seemed, he was in a deep sleep.

The youth leaned his breast against the brown dirt and peered over at the woods and up and down the line. Curtains of trees interfered with his ways of vision. He could see the low line of trenches but for a short distance. A few idle flags were perched on the dirt hills. Behind them were rows of dark bodies with a few heads sticking curiously over the top.

Always the noise of skirmishers came from the woods on the front and left, and the din on the right had grown to frightful proportions. The guns were roaring without an instant's pause for breath. It seemed that the cannon had come from all parts and were engaged in a stupendous wrangle. It became impossible to make a sentence heard.

The youth wished to launch a joke—a quotation from newspapers. He desired to say, "All quiet on the Rappahannock,"[1] but the guns refused to permit even a comment upon their uproar. He never successfully concluded the sentence. But at last the guns stopped, and among the men in the rifle pits rumors again flew, like birds, but they were now for the most part black creatures who flapped their wings drearily near to the ground and refused to rise on any wings of hope. The men's faces grew

---

1 A phrase used by northern newspapers to mock the lack of activity in the war in 1862-63. Union forces were massed together in Virginia, but the commanding officers were reluctant to attack. Weeks went by without any fighting.

doleful from the interpreting of omens. Tales of hesitation and uncertainty on the part of those high in place and responsibility came to their ears. Stories of disaster were borne into their minds with many proofs. This din of musketry on the right, growing like a released genie of sound, expressed and emphasized the army's plight.

The men were disheartened and began to mutter. They made gestures expressive of the sentence: "Ah, what more can we do?" And it could always be seen that they were bewildered by the alleged news and could not fully comprehend a defeat.

Before the gray mists had been totally obliterated by the sun rays, the regiment was marching in a spread column that was retiring carefully through the woods. The disordered, hurrying lines of the enemy could sometimes be seen down through the groves and little fields. They were yelling, shrill and exultant.

At this sight the youth forgot many personal matters and became greatly enraged. He exploded in loud sentences. "B'jiminey, we're generaled by a lot 'a lunkheads."

"More than one feller has said that t' day," observed a man.

His friend, recently aroused, was still very drowsy. He looked behind him until his mind took in the meaning of the movement. Then he sighed. "Oh, well, I s'pose we got licked," he remarked sadly.

The youth had a thought that it would not be handsome for him to freely condemn other men. He made an attempt to restrain himself, but the words upon his tongue were too bitter. He presently began a long and intricate denunciation of the commander of the forces.

"Mebbe, it wa'n't all his fault—not all together. He did th' best he knowed. It's our luck t' git licked often," said his friend in a weary tone. He was trudging along with stooped shoulders and shifting eyes like a man who has been caned and kicked.

"Well, don't we fight like the devil? Don't we do all that men can?" demanded the youth loudly.

He was secretly dumfounded at this sentiment when it came from his lips. For a moment his face lost its valor and he looked guiltily about him. But no one questioned his right to deal in such words, and presently he recovered his air of courage. He went on to repeat a statement he had heard going from group to group at the camp that morning. "The brigadier said he never saw a new reg'ment fight the way we fought yestirday, didn't he? And we didn't do better than many another reg'ment, did we? Well, then, you can't say it's th' army's fault, can you?"

In his reply, the friend's voice was stern. "'A course not," he said. "No man dare say we don't fight like th' devil. No man will ever dare say it. Th' boys fight like hell roosters. But still—still, we don't have no luck."

"Well, then, if we fight like the devil an' don't ever whip, it must be the general's fault," said the youth grandly and decisively. "And I don't see any sense in fighting and fighting and fighting, yet always losing through some derned old lunkhead of a general."

A sarcastic man who was tramping at the youth's side, then spoke lazily. "Mebbe yeh think yeh fit th' hull battle yestirday, Fleming," he remarked.

The speech pierced the youth. Inwardly he was reduced to an abject pulp by these chance words. His legs quaked privately. He cast a frightened glance at the sarcastic man.

"Why, no," he hastened to say in a conciliating voice, "I don't think I fought the whole battle yesterday."

But the other seemed innocent of any deeper meaning. Apparently, he had no information. It was merely his habit. "Oh!" he replied in the same tone of calm derision.

The youth, nevertheless, felt a threat. His mind shrank from going near to the danger, and thereafter he was silent. The significance of the sarcastic man's words took from him all loud moods that would make him appear prominent. He became suddenly a modest person.

There was low-toned talk among the troops. The officers were impatient and snappy, their countenances clouded with the tales of misfortune. The troops, sifting through the forest, were sullen. In the youth's company once a man's laugh rang out. A dozen soldiers turned their faces quickly toward him and frowned with vague displeasure.

The noise of firing dogged their footsteps. Sometimes, it seemed to be driven a little way, but it always returned again with increased insolence. The men muttered and cursed, throwing black looks in its direction.

In a clear space the troops were at last halted. Regiments and brigades, broken and detached through their encounters with thickets, grew together again and lines were faced toward the pursuing bark of the enemy's infantry.

This noise, following like the yellings of eager, metallic hounds, increased to a loud and joyous burst, and then, as the sun went serenely up the sky, throwing illuminating rays into the gloomy thickets, it broke forth into prolonged pealings. The woods began to crackle as if afire.

"Whoop-a-dadee," said a man, "here we are! Everybody fight-in'. Blood an' destruction."

"I was willin' t' bet they'd attack as soon as th' sun got fairly up," savagely asserted the lieutenant who commanded the youth's company. He jerked without mercy at his little mustache. He strode to and fro with dark dignity in the rear of his men, who were lying down behind whatever protection they had collected.

A battery had trundled into position in the rear and was thoughtfully shelling the distance. The regiment, unmolested as yet, awaited the moment when the gray shadows of the woods before them should be slashed by the lines of flame. There was much growling and swearing.

"Good Gawd," the youth grumbled, "we're always being chased around like rats! It makes me sick. Nobody seems to know where we go or why we go. We just get fired around from pillar to post and get licked here and get licked there, and nobody knows what it's done for. It makes a man feel like a damn' kitten in a bag. Now, I'd like to know what the eternal thunders we was marched into these woods for anyhow, unless it was to give the rebs a regular pot shot at us. We came in here and got our legs all tangled up in these cussed briers, and then we begin to fight and the rebs had an easy time of it. Don't tell me it's just luck! I know better. It's this derned old—"

The friend seemed jaded, but he interrupted his comrade with a voice of calm confidence. "It'll turn out all right in th' end," he said.

"Oh, the devil it will! You always talk like a dog-hanged parson. Don't tell me! I know—"

At this time there was an interposition by the savage-minded lieutenant, who was obliged to vent some of his inward dissatisfaction upon his men. "You boys shut right up! There no need 'a your wastin' your breath in long-winded arguments about this an' that an' th' other. You've been jawin' like a lot 'a old hens. All you've got t' do is to fight, an' you'll get plenty 'a that t' do in about ten minutes. Less talkin' an' more fightin' is what's best for you boys. I never saw sech gabbling jackasses."

He paused, ready to pounce upon any man who might have the temerity to reply. No words being said, he resumed his digni-fied pacing.

"There's too much chin music an' too little fightin' in this war, anyhow," he said to them, turning his head for a final remark.

The day had grown more white, until the sun shed his full radiance upon the thronged forest. A sort of a gust of battle came sweeping toward that part of the line where lay the youth's regiment. The front shifted a trifle to meet it squarely. There was a wait. In this part of the field there passed slowly the intense moments that precede the tempest.

A single rifle flashed in a thicket before the regiment. In an instant it was joined by many others. There was a mighty song of clashes and crashes that went sweeping through the woods. The guns in the rear, aroused and enraged by shells that had been thrown burlike at them, suddenly involved themselves in a hideous altercation with another band of guns. The battle roar settled to a rolling thunder, which was a single, long explosion.

In the regiment there was a peculiar kind of hesitation denoted in the attitudes of the men. They were worn, exhausted, having slept but little and labored much. They rolled their eyes toward the advancing battle as they stood awaiting the shock. Some shrank and flinched. They stood as men tied to stakes.

Chapter XVII

THIS advance of the enemy had seemed to the youth like a ruthless hunting. He began to fume with rage and exasperation. He beat his foot upon the ground, and scowled with hate at the swirling smoke that was approaching like a phantom flood. There was a maddening quality in this seeming resolution of the foe to give him no rest, to give him no time to sit down and think. Yesterday he had fought and had fled rapidly. There had been many adventures. For to-day he felt that he had earned opportunities for contemplative repose. He could have enjoyed portraying to uninitiated listeners various scenes at which he had been a witness or ably discussing the processes of war with other proved men. Too it was important that he should have time for physical recuperation. He was sore and stiff from his experiences. He had received his fill of all exertions, and he wished to rest.

But those other men seemed never to grow weary; they were fighting with their old speed. He had a wild hate for the relentless foe. Yesterday, when he had imagined the universe to be against him, he had hated it, little gods and big gods; to-day he hated the army of the foe with the same great hatred. He was not going to be badgered of his life, like a kitten chased by boys, he said. It was not well to drive men into final corners; at those moments they could all develop teeth and claws.

He leaned and spoke into his friend's ear. He menaced the woods with a gesture. "If they keep on chasing us, by Gawd, they'd better watch out. Can't stand *too* much."

The friend twisted his head and made a calm reply. "If they keep on a chasin' us they'll drive us all inteh th' river."

The youth cried out savagely at this statement. He crouched behind a little tree, with his eyes burning hatefully and his teeth set in a cur like snarl. The awkward bandage was still about his head, and upon it, over his wound, there was a spot of dry blood. His hair was wondrously tousled, and some straggling, moving locks hung over the cloth of the bandage down toward his forehead. His jacket and shirt were open at the throat, and exposed his young bronzed neck. There could be seen spasmodic gulpings at his throat.

His fingers twined nervously about his rifle. He wished that it was an engine of annihilating power. He felt that he and his companions were being taunted and derided from sincere convictions that they were poor and puny. His knowledge of his inability to take vengeance for it made his rage into a dark and stormy specter, that possessed him and made him dream of abominable cruelties. The tormentors were flies sucking insolently at his blood, and he thought that he would have given his life for a revenge of seeing their faces in pitiful plights.

The winds of battle had swept all about the regiment, until the one rifle, instantly followed by others, flashed in its front. A moment later the regiment roared forth its sudden and valiant retort. A dense wall of smoke settled slowly down. It was furiously slit and slashed by the knifelike fire from the rifles.

To the youth the fighters resembled animals tossed for a death struggle into a dark pit. There was a sensation that he and his fellows, at bay, were pushing back, always pushing fierce onslaughts of creatures who were slippery. Their beams of crimson seemed to get no purchase upon the bodies of their foes; the latter seemed to evade them with ease, and come through, between, around, and about with unopposed skill.

When, in a dream, it occurred to the youth that his rifle was an impotent stick, he lost sense of everything but his hate, his desire to smash into pulp the glittering smile of victory which he could feel upon the faces of his enemies.

The blue smoke-swallowed line curled and writhed like a snake stepped upon. It swung its ends to and fro in an agony of fear and rage.

The youth was not conscious that he was erect upon his feet. He did not know the direction of the ground. Indeed, once he even lost the habit of balance and fell heavily. He was up again immediately. One thought went through the chaos of his brain at the time. He wondered if he had fallen because he had been shot. But the suspicion flew away at once. He did not think more of it.

He had taken up a first position behind the little tree, with a direct determination to hold it against the world. He had not deemed it possible that his army could that day succeed, and from this he felt the ability to fight harder. But the throng had surged in all ways, until he lost directions and locations, save that he knew where lay the enemy.

The flames bit him, and the hot smoke broiled his skin. His rifle barrel grew so hot that ordinarily he could not have borne it upon his palms; but hc kept on stuffing cartridges into it, and pounding them with his clanking, bending ramrod. If he aimed at some changing form through the smoke, he pulled his trigger with a fierce grunt, as if he were dealing a blow of the fist with all his strength.

When the enemy seemed falling back before him and his fellows, he went instantly forward, like a dog who, seeing his foes lagging, turns and insists upon being pursued. And when he was compelled to retire again, he did it slowly, sullenly, taking steps of wrathful despair.

Once he, in his intent hate, was almost alone, and was firing, when all those near him had ceased. He was so engrossed in his occupation that he was not aware of a lull.

He was recalled by a hoarse laugh and a sentence that came to his ears in a voice of contempt and amazement. "Yeh infernal fool, don't yeh know enough t' quit when there ain't anything t' shoot at? Good Gawd!"

He turned then and, pausing with his rifle thrown half into position, looked at the blue line of his comrades. During this moment of leisure they seemed all to be engaged in staring with astonishment at him. They had become spectators. Turning to the front again he saw, under the lifted smoke, a deserted ground.

He looked bewildered for a moment. Then there appeared upon the glazed vacancy of his eyes a diamond point of intelligence. "Oh," he said, comprehending.

He returned to his comrades and threw himself upon the ground. He sprawled like a man who had been thrashed. His flesh seemed strangely on fire, and the sounds of the battle continued in his ears. He groped blindly for his canteen.

The lieutenant was crowing. He seemed drunk with fighting. He called out to the youth: "By heavens, if I had ten thousand wild cats like you I could tear th' stomach outa this war in less'n a week!" He puffed out his chest with large dignity as he said it.

Some of the men muttered and looked at the youth in awe-struck ways. It was plain that as he had gone on loading and firing and cursing without the proper intermission, they had found time to regard him. And they now looked upon him as a war devil.

The friend came staggering to him. There was some fright and dismay in his voice. "Are yeh all right, Fleming? Do yeh feel all right? There ain't nothin' th' matter with yeh, Henry, is there?"

"No," said the youth with difficulty. His throat seemed full of knobs and burs.

These incidents made the youth ponder. It was revealed to him that he had been a barbarian, a beast. He had fought like a pagan who defends his religion. Regarding it, he saw that it was fine, wild, and, in some ways, easy. He had been a tremendous figure, no doubt. By this struggle he had overcome obstacles which he had admitted to be mountains. They had fallen like paper peaks, and he was now what he called a hero. And he had not been aware of the process. He had slept and, awakening, found himself a knight.

He lay and basked in the occasional stares of his comrades. Their faces were varied in degrees of blackness from the burned powder. Some were utterly smudged. They were reeking with perspiration, and their breaths came hard and wheezing. And from these soiled expanses they peered at him.

"Hot work! Hot work!" cried the lieutenant deliriously. He walked up and down, restless and eager. Sometimes his voice could be heard in a wild, incomprehensible laugh.

When he had a particularly profound thought upon the science of war he always unconsciously addressed himself to the youth.

There was some grim rejoicing by the men. "By thunder, I bet this army'll never see another new reg'ment like us!"

"You bet!"

"A dog, a woman, an' a walnut tree,
Th' more yeh beat 'em, th' better they be!

That's like us."

"Lost a piler men, they did. If an' ol' woman swep' up th' woods she'd git a dustpanful."

"Yes, an' if she'll come around ag'in in 'bout an' hour she'll git a pile more."

The forest still bore its burden of clamor. From off under the trees came the rolling clatter of the musketry. Each distant thicket seemed a strange porcupine with quills of flame. A cloud of dark smoke, as from smoldering ruins, went up toward the sun now bright and gay in the blue, enameled sky.

Chapter XVIII

THE ragged line had respite for some minutes, but during its pause the struggle in the forest became magnified until the trees seemed to quiver from the firing and the ground to shake from the rushing of the men. The voices of the cannon were mingled in a long and interminable row. It seemed difficult to live in such an atmosphere. The chests of the men strained for a bit of freshness, and their throats craved water.

There was one shot through the body, who raised a cry of bitter lamentation when came this lull. Perhaps he had been calling out during the fighting also, but at that time no one had heard him. But now the men turned at the woeful complaints of him upon the ground.

"Who is it? Who is it?"

"It's Jimmie Rogers. Jimmie Rogers."

When their eyes first encountered him there was a sudden halt, as if they feared to go near. He was thrashing about in the grass, twisting his shuddering body into many strange postures. He was screaming loudly. This instant's hesitation seemed to fill him with a tremendous, fantastic contempt, and he damned them in shrieked sentences.

The youth's friend had a geographical illusion concerning a stream, and he obtained permission to go for some water. Immediately canteens were showered upon him. "Fill mine, will yeh?" "Bring me some, too." "And me, too." He departed, ladened. The youth went with his friend, feeling a desire to throw his heated body onto[1] the stream and, soaking there, drink quarts.

They made a hurried search for the supposed stream, but did not find it. "No water here," said the youth. They turned without delay and began to retrace their steps.

From their position as they again faced toward the place of the fighting, they could of course comprehend a greater amount of the battle than when their visions had been blurred by the hurling smoke of the line. They could see dark stretches winding along the land, and on one cleared space there was a row of guns making gray clouds, which were filled with large flashes of orange-colored flame. Over some foliage they could see the roof of a house. One window, ⌈glowing a deep murder red,⌋ shone

---

1 Crane's manuscript reads: into.

squarely through the leaves. From the edifice a tall leaning tower of smoke went far into the sky.

Looking over their own troops, they saw mixed masses slowly getting into regular form. The sunlight made twinkling points of the bright steel. To the rear there was a glimpse of a distant roadway as it curved over a slope. It was crowded with retreating infantry. From all the interwoven forest arose the smoke and bluster of the battle. The air was always occupied by a blaring.

Near where they stood shells were flip-flapping and hooting. Occasional bullets buzzed in the air and spanged into tree trunks. Wounded men and other stragglers were slinking through the woods.

Looking down an aisle of the grove, the youth and his companion saw a jangling general and his staff almost ride upon a wounded man, who was crawling on his hands and knees. The general reined strongly at his charger's opened and foamy mouth and guided it with dexterous horsemanship past the man. The latter scrambled in wild and torturing haste. His strength evidently failed him as he reached a place of safety. One of his arms suddenly weakened, and he fell, sliding over upon his back. He lay stretched out, breathing gently.

A moment later the small, creaking cavalcade was directly in front of the two soldiers. Another officer, riding with the skillful abandon of a cowboy, galloped his horse to a position directly before the general. The two unnoticed foot soldiers made a little show of going on, but they lingered near in the desire to overhear the conversation. Perhaps, they thought, some great inner historical things would be said.

The general, whom the boys knew as the commander of their division, looked at the other officer and spoke coolly, as if he were criticising his clothes. "Th' enemy's formin' over there for another charge," he said. "It'll be directed against Whiterside, an' I fear they'll break through there unless we work like thunder t' stop them."

The other swore at his restive horse, and then cleared his throat. He made a gesture toward his cap. "It'll be hell t' pay stoppin' them," he said shortly.

"I presume so," remarked the general. Then he began to talk rapidly and in a lower tone. He frequently illustrated his words with a pointing finger. The two infantrymen could hear nothing until finally he asked: "What troops can you spare?"

The officer who rode like a cowboy reflected for an instant. "Well," he said, "I had to order in th' 12th to help th' 76th, an' I haven't really got any. But there's th' 304th. They fight like a lot 'a mule drivers. I can spare them best of any."

The youth and his friend exchanged glances of astonishment.

The general spoke sharply. "Get 'em ready, then. I'll watch developments from here, an' send you word when t' start them. It'll happen in five minutes."

As the other officer tossed his fingers toward his cap and wheeling his horse, started away, the general called out to him in a sober voice: "I don't believe many of your mule drivers will get back."

The other shouted something in reply. He smiled.

With scared faces, the youth and his companion hurried back to the line.

These happenings had occupied an incredibly short time, yet the youth felt that in them he had been made aged. New eyes were given to him. And the most startling thing was to learn suddenly that he was very insignificant. The officer spoke of the regiment as if he referred to a broom. Some part of the woods needed sweeping, perhaps, and he merely indicated a broom in a tone properly indifferent to its fate. It was war, no doubt, but it appeared strange.

As the two boys approached the line, the lieutenant perceived them and swelled with wrath. "Fleming—Wilson—how long does it take yeh to git water, anyhow—where yeh been to."

But his oration ceased as he saw their eyes, which were large with great tales. "We're goin' t' charge—we're goin' t' charge!" cried the youth's friend, hastening with his news.

"Charge?" said the lieutenant. "Charge? Well, b'Gawd! Now, this is real fightin'." Over his soiled countenance there went a boastful smile. "Charge? Well, b'Gawd!"

A little group of soldiers surrounded the two youths. "Are we, sure 'nough? Well, I'll be derned! Charge? What fer? What at? Wilson, you're lyin'."

"I hope to die," said the youth, pitching his tones to the key of angry remonstrance. "Sure as shooting, I tell you."

And his friend spoke in re-enforcement. "Not by a blame sight, he ain't lyin'. We heard 'em talkin'."

They caught sight of two mounted figures a short distance from them. One was the colonel of the regiment and the other was the officer who had received orders from the commander of the division. They were gesticulating at each other. The soldier, pointing at them, interpreted the scene.

One man had a final objection: "How could yeh hear 'em

talkin'?" But the men, for a large part, nodded, admitting that previously the two friends had spoken truth.

They settled back into reposeful attitudes with airs of having accepted the matter. And they mused upon it, with a hundred varieties of expression. It was an engrossing thing to think about. Many tightened their belts carefully and hitched at their trousers.

A moment later the officers began to bustle among the men, pushing them into a more compact mass and into a better alignment. They chased those that straggled and fumed at a few men who seemed to show by their attitudes that they had decided to remain at that spot. They were like critical shepherds struggling with sheep.

Presently, the regiment seemed to draw itself up and heave a deep breath. None of the men's faces were mirrors of large thoughts. The soldiers were bended and stooped like sprinters before a signal. Many pairs of glinting eyes peered from the grimy faces toward the curtains of the deeper woods. They seemed to be engaged in deep calculations of time and distance.

They were surrounded by the noises of the monstrous altercation between the two armies. The world was fully interested in other matters. Apparently, the regiment had its small affair to itself.

The youth, turning, shot a quick, inquiring glance at his friend. The latter returned to him the same manner of look. They were the only ones who possessed an inner knowledge. "Mule drivers—hell t' pay—don't believe many will get back." It was an ironical secret. Still, they saw no hesitation in each other's faces, and they nodded a mute and unprotesting assent when a shaggy man near them said in a meek voice: "We'll git swallowed."

Chapter XIX

THE youth stared at the land in front of him. Its foliages now seemed to veil powers and horrors. He was unaware of the machinery of orders that started the charge, although from the corners of his eyes he saw an officer, who looked like a boy a-horseback, come galloping, waving his hat. Suddenly he felt a straining and heaving among the men. The line fell slowly forward like a toppling wall, and, with a convulsive gasp that was intended for a cheer, the regiment began its journey. The youth was pushed and jostled for a moment before he understood the movement at all, but directly he lunged ahead and began to run.

He fixed his eye upon a distant and prominent clump of trees where he had concluded the enemy were to be met, and he ran toward it as toward a goal. He had believed throughout that it was a mere question of getting over an unpleasant matter as quickly as possible, and he ran desperately, as if pursued for a murder. His face was drawn hard and tight with the stress of his endeavor. His eyes were fixed in a lurid glare. And with his soiled and disordered dress, his red and inflamed features surmounted by the dingy rag with its spot of blood, his wildly swinging rifle and banging accouterments, he looked to be an insane soldier.

As the regiment swung from its position out into a cleared space the woods and thickets before it awakened. Yellow flames leaped toward it from many directions. The forest made a tremendous objection.

The line lurched straight for a moment. Then the right wing swung forward; it in turn was surpassed by the left. Afterward the center careered to the front until the regiment was a wedge shaped mass, but an instant later the opposition of the bushes, trees, and uneven places on the ground split the command and scattered it into detached clusters.

The youth, light-footed, was unconsciously in advance. His eyes still kept note of the clump of trees. From all places near it the clannish yell of the enemy could be heard. The little flames of rifles leaped from it. The song of the bullets was in the air and shells snarled among the treetops. One tumbled directly into the middle of a hurrying group and exploded in crimson fury. There was an instant's spectacle of a man, almost over it, throwing up his hands to shield his eyes.

Other men, punched by bullets, fell in grotesque agonies. The regiment left a coherent trail of bodies.

They had passed into a clearer atmosphere. There was an effect like a revelation in the new appearance of the landscape. Some men working madly at a battery were plain to them, and the opposing infantry's lines were defined by the gray walls and fringes of smoke.

It seemed to the youth that he saw everything. Each blade of the green grass was bold and clear. He thought that he was aware of every change in the thin, transparent vapor that floated idly in sheets. The brown or gray trunks of the trees showed each roughness of their surfaces. And the men of the regiment, with their starting eyes and sweating faces, running madly, or falling, as if thrown headlong, to queer, heaped-up corpses—all were comprehended. His mind took a mechanical but firm impression, so that afterward everything was pictured and explained to him, save why he himself was there.

But there was a frenzy made from this furious rush. The men, pitching forward insanely, had burst into cheerings, moblike and barbaric, but tuned in strange keys that can arouse the dullard and the stoic. It made a mad enthusiasm that, it seemed, would be incapable of checking itself before granite and brass. There was the delirium that encounters despair and death, and is heedless and blind to the odds. It is a temporary but sublime absence of selfishness. And because it was of this order was the reason, perhaps, why the youth wondered, afterward, what reasons he could have had for being there.

Presently the straining pace ate up the energies of the men. As if by agreement, the leaders began to slacken their speed. The volleys directed against them had had a seeming windlike effect. The regiment snorted and blew. Among some stolid trees it began to falter and hesitate. The men, staring intently, began to wait for some of the distant walls of smoke to move and disclose to them the scene. Since much of their strength and their breath had vanished, they returned to caution. They were become men again.

The youth had a vague belief that he had run miles, and he thought, in a way, that he was now in some new and unknown land.

The moment the regiment ceased its advance the protesting splutter of musketry became a steadied roar. Long and accurate fringes of smoke spread out. From the top of a small hill came level belchings of yellow flame that caused an inhuman whistling in the air.

The men, halted, had opportunity to see some of their comrades dropping with moans and shrieks. A few lay under foot, still or wailing. And now for an instant the men stood, their rifles slack in their hands, and watched the regiment dwindle. They appeared dazed and stupid. This spectacle seemed to paralyze them, overcome them with a fatal fascination. They stared woodenly at the sights, and, lowering their eyes, looked from face to face. It was a strange pause, and a strange silence.

Then, above the sounds of the outside commotion, arose the roar of the lieutenant. He strode suddenly forth, his infantile features black with rage.

"Come on, yeh fools!" he bellowed. "Come on! Yeh can't stay here. Yeh must come on." He said more, but much of it could not be understood.

He started rapidly forward, with his head turned toward the men. "Come on," he was shouting. The men stared with blank and yokel like eyes at him. He was obliged to halt and retrace his steps. He stood then with his back to the enemy and delivered gigantic curses into the faces of the men. His body vibrated from the weight and force of his imprecations. And he could string oaths with the facility of a maiden who strings beads.

The friend of the youth aroused. Lurching suddenly forward and dropping to his knees, he fired an angry shot at the persistent woods. This action awakened the men. They huddled no more like sheep. They seemed suddenly to bethink them of their weapons, and at once commenced firing. Belabored by their officers, they began to move forward. The regiment, involved like a cart involved in mud and muddle, started unevenly with many jolts and jerks. The men stopped now every few paces to fire and load, and in this manner moved slowly on from trees to trees.

The flaming opposition in their front grew with their advance until it seemed that all forward ways were barred by the thin leaping tongues, and off to the right an ominous demonstration could sometimes be dimly discerned. The smoke lately generated was in confusing clouds that made it difficult for the regiment to proceed with intelligence. As he passed through each curling mass the youth wondered what would confront him on the farther side.

The command went painfully forward until an open space interposed between them and the lurid lines. Here, crouching and cowering behind some trees, the men clung with desperation, as if threatened by a wave. They looked wild-eyed, and as if amazed at this furious disturbance they had stirred. In the storm there was an ironical expression of their importance. The faces of the men, too, showed a lack of a certain feeling of responsibility for being there. It was as if they had been driven. It was the dominant animal failing to remember in the supreme moments the forceful causes of various superficial qualities. The whole affair seemed incomprehensible to many of them.

As they halted thus the lieutenant again began to bellow profanely. Regardless of the vindictive threats of the bullets, he went about coaxing, berating, and bedamning. His lips, that were habitually in a soft and childlike curve, were now writhed into unholy contortions. He swore by all possible deities.

Once he grabbed the youth by the arm. "Come on, yeh lunkhead!" he roared. "Come on! We'll all git killed if we stay here. We've on'y got t' go across that lot. An' then"—the remainder of his idea disappeared in a blue haze of curses.

The youth stretched forth his arm. "Cross there?" His mouth was puckered in doubt and awe.

"Certainly. Jest 'cross th' lot! We can't stay here," screamed the lieutenant. He poked his face close to the youth and waved his bandaged hand. "Come on!" Presently he grappled with him as if for a wrestling bout. It was as if he planned to drag the youth by the ear on to the assault.

The private felt a sudden unspeakable indignation against his officer. He wrenched fiercely and shook him off.

"Come on yerself, then," he yelled. There was a bitter challenge in his voice.

They galloped together down the regimental front. The friend scrambled after them. In front of the colors the three men began to bawl: "Come on! come on!" They danced and gyrated like tortured savages.

The flag, obedient to these appeals, bended its glittering form and swept toward them. The men wavered in indecision for a moment, and then with a long, wailful cry the dilapidated regiment surged forward and began its new journey.

Over the field went the scurrying mass. It was a handful of men splattered into the faces of the enemy. Toward it instantly sprang the yellow tongues. A vast quantity of blue smoke hung before them. A mighty banging made ears valueless.

The youth ran like a madman to reach the woods before a bullet could discover him. He ducked his head low, like a football player.[1] In his haste his eyes almost closed, and the scene was a wild blur. Pulsating saliva stood at the corners of his mouth.

---

1 Football was a new sport, but Crane had covered a college game as a journalist. In college, he had played baseball.

Within him, as he hurled himself forward, was born a love, a despairing fondness for this flag which was near him. It was a creation of beauty and invulnerability. It was a goddess, radiant, that bended its form with an imperious gesture to him. It was a woman, red and white, hating and loving, that called him with the voice of his hopes. Because no harm could come to it he endowed it with power. He kept near, as if it could be a saver of lives, and an imploring cry went from his mind.

In the mad scramble he was aware that the color sergeant flinched suddenly, as if struck by a bludgeon. He faltered, and then became motionless, save for his quivering knees.

He made a spring and a clutch at the pole. At the same instant his friend grabbed it from the other side. They jerked at it, stout and furious, but the color sergeant was dead, and the corpse would not relinquish its trust. For a moment there was a grim encounter. The dead man, swinging with bended back, seemed to be obstinately tugging, in ludicrous and awful ways, for the possession of the flag.

It was past in an instant of time. They wrenched the flag furiously from the dead man, and, as they turned again, the corpse swayed forward with bowed head. One arm swung high, and the curved hand fell with heavy protest on the friend's unheeding shoulder.

Chapter XX

WHEN the two youths turned with the flag they saw that much of the regiment had crumbled away, and the dejected remnant was coming slowly back. The men, having hurled themselves in projectile fashion, had presently expended their forces. They slowly retreated, with their faces still toward the spluttering woods, and their hot rifles still replying to the din. Several officers were giving orders, their voices keyed to screams.

"Where in hell yeh goin'?" the lieutenant was asking in a sarcastic howl. And a red-bearded officer, whose voice of triple brass could plainly be heard, was commanding: "Shoot into 'em! Shoot into 'em, Gawd damn their souls!" There was a *melée* of screeches, in which the men were ordered to do conflicting and impossible things.

The youth and his friend had a small scuffle over the flag. "Give it t' me!" "No, let me keep it!" Each felt satisfied with the other's possession of it, but each felt bound to declare, by an offer to carry the emblem, his willingness to further risk himself. The youth roughly pushed his friend away.

The regiment fell back to the stolid trees. There it halted for a moment to blaze at some dark forms that had begun to steal upon its track. Presently it resumed its march again, curving among the tree trunks. By the time the depleted regiment had again reached the first open space they were receiving a fast and merciless fire. There seemed to be mobs all about them.

The greater part of the men, discouraged, their spirits worn by the turmoil, acted as if stunned. They accepted the pelting of the bullets with bowed and weary heads. It was of no purpose to strive against walls. It was of no use to batter themselves against granite. And from this consciousness that they had attempted to conquer an unconquerable thing there seemed to arise a feeling that they had been betrayed. They glowered with bent brows, but dangerously, upon some of the officers, more particularly upon the red-bearded one with the voice of triple brass.

However, the rear of the regiment was fringed with men, who continued to shoot irritably at the advancing foes. They seemed resolved to make every trouble. The youthful lieutenant was perhaps the last man in the disordered mass. His forgotten back

---

1 Flag bearers were frequent targets for sharp shooters on both sides. The flag was a visual means of organization for a regiment.

was toward the enemy. He had been shot in the arm. It hung straight and rigid. Occasionally he would cease to remember it, and be about to emphasize an oath with a sweeping gesture. The multiplied pain caused him to swear with incredible power.

The youth went along with slipping, uncertain feet. He kept watchful eyes rearward. A scowl of mortification and rage was upon his face. He had thought of a fine revenge upon the officer who had referred to him and his fellows as mule drivers. But he saw that it could not come to pass. His dreams had collapsed when the mule drivers, dwindling rapidly, had wavered and hesitated on the little clearing, and then had recoiled. And now the retreat of the mule drivers was a march of shame to him.

A dagger-pointed gaze from without his blackened face was held toward the enemy, but his greater hatred was riveted upon the man, who, not knowing him, had called him a mule driver.

When he knew that he and his comrades had failed to do anything in successful ways that might bring the little pangs of a kind of remorse upon the officer, the youth allowed the rage of the baffled to possess him. This cold officer upon a monument, who dropped epithets unconcernedly down, would be finer as a dead man, he thought. So grievous did he think it that he could never possess the secret right to taunt truly in answer.

He had pictured red letters of curious revenge. "We *are* mule drivers, are we?" And now he was compelled to throw them away.

He presently wrapped his heart in the cloak of his pride and kept the flag erect. He harangued his fellows, pushing against their chests with his free hand. To those he knew well he made frantic appeals, beseeching them by name. Between him and the lieutenant, scolding and near to losing his mind with rage, there was felt a subtle fellowship and equality. They supported each other in all manner of hoarse, howling protests.

But the regiment was a machine run down. The two men babbled at a forceless thing. The soldiers who had heart to go slowly were continually shaken in their resolves by a knowledge that comrades were slipping with speed back to the lines. It was difficult to think of reputation when others were thinking of skins. Wounded men were left crying on this black journey.

The smoke fringes and flames blustered always. The youth, peering once through a sudden rift in a cloud, saw a brown mass of troops, interwoven and magnified until they appeared to be thousands. A fierce-hued flag flashed before his vision.

Immediately, as if the uplifting of the smoke had been prearranged, the discovered troops burst into a rasping yell, and a hundred flames jetted toward the retreating band. A rolling gray cloud again interposed as the regiment doggedly replied. The youth had to depend again upon his misused ears, which were trembling and buzzing from the *melée* of musketry and yells.

The way seemed eternal. In the clouded haze men became panic-stricken with the thought that the regiment had lost its path, and was proceeding in a perilous direction. Once the men who headed the wild procession turned and came pushing back against their comrades, screaming that they were being fired upon from points which they had considered to be toward their own lines. At this cry a hysterical fear and dismay beset the troops. A soldier, who heretofore had been ambitious to make the regiment into a wise little band that would proceed calmly amid the huge appearing difficulties, suddenly sank down and buried his face in his arms with an air of bowing to a doom. From another a shrill lamentation rang out filled with profane allusions to a general. Men ran hither and thither, seeking with their eyes roads of escape. With serene regularity, as if controlled by a schedule, bullets buffed into men.

The youth walked stolidly into the midst of the mob, and with his flag in his hands took a stand as if he expected an attempt to push him to the ground. He unconsciously assumed the attitude of the color bearer in the fight of the preceding day. He passed over his brow a hand that trembled. His breath did not come freely. He was choking during this small wait for the crisis.

His friend came to him. "Well, Henry, I guess this is good-by-John."[1]

"Oh, shut up, you damned fool!" replied the youth, and he would not look at the other.

The officers labored like politicians to beat the mass into a proper circle to face the menaces. The ground was uneven and torn. The men curled into depressions and fitted themselves snugly behind whatever would frustrate a bullet.

The youth noted with vague surprise that the lieutenant was standing mutely with his legs far apart and his sword held in the manner of a cane. The youth wondered what had happened to his vocal organs that he no more cursed.

There was something curious in this little intent pause of the lieutenant. He was like a babe which, having wept its fill, raises its eyes and fixes upon a distant toy. He was engrossed in this contemplation, and the soft under lip quivered from self-whispered words.

---

1 Henry's friend is certain that he will be killed in the upcoming battle.

Some lazy and ignorant smoke curled slowly. The men, hiding from the bullets, waited anxiously for it to lift and disclose the plight of the regiment.

The silent ranks were suddenly thrilled by the eager voice of the youthful lieutenant bawling out: "Here they come! Right onto us, b'Gawd!" His further words were lost in a roar of wicked thunder from the men's rifles.

The youth's eyes had instantly turned in the direction indicated by the awakened and agitated lieutenant, and he had seen the haze of treachery disclosing a body of soldiers of the enemy. They were so near that he could see their features. There was a recognition as he looked at the types of faces. Also he perceived with dim amazement that their uniforms were rather gay in effect, being light gray, accented with a brilliant hued facing. Too, the clothes seemed new.

These troops had apparently been going forward with caution, their rifles held in readiness, when the youthful lieutenant had discovered them and their movement had been interrupted by the volley from the blue regiment. From the moment's glimpse, it was derived that they had been unaware of the proximity of their dark-suited foes or had mistaken the direction. Almost instantly they were shut utterly from the youth's sight by the smoke from the energetic rifles of his companions. He strained his vision to learn the accomplishment of the volley, but the smoke hung before him.

The two bodies of troops exchanged blows in the manner of a pair of boxers. The fast angry firings went back and forth. The men in blue were intent with the despair of their circumstances and they seized upon the revenge to be had at close range. Their thunder swelled loud and valiant. Their curving front bristled with flashes and the place resounded with the clangor of their ramrods. The youth ducked and dodged for a time and achieved a few unsatisfactory views of the enemy. There appeared to be many of them and they were replying swiftly. They seemed moving toward the blue regiment, step by step. He seated himself gloomily on the ground with his flag between his knees.

As he noted the vicious, wolflike temper of his comrades he had a sweet thought that if the enemy was about to swallow the regimental broom as a large prisoner, it could at least have the consolation of going down with bristles forward.

But the blows of the antagonist began to grow more weak. Fewer bullets ripped the air, and finally, when the men slackened to learn of the fight, they could see only dark, floating smoke. The regiment lay still and gazed. Presently some chance whim came to the pestering blur, and it began to coil heavily away. The men saw a ground vacant of fighters. It would have been an empty stage if it were not for a few corpses that lay thrown and twisted into fantastic shapes upon the sward.

At sight of this tableau, many of the men in blue sprang from behind their covers and made an ungainly dance of joy. Their eyes burned and a hoarse cheer of elation broke from their dry lips.

 It had begun to seem to them that events were trying to prove that they were impotent. These little battles had evidently endeavored to demonstrate that the men could not fight well. When on the verge of submission to these opinions, the small duel had showed them that the proportions were not impossible, and by it they had revenged themselves upon their misgivings and upon the foe.

The impetus of enthusiasm was theirs again. They gazed about them with looks of uplifted pride, feeling new trust in the grim, always confident weapons in their hands. And they were men.

Chapter XXI

PRESENTLY they knew that no firing threatened them. All ways seemed once more opened to them. The dusty blue lines of their friends were disclosed a short distance away. In the distance there were many colossal noises, but in all this part of the field there was a sudden stillness.

They perceived that they were free. The depleted band drew a long breath of relief and gathered itself into a bunch to complete its trip.

In this last length of journey the men began to show strange emotions. They hurried with nervous fear. Some who had been dark and unfaltering in the grimmest moments now could not conceal an anxiety that made them frantic. It was perhaps that they dreaded to be killed in insignificant ways after the times for proper military deaths had passed. Or, perhaps, they thought it would be too ironical to get killed at the portals of safety. With backward looks of perturbation, they hastened.

As they approached their own lines there was some sarcasm exhibited on the part of a gaunt and bronzed regiment that lay resting in the shade of trees. Questions were wafted to them.

"Where th' hell yeh been?"

"What yeh comin' back fer?"

"Why didn't yeh stay there?"

"Was it warm out there, sonny?"

"Goin' home now, boys?"

One shouted in taunting mimicry: "Oh, mother, come quick an' look at th' sojers!"

There was no reply from the bruised and battered regiment, save that one man made broadcast challenges to fist fights and the red-bearded officer walked rather near and glared in great swashbuckler style at a tall captain in the other regiment. But the lieutenant suppressed the man who wished to fist fight, and the tall captain, flushing at the little fanfare of the red-bearded one, was obliged to look intently at some trees.

The youth's tender flesh was deeply stung by these remarks. From under his creased brows he glowered with hate at the mockers. He meditated upon a few revenges. Still, many in the regiment hung their heads in criminal fashion, so that it came to pass that the men trudged with sudden heaviness, as if they bore upon their bended shoulders the coffin of their honor. And the youthful lieutenant, recollecting himself, began to mutter softly in black curses.

They turned when they arrived at their old position to regard the ground over which they had charged.

The youth in this contemplation was smitten with a large astonishment. He discovered that the distances, as compared with the brilliant measurings of his mind, were trivial and ridiculous. The stolid trees, where much had taken place, seemed incredibly near. The time, too, now that he reflected, he saw to have been short. He wondered at the number of emotions and events that had been crowded into such little spaces. Elfin thoughts must have exaggerated and enlarged everything, he said.

It seemed, then, that there was bitter justice in the speeches of the gaunt and bronzed veterans. He veiled a glance of disdain at his fellows who strewed the ground, choking with dust, red from perspiration, misty eyed, disheveled.

They were gulping at their canteens, fierce to wring every mite of water from them, and they polished at their swollen and watery features with coat sleeves and bunches of grass.

However, to the youth there was a considerable joy in musing upon his performances during the charge. He had had very little time previously in which to appreciate himself, so that there was now much satisfaction in quietly thinking of his actions. He recalled bits of color that in the flurry had stamped themselves unawares upon his engaged senses.

As the regiment lay heaving from its hot exertions the officer who had named them as mule drivers came galloping along the line. He had lost his cap. His tousled hair streamed wildly, and his face was dark with vexation and wrath. His temper was displayed with more clearness by the way in which he managed his horse. He jerked and wrenched savagely at his bridle, stopping the hard-breathing animal with a furious pull near the colonel of the regiment. He immediately exploded in reproaches which came unbidden to the ears of the men. They were suddenly alert, being always curious about black words between officers.

"Oh, thunder, MacChesnay, what an awful bull you made of this thing!" began the officer. He attempted low tones, but his indignation caused certain of the men to learn the sense of his words. "What an awful mess you made! Good Lord, man, you stopped about a hundred feet this side of a very pretty success! If your men had gone a hundred feet farther you would have made a great charge, but as it is—what a lot of mud diggers you've got anyway!"

The men, listening with bated breath, now turned their curious eyes upon the colonel. They had a ragamuffin interest in this affair.

The colonel was seen to straighten his form and put one hand forth in oratorical fashion. He wore an injured air; it was as if a deacon had been accused of stealing. The men were wiggling in an ecstasy of excitement.

But of a sudden the colonel's manner changed from that of a deacon to that of a Frenchman. He shrugged his shoulders. "Oh, well, general, we went as far as we could," he said calmly.

"As far as you could? Did you, b'Gawd?" snorted the other. "Well, that wasn't very far, was it?" he added, with a glance of cold contempt into the other's eyes. "Not very far, I think. You were intended to make a diversion in favor of Whiterside. How well you succeeded your own ears can now tell you." He wheeled his horse and rode stiffly away.

The colonel, bidden to hear the jarring noises of an engagement in the woods to the left, broke out in vague damnations.

The lieutenant, who had listened with an air of impotent rage to the interview, spoke suddenly in firm and undaunted tones. "I don't care what a man is—whether he is a general or what—if he says th' boys didn't put up a good fight out there he's a damned fool."

"Lieutenant," began the colonel, severely, "this is my own affair, and I'll trouble you   "

The lieutenant made an obedient gesture. "All right, colonel, all right," he said. He sat down with an air of being content with himself.

The news that the regiment had been reproached went along the line. For a time the men were bewildered by it. "Good thunder!" they ejaculated, staring at the vanishing form of the general. They conceived it to be a huge mistake.

Presently, however, they began to believe that in truth their efforts had been called light. The youth could see this conviction weigh upon the entire regiment until the men were like cuffed and cursed animals, but withal rebellious.

The friend, with a grievance in his eye, went to the youth. "I wonder what he does want," he said. "He must think we went out there an' played marbles! I never see sech a man!"

The youth developed a tranquil philosophy for these moments of irritation. "Oh, well," he rejoined, "he probably didn't see nothing of it at all and got mad as blazes, and concluded we were a lot of sheep, just because we didn't do what he wanted done.

It's a pity old Grandpa Henderson got killed yestirday—he'd have known that we did our best and fought good. It's just our awful luck, that's what."

"I should say so," replied the friend. He seemed to be deeply wounded at an injustice. "I should say we did have awful luck! There's no fun in fightin' fer people when everything yeh do—no matter what—ain't done right. I have a notion t' stay behind next time an' let 'em take their ol' charge an' go t' th' devil with it."

The youth spoke soothingly to his comrade. "Well, we both did good. I'd like to see the fool what'd say we both didn't do as good as we could!"

"Of course we did," declared the friend stoutly. "An' I'd break th' feller's neck if he was as big as a church. But we're all right, anyhow, for I heard one feller say that we two fit th' best in th' reg'ment, an' they had a great argument 'bout it. Another feller, 'a course, he had t' up an' say it was a lie—he seen all what was goin' on an' he never seen us from th' beginnin' t' th' end. An' a lot more struck in an' ses it wasn't a lie—we did fight like thunder, an' they give us quite a send off. But this is what I can't stand—these everlastin' ol' soldiers, titterin' an' laughin', an' then that general, he's crazy."

The youth exclaimed with sudden exasperation: "He's a lunkhead! He makes me mad. I wish he'd come along next time. We'd show 'im what—"

He ceased because several men had come hurrying up. Their faces expressed a bringing of great news.

"O Flem, yeh jest oughta heard!" cried one, eagerly.

"Heard what?" said the youth.

"Yeh jest oughta heard!" repeated the other, and he arranged himself to tell his tidings. The others made an excited circle. "Well, sir, th' colonel met your lieutenant right by us—it was damnedest thing I ever heard—an' he ses: 'Ahem! ahem!' he ses. 'Mr. Hasbrouck!' he ses, 'by th' way, who was that lad what carried th' flag?' he ses. There, Flemin', what d' yeh think 'a that? 'Who was th' lad what carried th' flag?' he ses, an' th' lieutenant, he speaks up right away: 'That's Flemin', an' he's a jimhickey,' he ses, right away. What? I say he did. 'A jimhickey,' he ses—those 'r his words. He did, too. I say he did. If you kin tell this story better than I kin, go ahead an' tell it. Well, then, keep yer mouth shet. Th' lieutenant, he ses: 'He's a jimhickey,' an' th' colonel, he ses: 'Ahem! ahem! he is, indeed, a very good man t' have, ahem! He kep' th' flag 'way t' th' front. I saw 'im. He's a good un,' ses th' colonel. 'You bet,' ses th' lieutenant, 'he an' a feller named Wilson was at th' head 'a th' charge, an' howlin' like Indians all th' time,' he ses. 'Head 'a th' charge all th' time,' he ses. 'A feller named Wilson,' he ses. There, Wilson, m'boy, put that in a letter an' send it hum t' yer mother, hay? 'A feller named Wilson,' he ses. An' th' colonel, he ses: 'Were they, indeed? Ahem! ahem! My sakes!' he ses. 'At th' head 'a th' reg'ment?' he ses. 'They were,' ses th' lieutenant. 'My sakes!' ses th' colonel. He ses: 'Well, well, well,' he ses, 'those two babies?' 'They were,' ses th' lieutenant. 'Well, well,' ses th' colonel, 'they deserve t' be major generals,' he ses. 'They deserve t' be major generals.'"

The youth and his friend had said: "Huh!" "Yer lyin', Thompson." "Oh, go t' blazes!" "He never sed it." "Oh, what a lie!" "Huh!" But despite these youthful scoffings and embarrassments, they knew that their faces were deeply flushing from thrills of pleasure. They exchanged a secret glance of joy and congratulation.

They speedily forgot many things. The past held no pictures of error and disappointment. They were very happy, and their hearts swelled with grateful affection for the colonel and the youthful lieutenant.

Chapter XXII

WHEN the woods again began to pour forth the dark-hued masses of the enemy the youth felt serene self-confidence. He smiled briefly when he saw men dodge and duck at the long screechings of shells that were thrown in giant handfuls over them. He stood, erect and tranquil, watching the attack begin against a part of the line that made a blue curve along the side of an adjacent hill. His vision being unmolested by smoke from the rifles of his companions, he had opportunities to see parts of the hard fight. It was a relief to perceive at last from whence came some of these noises which had been roared into his ears.

Off a short way he saw two regiments fighting a little separate battle with two other regiments. It was in a cleared space, wearing a set-apart look. They were blazing as if upon a wager, giving and taking tremendous blows. The firings were incredibly fierce and rapid. These intent regiments apparently were oblivious of all larger purposes of war, and were slugging each other as if at a matched game.

In another direction he saw a magnificent brigade going with the evident intention of driving the enemy from a wood. They passed in out of sight and presently there was a most awe-inspiring racket in the wood. The noise was unspeakable. Having stirred this prodigious uproar, and, apparently, finding it too prodigious, the brigade, after a little time, came marching airily out again with its fine formation in nowise disturbed. There were no traces of speed in its movements. The brigade was jaunty and seemed to point a proud thumb at the yelling wood.

On a slope to the left there was a long row of guns, gruff and maddened, denouncing the enemy, who, down through the woods, were forming for another attack in the pitiless monotony of conflicts. The round red discharges from the guns made a crimson flare and a high, thick smoke. Occasional glimpses could be caught of groups of the toiling artillerymen. In the rear of this row of guns stood a house, calm and white, amid bursting shells. A congregation of horses, tied to a long railing, were tugging frenziedly at their bridles. Men were running hither and thither.

The detached battle between the four regiments lasted for some time. There chanced to be no interference, and they settled their dispute by themselves. They struck savagely and powerfully at each other for a period of minutes, and then the lighter-hued regiments faltered and drew back, leaving the dark-blue lines shouting. The youth could see the two flags shaking with laughter amid the smoke remnants.

Presently there was a stillness, pregnant with meaning. The blue lines shifted and changed a trifle and stared expectantly at the silent woods and fields before them. The hush was solemn and churchlike, save for a distant battery that, evidently unable to remain quiet, sent a faint rolling thunder over the ground. It irritated, like the noises of unimpressed boys. The men imagined that it would prevent their perched ears from hearing the first words of the new battle.

Of a sudden the guns on the slope roared out a message of warning. A spluttering sound had begun in the woods. It swelled with amazing speed to a profound clamor that involved the earth in noises. The splitting crashes swept along the lines until an interminable roar was developed. To those in the midst of it it became a din fitted to the universe. It was the whirring and thumping of gigantic machinery, complications among the smaller stars. The youth's ears were filled up. They were incapable of hearing more.

On an incline over which a road wound he saw wild and desperate rushes of men perpetually backward and forward in riotous surges. These parts of the opposing armies were two long waves that pitched upon each other madly at dictated points. To and fro they swelled. Sometimes, one side by its yells and cheers would proclaim decisive blows, but a moment later the other side would be all yells and cheers. Once the youth saw a spray of light forms go in houndlike leaps toward the waving blue lines. There was much howling, and presently it went away with a vast mouthful of prisoners. Again, he saw a blue wave dash with such thunderous force against a gray obstruction that it seemed to clear the earth of it and leave nothing but trampled sod. And always in their swift and deadly rushes to and fro the men screamed and yelled like maniacs.

Particular pieces of fence or secure positions behind collections of trees were wrangled over, as gold thrones or pearl bedsteads. There were desperate lunges at these chosen spots seemingly every instant, and most of them were bandied like light toys between the contending forces. The youth could not tell from the battle flags flying like crimson foam in many directions which color of cloth was winning.

His emaciated regiment bustled forth with undiminished fierceness when its time came. When assaulted again by bullets, the men burst out in a barbaric cry of rage and pain. They bent their heads in aims of intent hatred behind the projected hammers of their guns. Their ramrods clanged loud with fury as their eager arms pounded the cartridges into the rifle barrels. The front of the regiment was a smokewall penetrated by the flashing points of yellow and red.

Wallowing in the fight, they were in an astonishingly short time resmudged. They surpassed in stain and dirt all their previous appearances. Moving to and fro with strained exertion, jabbering the while, they were, with their swaying bodies, black faces, and glowing eyes, like strange and ugly friends[1] jigging heavily in the smoke.

The lieutenant, returning from a tour after a bandage, produced from a hidden receptacle of his mind new and portentous oaths suited to the emergency. Strings of expletives he swung lashlike over the backs of his men, and it was evident that his previous efforts had in nowise impaired his resources.

The youth, still the bearer of the colors, did not feel his idleness. He was deeply absorbed as a spectator. The crash and swing of the great drama made him lean forward, intent-eyed, his face working in small contortions. Sometimes he prattled, words coming unconsciously from him in grotesque exclamations. He did not know that he breathed; that the flag hung silently over him, so absorbed was he.

A formidable line of the enemy came within dangerous range. They could be seen plainly—tall, gaunt men with excited faces running with long strides toward a wandering fence.

At sight of this danger the men suddenly ceased their cursing monotone. There was an instant of strained silence before they threw up their rifles and fired a plumping volley at the foes. There had been no order given; the men, upon recognizing the menace, had immediately let drive their flock of bullets without waiting for word of command.

But the enemy were quick to gain the protection of the wandering line of fence. They slid down behind it with remarkable celerity, and from this position they began briskly to slice up the blue men.

These latter braced their energies for a great struggle. Often, white clinched teeth shone from the dusky faces. Many heads surged to and fro, floating upon a pale sea of smoke. Those behind the fence frequently shouted and yelped in taunts and gibelike cries, but the regiment maintained a stressed silence.

---

1 Crane's manuscript reads: fiends.

Perhaps, at this new assault the men recalled the fact that they had been named mud diggers, and it made their situation thrice bitter. They were breathlessly intent upon keeping the ground and thrusting away the rejoicing body of the enemy. They fought swiftly and with a despairing savageness denoted in their expressions.

The youth had resolved not to budge whatever should happen. Some arrows of scorn that had buried themselves in his heart had generated strange and unspeakable hatred. It was clear to him that his final and absolute revenge was to be achieved by his dead body lying, torn and gluttering,[1] upon the field. This was to be a poignant retaliation upon the officer who had said "mule drivers," and later "mud diggers," for in all the wild graspings of his mind for a unit responsible for his sufferings and commotions he always seized upon the man who had dubbed him wrongly. And it was his idea, vaguely formulated, that his corpse would be for those eyes a great and salt reproach.

The regiment bled extravagantly. Grunting bundles of blue began to drop. The orderly sergeant of the youth's company was shot through the cheeks. Its supports being injured, his jaw hung afar down, disclosing in the wide cavern of his mouth a pulsing mass of blood and teeth. And with it all he made attempts to cry out. In his endeavor there was a dreadful earnestness, as if he conceived that one great shriek would make him well.

The youth saw him presently go rearward. His strength seemed in nowise impaired. He ran swiftly, casting wild glances for succor.

Others fell down about the feet of their companions. Some of the wounded crawled out and away, but many lay still, their bodies twisted into impossible shapes.

The youth looked once for his friend. He saw a vehement young man, powder-smeared and frowzled, whom he knew to be him. The lieutenant, also, was unscathed in his position at the rear. He had continued to curse, but it was now with the air of a man who was using his last box of oaths.

For the fire of the regiment had begun to wane and drip. The robust voice, that had come strangely from the thin ranks, was growing rapidly weak.

---

1 Most likely a spelling error for "guttering," the pool formed by melted wax from a candle.

Chapter XXIII

THE colonel came running along back of the line. There were other officers following him. "We must charge'm!" they shouted. "We must charge'm!" they cried with resentful voices, as if anticipating a rebellion against this plan by the men.

The youth, upon hearing the shouts, began to study the distance between him and the enemy. He made vague calculations. He saw that to be firm soldiers they must go forward. It would be death to stay in the present place, and with all the circumstances to go backward would exalt too many others. Their hope was to push the galling foes away from the fence.

He expected that his companions, weary and stiffened, would have to be driven to this assault, but as he turned toward them he perceived with a certain surprise that they were giving quick and unqualified expressions of assent. There was an ominous, clanging overture to the charge when the shafts of the bayonets rattled upon the rifle barrels. At the yelled words of command the soldiers sprang forward in eager leaps. There was new and unexpected force in the movement of the regiment. A knowledge of its faded and jaded condition made the charge appear like a paroxysm, a display of the strength that comes before a final feebleness. The men scampered in insane fever of haste, racing as if to achieve a sudden success before an exhilarating fluid should leave them. It was a blind and despairing rush by the collection of men in dusty and tattered blue, over a green sward and under a sapphire sky, toward a fence, dimly outlined in smoke, from behind which spluttered the fierce rifles of enemies.

The youth kept the bright colors to the front. He was waving his free arm in furious circles, the while shrieking mad calls and appeals, urging on those that did not need to be urged, for it seemed that the mob of blue men hurling themselves on the dangerous group of rifles were again grown suddenly wild with an enthusiasm of unselfishness. From the many firings starting toward them, it looked as if they would merely succeed in making a great sprinkling of corpses on the grass between their former position and the fence. But they were in a state of frenzy, perhaps because of forgotten vanities, and it made an exhibition of sublime recklessness. There was no obvious questioning, nor figurings, nor diagrams. There was, apparently, no considered loopholes. It appeared that the swift wings of their desires would have shattered against the iron gates of the impossible.

He himself felt the daring spirit of a savage religion-mad. He was capable of profound sacrifices, a tremendous death. He had no time for dissections, but he knew that he thought of the bullets only as things that could prevent him from reaching the place of his endeavor. There were subtle flashings of joy within him that thus should be his mind.

He strained all his strength. His eyesight was shaken and dazzled by the tension of thought and muscle. He did not see anything excepting the mist of smoke gashed by the little knives of fire, but he knew that in it lay the aged fence of a vanished farmer protecting the snuggled bodies of the gray men.

As he ran a thought of the shock of contact gleamed in his mind. He expected a great concussion when the two bodies of troops crashed together. This became a part of his wild battle madness. He could feel the onward swing of the regiment about him and he conceived of a thunderous, crushing blow that would prostrate the resistance and spread consternation and amazement for miles. The flying regiment was going to have a catapult-ian effect. This dream made him run faster among his comrades, who were giving vent to hoarse and frantic cheers.

But presently he could see that many of the men in gray did not intend to abide the blow. The smoke, rolling, disclosed men who ran, their faces still turned. These grew to a crowd, who retired stubbornly. Individuals wheeled frequently to send a bullet at the blue wave.

But at one part of the line there was a grim and obdurate group that made no movement. They were settled firmly down behind posts and rails. A flag, ruffled and fierce, waved over them and their rifles dinned fiercely.

The blue whirl of men got very near, until it seemed that in truth there would be a close and frightful scuffle. There was an expressed disdain in the opposition of the little group, that changed the meaning of the cheers of the men in blue. They became yells of wrath, directed, personal. The cries of the two parties were now in sound an interchange of scathing insults.

They in blue showed their teeth; their eyes shone all white. They launched themselves as at the throats of those who stood resisting. The space between dwindled to an insignificant distance.

The youth had centered the gaze of his soul upon that other flag. Its possession would be high pride. It would express bloody minglings, near blows. He had a gigantic hatred for those who made great difficulties and complications. They caused it to be as a craved treasure of mythology, hung amid tasks and contrivances of danger.

He plunged like a mad horse at it. He was resolved it should not escape if wild blows and darings of blows could seize it. His own emblem, quivering and aflare, was winging toward the other. It seemed there would shortly be an encounter of strange beaks and claws, as of eagles.

The swirling body of blue men came to a sudden halt at close and disastrous range and roared a swift volley. The group in gray was split and broken by this fire, but its riddled body still fought. The men in blue yelled again and rushed in upon it.

The youth, in his leapings, saw, as through a mist, a picture of four or five men stretched upon the ground or writhing upon their knees with bowed heads as if they had been stricken by bolts from the sky. Tottering among them was the rival color bearer, whom the youth saw had been bitten vitally by the bullets of the last formidable volley. He perceived this man fighting a last struggle, the struggle of one whose legs are grasped by demons. It was a ghastly battle. Over his face was the bleach of death, but set upon it was the dark and hard lines of desperate purpose. With this terrible grin of resolution he hugged his precious flag to him and was stumbling and staggering in his design to go the way that led to safety for it.

But his wounds always made it seem that his feet were retarded, held, and he fought a grim fight, as with invisible ghouls fastened greedily upon his limbs. Those in advance of the scampering blue men, howling cheers, leaped at the fence. The despair of the lost was in his eyes as he glanced back at them.

The youth's friend went over the obstruction in a tumbling heap and sprang at the flag as a panther at prey. He pulled at it and, wrenching it free, swung up its red brilliancy with a mad cry of exultation even as the color bearer, gasping, lurched over in a final throe and, stiffening convulsively, turned his dead face to the ground. There was much blood upon the grass blades.

At the place of success there began more wild clamorings of cheers. The men gesticulated and bellowed in an ecstasy. When they spoke it was as if they considered their listener to be a mile away. What hats and caps were left to them they often slung high in the air.

At one part of the line four men had been swooped upon, and they now sat as prisoners. Some blue men were about them in an eager and curious circle. The soldiers had trapped strange birds, and there was an examination. A flurry of fast questions was in the air.

(1) One of the prisoners was nursing a superficial wound in the foot. He cuddled it, baby-wise, but he looked up from it often to curse with an astonishing utter abandon straight at the noses of his captors. He consigned them to red regions; he called upon the pestilential wrath of strange gods. And with it all he was singularly free from recognition of the finer points of the conduct of prisoners of war. It was as if a clumsy clod had trod upon his toe and he conceived it to be his privilege, his duty, to use deep, resentful oaths.

(2) Another, who was a boy in years, took his plight with great calmness and apparent good nature. He conversed with the men in blue, studying their faces with his bright and keen eyes. They spoke of battles and conditions. There was an acute interest in all their faces during this exchange of view points. It seemed a great satisfaction to hear voices from where all had been darkness and speculation.

(3) The third captive sat with a morose countenance. He preserved a stoical and cold attitude. To all advances he made one reply without variation, "Ah, go t' hell!"

(4) The last of the four was always silent and, for the most part, kept his face turned in unmolested directions. From the views the youth received he seemed to be in a state of absolute dejection. Shame was upon him, and with it profound regret that he was, perhaps, no more to be counted in the ranks of his fellows. The youth could detect no expression that would allow him to believe that the other was giving a thought to his narrowed future, the pictured dungeons, perhaps, and starvations and brutalities, liable to the imagination. All to be seen was shame for captivity and regret for the right to antagonize.

After the men had celebrated sufficiently they settled down behind the old rail fence, on the opposite side to the one from which their foes had been driven. A few shot perfunctorily at distant marks.

There was some long grass. The youth nestled in it and rested, making a convenient rail support the flag. His friend, jubilant and glorified, holding his treasure with vanity, came to him there. They sat side by side and congratulated each other.

Chapter XXIV

THE roarings that had stretched in a long line of sound across the face of the forest began to grow intermittent and weaker. The stentorian speeches of the artillery continued in some distant encounter, but the crashes of the musketry had almost ceased. The youth and his friend of a sudden looked up, feeling a deadened form of distress at the waning of these noises, which had become a part of life. They could see changes going on among the troops. There were marchings this way and that way. A battery wheeled leisurely. On the crest of a small hill was the thick gleam of many departing muskets.

The youth arose. "Well, what now, I wonder?" he said. By his tone he seemed to be preparing to resent some new monstrosity in the way of dins and smashes. He shaded his eyes with his grimy hand and gazed over the field.

His friend also arose and stared. "I bet we're goin' t' git along out of this an' back over th' river," said he.

"Well, I swan!" said the youth.

They waited, watching. Within a little while the regiment received orders to retrace its way. The men got up grunting from the grass, regretting the soft repose. They jerked their stiffened legs, and stretched their arms over their heads. One man swore as he rubbed his eyes. They all groaned "O Lord!" They had as many objections to this change as they would have had to a proposal for a new battle.

They trampled[1] slowly back over the field across which they had run in a mad scamper.

The regiment marched until it had joined its fellows. The reformed brigade, in column, aimed through a wood at the road. Directly they were in a mass of dust-covered troops, and were trudging along in a way parallel to the enemy's lines as these had been defined by the previous turmoil.

They passed within view of a stolid white house, and saw in front of it groups of their comrades lying in wait behind a neat breastwork. A row of guns were booming at a distant enemy. Shells thrown in reply were raising clouds of dust and splinters. Horsemen dashed along the line of intrenchments.

At this point of its march the division curved away from the field and went winding off in the direction of the river. When the

---

1   Crane's manuscript reads: tramped.

significance of this movement had impressed itself upon the youth he turned his head and looked over his shoulder toward the trampled and *débris*-strewed ground. He breathed a breath of new satisfaction. He finally nudged his friend. "Well, it's all over," he said to him.

His friend gazed backward. "B'Gawd, it is," he assented. They mused.

For a time the youth was obliged to reflect in a puzzled and uncertain way. His mind was undergoing a subtle change. It took moments for it to cast off its battleful ways and resume its accustomed course of thought. Gradually his brain emerged from the clogged clouds, and at last he was enabled to more closely comprehend himself and circumstance.

He understood then that the existence of shot and counter shot was in the past. He had dwelt in a land of strange, squalling upheavals and had come forth. He had been where there was red of blood and black of passion, and he was escaped. His first thoughts were given to rejoicings at this fact.

Later he began to study his deeds, his failures, and his achievements. Thus, fresh from scenes where many of his usual machines of reflection had been idle, from where he had proceeded sheeplike, he struggled to marshal all his acts.

At last they marched before him clearly. From this present view point he was enabled to look upon them in spectator fashion and to criticise them with some correctness, for his new condition had already defeated certain sympathies.

Regarding his procession of memory he felt gleeful and unregretting, for in it his public deeds were paraded in great and shining prominence. Those performances which had been witnessed by his fellows marched now in wide purple and gold, having various deflections. They went gayly with music. It was pleasure to watch these things. He spent delightful minutes viewing the gilded images of memory.

He saw that he was good. He recalled with a thrill of joy the respectful comments of his fellows upon his conduct.

Nevertheless, the ghost of his flight from the first engagement appeared to him and danced. There were small shoutings in his brain about these matters. For a moment he blushed, and the light of his soul flickered with shame.

A specter of reproach came to him. There loomed the dogging memory of the tattered soldier—he who, gored by bullets and faint for blood, had fretted concerning an imagined wound in another; he who had loaned his last of strength and intellect for the tall soldier; he who, blind with weariness and pain, had been deserted in the field.

For an instant a wretched chill of sweat was upon him at the thought that he might be detected in the thing. As he stood persistently before his vision, he gave vent to a cry of sharp irritation and agony.

His friend turned. "What's the matter, Henry?" he demanded. The youth's reply was an outburst of crimson oaths.

As he marched along the little branch hung roadway among his prattling companions this vision of cruelty brooded over him. It clung near him always and darkened his view of these deeds in purple and gold. Whichever way his thoughts turned they were followed by the somber phantom of the desertion in the fields. He looked stealthily at his companions, feeling sure that they must discern in his face evidences of this pursuit. But they were plodding in ragged array, discussing with quick tongues the accomplishments of the late battle.

"Oh, if a man should come up an' ask me, I'd say we got a dum good lickin'."

"Lickin'—in yer eye! We ain't licked, sonny. We're goin' down here aways, swing aroun', an' come in behint 'em."

"Oh, hush, with your comin' in behint 'em. I've seen all 'a that I wanta. Don't tell me about comin' in behint—"

"Bill Smithers, he ses he'd rather been in ten hundred battles than been in that heluva hospital. He ses they got shootin' in th' nighttime, an' shells dropped plum among 'em in th' hospital. He ses sech hollerin' he never see."

"Hasbrouck? He's th' best off'cer in this here reg'ment. He's a whale."

"Didn't I tell yeh we'd come aroun' in behint 'em? Didn't I tell yeh so? We—"

"Oh, shet yeh mouth!"

For a time this pursuing recollection of the tattered man took all elation from the youth's veins. He saw his vivid error, and he was afraid that it would stand before him all his life. He took no share in the chatter of his comrades, nor did he look at them or know them, save when he felt sudden suspicion that they were seeing his thoughts and scrutinizing each detail of the scene with the tattered soldier.

Yet gradually he mustered force to put the sin at a distance. And at last his eyes seemed to open to some new ways. He found that he could look back upon the brass and bombast of his earlier gospels and see them truly. He was gleeful when he discovered that he now despised them.

With this conviction came a store of assurance. He felt a quiet manhood, nonassertive but of sturdy and strong blood. He knew that he would no more quail before his guides wherever they should point. He had been to touch the great death, and found that, after all, it was but the great death. He was a man.

So it came to pass that as he trudged from the place of blood and wrath his soul changed. He came from hot plowshares to prospects of clover tranquilly, and it was as if hot plowshares were not. Scars faded as flowers.

It rained. The procession of weary soldiers became a bedraggled train, despondent and muttering, marching with churning effort in a trough of liquid brown mud under a low, wretched sky. Yet the youth smiled, for he saw that the world was a world for him, though many discovered it to be made of oaths and walking sticks. He had rid himself of the red sickness of battle. The sultry nightmare was in the past. He had been an animal blistered and sweating in the heat and pain of war. He turned now with a lover's thirst to images of tranquil skies, fresh meadows, cool brooks—an existence of soft and eternal peace.

Over the river a golden ray of sun came through the hosts of leaden rain clouds.

THE END.

Appendix A: Reminiscences of Stephen Crane

1. Hamlin Garland, "Stephen Crane: A Soldier of Fortune" (1900)

[Hamlin Garland's reminiscence of Stephen Crane was first published in *The Saturday Evening Post* 173 (July 28, 1900): 16-17, and later incorporated into *Roadside Meetings* (1930). Crane met Garland in the summer of 1891 in Avon-by-the-Sea, New Jersey, where Garland was lecturing on William Dean Howells and Realism. Crane asked the famous author of *Main-Travelled Roads* if he could consult his notes for a newspaper article, and Garland concurred. The result was Crane's "Howells Discussed at Avon-by-the-Sea," *New York Tribune* (August 18, 1891): 5. The two men quickly became friends, talking about baseball and literature. They saw one another again in 1892, and more frequently beginning in March 1893, when Crane was living in New York in the old Art Students League on East 23rd Street, where he wrote *The Red Badge of Courage*.

Crane apparently respected the older writer because in April of 1894 he took part of the manuscript of the novel to Hamlin Garland, asking for not only advice but for fifteen dollars so that he could retrieve the rest of it from the typist. It is not clear if Hamlin or his brother, Franklin, gave Crane the money, but the next day he was back with the entire typed draft. Garland read it carefully and offered a number of suggestions, including removing the names of the characters from the early chapters and softening the use of dialect. Crane responded by creating epithets rather than names for the characters (Henry Fleming became "the youthful soldier," Wilson "the loud soldier," Jim Conklin "the tall soldier") and he revised Henry's dialogue so that, in general, he speaks in standard English. He left many of the dialect indicators for Wilson and Conklin.

Garland was very active in professional organizations, and he knew virtually all of the leading American writers of his day. It is clear from his comments that he liked Crane from the beginning and thought highly of his promise. His account of Crane in the early 1890s is generous but honest, and he is frank in describing Crane's slovenly appearance and unkempt rooms. That Crane died in 1900, at the early age of twenty-eight, seems to have touched Garland a great deal, and he wrote several times about his memories of the young author.]

The death of Stephen Crane, far away in the mountains of Bavaria, seems to me at this moment a very sorrowful thing. He should have continued to be one of our most distinctive literary workers for many years to come. And yet I cannot say I am surprised. His was not the physical organization that runs to old age. He was old at twenty.

It happened that I knew Crane when he was a boy and have had some years exceptional opportunities for studying him. In the summer of 1888 or 1889 I was lecturing for a seaside assembly at Avon, New Jersey. The report of my first lecture (on "The Local Novelists," by the way) was exceedingly well done in the "Tribune," and I asked for the name of the reporter. "He is a mere boy," was the reply of Mr. Albert, the manager of the assembly, "and his name is Stephen Crane."

Crane came to see me the following evening, and turned out to be a reticent young fellow, with a big German pipe in his mouth. He was small, sallow and inclined to stoop, but sinewy and athletic for all that—for we fell to talk of sports, and he consented to practice baseball pitching with me. I considered him at this time a very good reporter, and a capital catcher of curved balls—no more, and I said goodby to him two weeks later with no expectation of ever seeing him again.

In the summer of '91, if I do not mistake, I was visiting Mr. and Mrs. Albert at their school in New York City, when a curious book came to me by mail. It was a small yellow-covered volume, hardly more than a pamphlet, without a publisher's imprint. The author's name was Johnston Smith.[1] The story was called "Maggie, a Girl of the Streets," and the first paragraph described the battle of some street urchins with so much insight and with such unusual and vivid use of English that I became very much excited about it. Next day I mailed the book to Mr. Howells, in order that he might share the discovery with me. The author had the genius which makes an old world new.

On that very afternoon Crane called upon me and confessed that he had written the book and had not been able to get any one to publish it. Even the firm of printers that put it together refused to place their imprint upon it. He said that the bulk of the edition

---

1 Garland is off on the year. In 1893 Crane paid a printer in New York to publish *Maggie: A Girl of the Streets*, which did not sell well but impressed both Garland and Howells. Both of those writers encouraged Crane in the early years of his career.

remained unsold, and that he had sent the book to a number of critics and also to several ministers. On the cover of each copy (as on mine) was written, in diagonal lines, these words or their substance in Crane's beautiful script: "The reader of this story must inevitably be shocked, but let him persist, and in the end he will find this story to be moral." I cannot remember exactly the quaint terms of this admonition, but these words give the idea.

I said to him: "I hardly dare tell you how good that story is. I have sent it to Mr. Howells as a 'find.' Go and see him when he has read it. I am sure he will like it."

He then told me that he had been discharged from the staff of the "Tribune." He seemed to be greatly encouraged by our conversation, and when he went away I talked with his friends about the book, which appealed to me with great power. I have it still. This desperate attempt of a young author to get a hearing is amusing to an outsider, but it was serious business with Crane then.

I did not see him again until the autumn of 1892, when I went to New York to spend the winter. He wrote occasionally, saying, "Things go pretty slow with me, but I manage to live."

My brother Franklin was in Mr. Herne's Shore Acres Company in those days, and as they were playing an all-season engagement at Daly's theater we decided to take a little flat and camp together for the winter. Our flat was on One Hundred and Fifth street, and there Crane visited us two or three times a week. He was always hungry and a little gloomy when he came, but my brother made a point of having an extra chop or steak ready for a visitor and Crane often chirped like a bird when he had finished dinner. We often smiled over it then, but it is a pleasure to us now to think we were able to cheer him when he needed it most.

He was living at this time with a group of artists—"Indians," he called them—in the old studio building on East Twenty-third street. I never called to see him there, but he often set forth their doings with grim humor. Most of them slept on the floor and painted on towels, according to his report. Sometimes they ate, but they all smoked most villainous tobacco, for Crane smelled so powerfully of their "smoke-talks" that he filled our rooms with the odor. His fingers were yellow with cigarette reek, and he looked like a man badly nourished.

This crowd of artists, according to his story, spent their days in sleep and their nights in "pow-wows" around a big table where they beat and clamored and assaulted each other under a canopy of tobacco smoke. They hated the world. They were infuriated with all hanging committees[1] and art editors, and each man believed religiously in his own genius. Linson was one of those Crane mentioned, and Vosburg and Green.[2] Together they covenanted to go out some bleak day and slay all the editors and art critics of the city.

Crane at this time wore a light check suit and over it a long gray ulster[3] which had seen much service. His habitual expression was a grim sort of smile. One day he appeared in my study with his outside pockets bulging with two rolls of manuscript. As he entered he turned ostentatiously to put down his hat, and so managed to convey to my mind an impression that he was concealing something. His manner was embarrassed, as if he had come to do a thing and was sorry about it.

"Come now, out with it," I said. "What is the roll I see in your pocket?"

With a sheepish look he took out a fat roll of legal cap paper and handed it to me with a careless, boyish gesture.

"There's another," I insisted, and he still more abruptly delivered himself of another but smaller parcel.

I unrolled the first package, and found it to be a sheaf of poems. I can see the initial poem now, exactly as it was then written, without a blot or erasure—almost without punctuation—in blue ink. It was beautifully legible and clean of outline.

It was the poem which begins thus:

"God fashioned the ship of the world carefully."

I read this with delight and amazement. I rushed through the others, some thirty in all, with growing wonder. I could not believe they were the work of the pale, reticent boy moving restlessly about the room.

"Have you any more?" I asked.

"I've got five or six all in a little row up here," he quaintly replied, pointing to his temple. "That's the way they come—in little rows, all made up, ready to be put down on paper."

"When did you write these?"

"Oh! I've been writing five or six every day. I wrote nine yesterday. I wanted to write some more last night, but those 'Indians'

---

1 The group that choses which works of art will be in the show.
2 Garland misspells both names. R.G. Vosburgh was one of Crane's roommates in the old Art Students League building in New York. He was an artist who provided the illustrations for some of Crane's short stories. Nelson Greene was another roommate who was also an artist. He had studied at the League with William M. Chase, an Impressionist, and the ideas of that movement had an important influence of Crane's artistic credo.
3 An Irish wool coat.

wouldn't let me do it. They howled over the other verses so loud they nearly cracked my ears. You see, we all live in a box together, and I've no place to write, except in the general squabble. They think my lines are funny. They make a circus of me." All this with a note of exaggeration, of course.

"Never you mind," I replied; "don't you do a thing till you put all these verses down on paper."

"I've got to eat," he said, and his smile was not pleasant.

"Well, let's consider. Can't we get some work for you to do? Some of these press syndicate men have just been after me to do short stories for them. Can't you do something there?"

"I'll try," he said, without much resolution. "I don't seem to be the kind of writer they want. The newspapers can't see me at all."

"Well, now, let's see what can be done. I'll give you a letter to Mr. Flower,[1] of the 'Arena,' and one to Mr. Howells. And I want to take these poems to Mr. Howells to-morrow; I'm sure he'll help you. He's kind to all who struggle."

Later in the meal I said: "Why don't you go down and do a study of this midnight bread distribution which the papers are making so much of? Mr. Howells suggested it to me, but it isn't my field. It is yours. You could do it beyond anybody."[2]

"I might do that," he said; "it interests me."

"Come to-morrow to luncheon," I said, as he went away visibly happier. "Perhaps I'll have something to report."

I must confess I took the lines seriously. If they were [a] direct output of this unaccountable boy, then America had produced another genius, singular as Poe. I went with them at once to Mr. Howells, whose wide reading I knew and relied upon. He read them with great interest, and immediately said:

"They do not seem to relate directly to the work of any other writer. They seem to be the work of a singularly creative mind. Of course they reflect the author's reading and sympathies, but they are not imitations."

When Crane came next day he brought the first part of a war story which was at that time without a name. The first page of this was as original as the verses, and it passed at once to the description of a great battle. Such mastery of details of war was sufficiently

---

1 Benjamin Orange Flower was the editor of *The Arena*, a magazine devoted to Populist social reforms. Garland published many of his early Naturalistic stories in that magazine, and he would have had a good deal of influence with Flower.

2 The story Crane later produced from this idea was entitled "The Men in the Storm."

startling in a youth of twenty-one who had never smelled any more carnage than a firecracker holds, but the seeing was so keen, the phrases so graphic, so fresh, so newly coined, that I dared not express to the boy's face my admiration. I asked him to leave the story with me. I said:

"Did you do any more 'lines'?"

He looked away bashfully.

"Only six."

"Let me see them."

As he handed them to me he said: "Got three more waiting in line. I could do one now."

"Sit down and try," I said, glad of his offer, for I could not relate the man to his work.

He took a seat and began to write steadily, composedly, without hesitation or blot or interlineation, and so produced in my presence one of his most powerful verses. It flowed from his pen as smooth as oil.

The next day I asked for the other half of the novel. "We must get it published at once," I said. "It is a wonderful study. A mysterious product for you to have in hand. Where is the other part?"

He looked very much embarrassed. "It's in 'hock,'" he said.

"To whom?"

"To the typewriter."

We all laughed, but it was serious business to him. He could see the humor of the situation, but there was a bitter rebellion in his voice.

"How much is it 'hung up' for?"

"Fifteen dollars."

I looked at my brother. "I guess we can spare that, don't you think?"

So Crane went away joyously and brought the last half of "The Red Badge of Courage," still unnamed at the time. He told us that the coming of that story was just as mysterious as in the case of the verses, and I can believe it. It literally came of its own accord like sap flowing from a tree.

I gave him such words of encouragement as I could. "Your future is secure. A man who can write 'The Red Badge of Courage' can not be forever a lodger in a bare studio."

He replied: "That may be, but if I had some money to buy a new suit of clothes I'd feel my grip tighten on the future."

"You'll laugh at all this—we all go through it," said I.

"It's ridiculous, but it doesn't make me laugh," he said, soberly.

My predictions of his immediate success did not come true. "The Red Badge of Courage" and "Maggie" were put through the

Syndicate with very slight success. They left Crane almost as poor as before.

In one of his letters, in April, he wrote: "I have not been up to see you because of various strange conditions—notably my toes coming through one shoe, and I have not been going out into society as much as I might. I mail you last Sunday's 'Press.' I've moved now—live in a flat. People can come to see me now. They come in shoals, and say I am a great writer. Counting five that are sold, four that are unsold and six that are mapped out, I have fifteen short stories in my head and out of it. They'll make a book. The 'Press' people pied some of 'Maggie,' as you will note."

I saw little of him during '93 and '94, but a letter written in May, '94, revealed his condition:

"I have not written you because there has been little to tell of late. I am plodding along on the 'Press' in a quiet and effective way. We now eat with charming regularity at least two times a day. I am content and am now writing another novel which is a bird. . . . I am getting lots of free advertising. Everything is coming along nicely now. I have got the poetic spout so that I can turn it on and off. I wrote a Decoration Day[1] thing for the 'Press' which aroused them to enthusiasm. They said in about a minute, though, that I was firing over the heads of the soldiers."

His allusion to free advertising means that the critics were wrangling over "The Black Riders" and "Maggie." But the public was not interested. I had given him a letter to a Syndicate Press Company, and with them he had left the manuscript of his war novel. In a letter written in November, 1894, he makes sad mention of his lack of success:

"My Dear Friend: So much of my row with the world has to be silence and endurance that sometimes I wear the appearance of having forgotten my best friends, those to whom I am indebted for everything. As a matter of fact, I have just crawled out of the fifty-third ditch into which I have been cast, and now I feel that I can write you a letter which will not make you ill.   —— put me in one of the ditches. He kept 'The Red Badge' six months until I was near mad. Oh, yes—he was going to use it but—Finally I took it to B. They used it in January in a shortened form. I have just completed a New York book that leaves 'Maggie' at the post. It is my best thing. Since you are not here I am going to see if Mr. Howells will not read it. I am still working for the 'Press.'"

---

1   A day for honoring fallen soldiers. The holiday was begun during the Civil War. The name was later changed to Memorial Day.

At this point his affairs took a sudden turn, and he was made the figure I had hoped to see him two years before. The English critics spoke in highest praise of "The Red Badge," and the book became the critical bone of contention between military objectors and literary enthusiasts here at home, and Crane became the talk of the day. He was accepted as a very remarkable literary man of genius.

He was too brilliant, too fickle, too erratic to last. Men cannot go on doing stories like "The Red Badge of Courage." The danger with such highly individual work lies in this—the words which astonish, the phrases which excite wonder and admiration, come eventually to seem like tricks. They lose force with repetition, and come at last to be absolutely distasteful. "The Red Badge of Courage" was marvelous, but manifestly Crane could not go on doing such work. If he wrote in conventional phrase, his power lessened. If he continued to write in his own phrases he came under the charge of repeating himself.

It seems now that he was destined from the first to be a sort of present-day Poe. His was a singular and daring soul, as irresponsible as the wind. He was a man to be called a genius, for we call that power genius which we do not easily understand or measure. I have never known a man whose source of power was so unaccounted for.

The fact of the matter seems to be this. Crane's mind was more largely subconscious in its workings than that of most men. He did not understand his own mental processes or resources. When he put pen to paper he found marvelous words, images, sentences, pictures already[1] to be drawn off and fixed upon paper. His pen was "a spout," as he says. The farther he got from his own field, his own inborn tendency, the weaker he became. Such a man cannot afford to enter the white-hot public thoroughfare, for his genius is of the lonely and the solitary shadow-land.

2. Joseph Conrad, "Stephen Crane: A Note without Dates," *The London Mercury* 1 (December 1919): 192-93

[Joseph Conrad (1857-1924) was a Polish immigrant who came to England in 1894 determined to become a writer in a language he spoke poorly. Within a year he had published his first novel, *Almayer's Folly,* and he went on to establish himself as one of the most important authors in English. His career included both *Lord Jim* (1900) and *Heart of Darkness* (1899). When Stephen Crane moved to England in

---

1 Garland would seem to have meant "all ready."

the late 1890s, Conrad became part of his circle of friends, a relationship reflected in his reminiscence.]

My acquaintance with Crane was brought about by Mr. S. S. Pawling, partner in the publishing firm of Mr. William Heinemann.

One day Mr. Pawling said to me: "Stephen Crane has arrived in England. I asked him if there was anybody he wanted to meet and he mentioned two names. One of them was yours." I had then just been reading, like the rest of the world, Crane's *Red Badge of Courage*. The subject of that story was war, from the point of view of an individual soldier's emotions. That individual (he remains nameless throughout)[1] was interesting enough in himself, but on turning over the pages of that little book which had for the moment secured such a noisy recognition I had been even more interested in the personality of the writer. The picture of a simple and untried youth becoming through the needs of his country part of a great fighting machine was presented with an earnestness of purpose, a sense of tragic issues, and an imaginative force of expression which struck me as quite uncommon and altogether worthy of admiration.

Apparently Stephen Crane had received a favourable impression from reading *The Nigger of the Narcissus* (1897), a book of mine which had also been published lately. I was truly pleased to hear this.

On my next visit to town we met at a lunch. I saw a young man of medium stature and slender build, with very steady, penetrating blue eyes, the eyes of a being who not only sees visions but can brood over them to some purpose.

He had indeed a wonderful power of vision, which he applied to the things of this earth and of our mortal humanity with a penetrating force that seemed to reach within life's appearances and forms the very spirit of their truth. His ignorance of the world at large—he had seen very little of it—did not stand in the way of his imaginative grasp of facts, events, and picturesque men.

His manner was very quiet, his personality at first sight interesting, and he talked slowly with an intonation which on some people, mainly Americans, had, I believe, a jarring effect. But not on me. Whatever he said had a personal note, and he expressed himself with a graphic simplicity which was extremely engaging. He knew little of literature, either of his own country or of any other, but he was himself a wonderful artist in words whenever he took a pen into his hand. Then his gift came out—and it was seen to be much more than mere felicity of

1   Conrad, of course, is in error on this point. The protagonist's name is Henry Fleming.

language. His impressionism of phrase went really deeper than the surface. In his writing he was very sure of his effects. I don't think he was ever in doubt about what he could do. Yet it often seemed to me that he was but half aware of the exceptional quality of his achievement.

This achievement was curtailed by his early death. It was a great loss to his friends, but perhaps not so much to literature. I think that he had given his measure fully in the few books he had the time to write. Let me not be misunderstood: the loss was great, but it was the loss of the delight his art could give, not the loss of any further possible revelation. As to himself, who can say how much he gained or lost by quitting so early this world of the living, which he knew how to set before us in terms of his own artistic vision? Perhaps he did not lose a great deal. The recognition he was accorded was rather languid and given him grudgingly. The worthiest welcome he secured for his tales in this country was from Mr. W. Henley in the *New Review*[1] and later, towards the end of his life, from the late Mr. William Blackwood in his magazine.[2] For the rest I must say that during his sojourn in England he had the misfortune to be, as the French say, *mal entouré*.[3] He was beset by people who understood not the quality of his genius and were antagonistic to the deeper fineness of his nature. Some of them have died since, but dead or alive they are not worth speaking about now. I don't think he had any illusions about them himself; yet there was a strain of good-nature and perhaps of weakness in his character which prevented him from shaking himself free from their worthless and patronising attentions, which in those days caused me much secret irritation whenever I stayed with him in either of his English homes. My wife and I like best to remember him riding to meet us at the gate of the Park at Brede.[4] Born master of his sincere impressions he was also a born horseman. He never appeared so happy or so much to advantage as on the back of a horse. He had formed the project of teaching my eldest boy to ride and meantime, when the child was about two years old, presented him with his first dog.

I saw Stephen Crane a few days after his first arrival in London. I saw him for the last time on his last day in England. It was in Dover, in a big hotel, in a bedroom with a large window looking on to the sea.

---

1 William Ernest Henley, a writer and editor, published a positive review of Crane's fiction in the influential magazine *The New Review.*
2 William Blackwood owned and edited *Blackwood's Magazine* in Edinburgh, a publication that often offered encouragement to young authors.
3 Literally, "badly sourrounded" (French). Conrad's point is that Crane was popular for the wrong reasons, and it had a negative effect on him.
4 Joseph Conrad visited Crane often at his home in England, Brede Place.

He had been very ill and Mrs. Crane was taking him to some place in Germany, but one glance at that wasted face was enough to tell me that it was the most forlorn of all hopes. The last words he breathed out to me were: "I am tired. Give my love to your wife and child." When I stopped at the door for another look I saw that he had turned his head on the pillow and was staring wistfully out of the window at the sails of a cutter yacht that glided slowly across the frame, like a dim shadow against a grey sky.

Those who have read his little tale, *Horses*,[1] and the story, *The Open Boat*, in the volume of that name, know with what fine understanding he loved horses and the sea. And his passage on this earth was like that of a horseman riding swiftly in the dawn of a day fated to be short and without sunshine.

---

1   The actual title is "One Dash—Horses."

Appendix B: Reviews of The Red Badge of Courage

1. William Dean Howells, *Harper's Weekly* 39 (26 October 1895): 1013

[In 1895, William Dean Howells was the foremost literary figure in the United States. He had already published a score of novels, among them the widely admired *A Modern Instance* (1882) and *The Rise of Silas Lapham* (1885), and he was immensely influential as the editor of *The Atlantic Monthly* and as an advisor to major publishing companies.]

Of our own smaller fiction I have been reading several books without finding a very fresh note except in *The Red Badge of Courage*, by Mr. Stephen Crane. He is the author of that story of New York tough life, *Maggie*, which I mentioned some time ago as so good but so impossible of general acceptance because of our conventional limitations in respect of swearing, and some other traits of the common parlance. He has now attempted to give a close-at-hand impression of battle as seen by a young volunteer in the civil war, and I cannot say that to my inexperience of battle he has given such a vivid sense of it as one gets from some other authors. The sense of deaf and blind turmoil he does indeed give, but we might get that from fewer pages than Mr. Crane employs to impart it. The more valuable effect of the book is subjective: the conception of character in the tawdry-minded youth whom the slight story gathers itself about, and in his comrades and superiors of all sorts. The human commonness (which we cannot shrink from without vulgarity) is potently illustrated throughout in their speech and action and motive; and the cloud of bewilderment in which they all have their being after the fighting begins, the frenzy, the insensate resentment, are graphically and probably suggested. The dialect employed does not so much convince me; I have not heard people speak with those contractions, though perhaps they do it; and in commending the book I should dwell rather upon the skill shown in evolving from the youth's crude expectations and ambitions a quiet honesty and self-possession manlier and nobler than any heroism he had imagined. There are divinations of motive and experience which cannot fail to strike the critical reader, from time to time; and decidedly on the psychological side the book is worth while as an earnest of the greater things that we may hope from a new talent working upon a high level, not quite clearly as yet, but strenuously.

2. H.B. Marriott Watson, *Pall Mall Gazette* 11 (26 November 1895): 4

[Henry Brereton Marriott Watson was a prolific writer of swashbuck-ling historical romances and an influential literary figure who was the assistant editor of the *Pall Mall Gazette*. His enthusiastic review of *The Red Badge* appeared prior to the publication of the English edition of the novel and helped establish a British audience for Crane's work. Three years later, when Crane had settled in England, he and Watson became part of a literary circle that included Henry James, H.G. Wells, and Joseph Conrad. When Crane died leaving an unfinished novel, *The O'Ruddy*, behind, Cora, who lived with Crane as his wife, asked Watson to complete the book, but he declined.]

Mr. Crane has certainly written a remarkable book. He has deliber-ately synthesized the particular emotions of warfare, which, it is plain, he had been at pains to analyze fastidiously. To a curious reader it may appear that the synthesis is better than the analysis, but in reality we may well halt and doubt on reaching this conclusion definitely. Certainly at times Mr. Crane would seem to wander slightly; his psy-chology has now and then an aberrant air; he moves with a sureness, but it is sometimes a sureness that does not convince. It is as though he built upon the current passions and fears too insistently. The scheme is a trifle too logical, too methodic. It is not ecstatic, it is not extravagant; nay, its very coolness and deliberation seem studied and articulate. It is wholly cold-blooded. But it is a gallant endeavour, and in truth and beyond question a very singular performance. Not the least of Mr. Crane's gifts is that this narrative, with scarce a name to hang upon a single character, and no plot whatsoever, holds one irrevocably. There is no possibility of resistance, when once you are in its grip, from the first march of the troops to the closing scenes. The hero is the "youth." His comrades call him Henry, but to Mr. Crane and the reader he remains the "youth." He goes into battle a coward; he is among the deserters on the first day of fighting; he comes out of the three days' campaign with the red badge. How much of his inspi-ration Mr. Crane has derived from Tolstoi it would be hard to say, but the works bear signal comparison. There is another writer, much neg-lected, if we remember rightly, who has treated war in much the same way, and strangely enough his episodes were taken from the Ameri-can Civil War; but Mr. Ambrose Bierce[1] never prosecuted analysis so

---

1 Ambrose Bierce (1842-1914) was a famous journalist and writer of fiction. His *The Devil's Dictionary* (1911) has entertained millions of readers, and his story "An Occurrence at Owl Creek Bridge" is one of the most famous in English.

staunchly as Mr. Crane. This is an integral attempt to embody in language the detail of a soldier's mind in his first action. Let us see how Mr. Crane makes his essay, for the study will repay rigid attention.

Upon hearing the battle was imminent the youth was in a trance of astonishment, wondering if he would be brave. This mood passed, and he "saw visions of a thousand-tongued fear that would babble at his back and cause him to flee, while others were going coolly about their country's business." The regiment started for action, but there was the indefinite delay of warfare. He now panted for battle; he wanted to get it over, and to know whether he was to be a coward or not. Still there was no fighting, but the line encountered a dead body. "The ranks opened covertly to avoid the corpse. The invulnerable dead man forced a way for himself. The youth looked keenly at the ashen face. The wind raised the tawny beard. It moved as if a hand were stroking it. He vaguely desired to walk around and around the body and stare; the impulse of the living to try to read in dead eyes the answer to the Question." The whole of this scene is remarkable, as remarkable as that later period of panic which perhaps covers the most important episode in the volume. The regiment was shifted, shifted constantly; the soldiers raised little heaps of stones for protection before them, and were moved away. The act became mechanical. The regiment came into action; bullets whistled in the trees. After the first shot the youth "was working at his weapon like an automatic affair. He suddenly lost concern for himself; and forgot to look at a menacing fate.... If he had thought the regiment was about to be annihilated, perhaps he would have amputated himself from it. But its noise gave him assurance. The regiment was like a firework that, once ignited, proceeds superior to circumstances until its blazing vitality fades." But after this first frenzy it is that he runs. Panic seizes him and he scuttles past the furious lieutenant. We have no space for quotation, otherwise we should like to have quoted from the horrible passages which describe his encounter with the train of wounded. Verestschagin[1] painted such scenes, but Verestschagin's canvas testified merely to fact, and not to emotion. A more gruesome reality was never adventured on paper than the description in Chapters IX. and X. of Jim Conklin and the "tattered man." Mr. Crane's imagination adumbrates the horrible confusion and vagueness of the battlefield. You will pick from his pages nothing of the campaign, nothing of any certainty, save the terrors and

---

1 Vasili Verestschagin (1842-1904) was an artist who specialized in scenes of war. He was particularly adept in the handling of color, and some reviewers compared his work to Crane's novel in this regard.

passions of the characters he employs. The reader is befogged with the bewildered "youth," and wanders from camp to camp in the mellay. Finally, out of this panic comes the redemption. It is excellently managed⌈The heroic has no place in the mental evolution. It is by the baptism of fire alone that the soldier regains his nerve.⌋If the concluding portions of the analysis are less sensational, they are none the less interesting. In the new peace that comes of accomplishment the youth is pursued by images of the "tattered" soldier, whom he had deserted in the extremity of death. But slowly he put the shame of his cowardice from him. "He found that he could look back upon the brass and bombast of his earlier gospels and see them truly. He was gleeful when he discovered that he now despised them. With this conviction came a store of assurance. He felt a quiet manhood, non-assertive, but of sturdy and strong blood. . . . He had been to touch the great death, and found that, after all, it was but the great death. He was a man." Mr. Crane, we repeat, has written a remarkable book. His insight and his power of realization amount to genius.

(3.) Harold Frederic, *The New York Times* (26 January 1896): 22

[Harold Frederic (1856-98) was the London correspondent for *The New York Times* and an important writer of Realism in the United States. His novel *The Damnation of Theron Ware* (1896) outsold *The Red Badge of Courage*, but its appeal diminished over the years. Frederic had never met Stephen Crane when he wrote this review, but they later became good friends in England. Both of these writers were to die young: Frederic in 1898, Crane in 1900.]

Who in London knows about Stephen Crane? The question is one of genuine interest here. It happens, annoyingly enough, that the one publishing person who might throw some light on the answer is for the moment absent from town. Other sources yield only the meagre information that the name is believed to be a real, and not an assumed, one, and that its owner is understood to be a very young man, indeed. That he is an American, or, at least, learned to read and write in America, is obvious enough. The mere presence in his vocabulary of the verb "loan" would settle that, if the proof were not otherwise blazoned on every page of his extraordinary book. For this mysteriously unknown youth has really written an extraordinary book.

The Red Badge of Courage appeared a couple of months ago, unheralded and unnoticed, in a series which, under the distinctive label of "Pioneer," is popularly supposed to present fiction more or less after the order of *The Green Carnation*,[1] which was also of that lot. The first one who mentioned in my hearing that this *Red Badge* was well worth reading happened to be a person whose literary admirations serve me generally as warnings what to avoid, and I remembered the title languidly from that standpoint of self-protection. A little later others began to speak of it. All at once, every bookish person had it at his tongue's end. It was clearly a book to read, and I read it. Even as I did so, reviews burst forth in a dozen different quarters, hailing it as extraordinary. Some were naturally more excited and voluble than others, but all the critics showed, and continue to show, their sense of being in the presence of something not like other things. George Wyndham, M.P., has already written of it in *The New Review* as "a remarkable book." Other magazine editors have articles about it in preparation, and it is evident that for the next few months it is to be more talked about than anything else in current literature. It seems almost equally certain that it will be kept alive, as one of the deathless books which must be read by everybody who desires to be, or to seem, a connoisseur of modern fiction.

If there were in existence any books of a similar character, one could start confidently by saying that it was the best of its kind. But it has no fellows. It is a book outside of all classification. So unlike anything else is it that the temptation rises to deny that it is a book at all. When one searches for comparisons, they can only be found by culling out selected portions from the trunks of masterpieces, and considering these detached fragments, one by one, with reference to the *Red Badge*, which is itself a fragment, and yet is complete. "Thus one lifts the best battle pictures from Tolstoi's great *War and Peace*, from Balzac's *Chouans*, from Hugo's *Les Miserables*, and the forest fight in '93," from Prosper Mérimée's assault of the redoubt, from Zola's *La Débacle* and *Attack on the Mill*,[2] (it is strange enough that equivalents in the literature of our own language do not suggest themselves) and studies them side by side with this tremendously effective battle painting by the unknown youngster. Positively they are cold and ineffectual

---

1 Robert Hichens' novel *The Green Carnation* created a scandal when it appeared in 1894, since it portrayed famous people who were easily identified. It became enormously popular in both England and the United States.

2 Prosper Mérimée (1803-70) was famous as the author of the novella *Carmen* (1845). His story "L'enlèvement de la redoute" was included in the collection *Mosaïque* (1833). Leo Tolstoy (1828-1910) published his most famous novel, *War and Peace*, in 1869. Honoré de Balzac (1799-1850) was the author of *Les Chouans* (1829). Victor Hugo (1802-85) wrote *Les Misérables* (1862).

beside it. The praise may sound exaggerated, but really it is inadequate. These renowned battle descriptions of the big men are made to seem all wrong. The *Red Badge* impels the feeling that the actual truth about a battle has never been guessed before.

In construction the book is as original as in its unique grasp of a new grouping of old materials. All the historic and prescribed machinery of the romance is thrust aside. One barely knows the name of the hero; it is only dimly sketched in that he was a farm boy and had a mother when he enlisted. These facts recur to him once or twice, they play no larger part in the reader's mind. Only two other characters are mentioned by name—Jim Conklin and Wilson; more often even they are spoken of as the tall soldier and the loud soldier. Not a word is expended on telling where they come from, or who they are. They pass across the picture, or shift from one posture to another in its moving composition, with the impersonality of one's chance fellow-passengers in a railroad car. There is a lieutenant who swears new oaths all the while, another officer with a red beard, and two or three still vaguer figures, revealed here and there through the smoke. We do not know, or seek to know, their names, or anything about them except what, staring through the eyes of Henry Fleming, we are permitted to see. The regiment itself, the refugees from other regiments in the crowded flight, and the enemy on the other side of the fence, are differentiated only as they wear blue or gray. We never get their color out of our mind's eye. This exhausts the dramatis personae of the book, and yet it is more vehemently alive and heaving with dramatic human action than any other book of our time. The people are all strangers to us, but the sight of them stirs the profoundest emotions of interest in our breasts. What they do appeals as vividly to our consciousness as if we had known them all our life.

The central idea of the book is of less importance than the magnificent graft of externals upon it. We begin with the young raw recruit, hearing that at last his regiment is going to see some fighting, and brooding over the problem of his own behavior under fire. We follow his perturbed meditations through thirty pages, which cover a week or so of this menace of action. Then suddenly, with one gray morning, the ordeal breaks abruptly over the youngster's head. We go with him, so close that he is never out of sight, for two terribly crowded days, and then the book is at an end. This cross-section of his experience is made a part of our own. We see with his eyes, think with his mind, quail or thrill with his nerves. He strives to argue himself into the conventional soldier's bravery; he runs ingloriously away; he excuses, defends, and abhors himself in turn; he tremblingly yields to the sinister fascination of creeping near the battle; he basely allows his comrades to ascribe to heroism the wound he received in the frenzied 'sauve qui peut'[1] of the fight, he gets at last the fire of combat in his veins, and blindly rushing in deports himself with such hardy and temerarious valor that even the Colonel notes him, and admits that he is a "jimhickey." These sequent processes, observed with relentless minutiae, are so powerfully and speakingly portrayed that they seem the veritable actions of our own minds. To produce the effect is a notable triumph, but it is commonplace by comparison with the other triumph of making us realize what Henry saw and heard as well as what he felt. The value of the former feat has the limitations of the individual. No two people are absolutely alike; any other young farm boy would have passed through the trial with something different somewhere. Where Henry fluttered, he might have been obtuse; neither the early panic nor the later irrational ferocity would necessarily have been just the same. But the picture of the trial itself seems to me never to have been painted as well before.

Oddly enough, *The Saturday Review* and some other of the commentators take it for granted that the writer of the *Red Badge* must have seen real warfare. "The extremely vivid touches of detail convince us," says *The Review*, "that he has had personal experience of the scenes he depicts. Certainly, if his book were altogether a work of imagination, unbased on personal experience, his realism would be nothing short of a miracle." This may strike the reader who has not thought much about it as reasonable, but I believe it to be wholly fallacious. Some years ago I had before me the task of writing some battle chapters in a book I was at work upon. The novel naturally led up to the climax of a battle, and I was excusably anxious that when I finally got to this battle, I should be as fit to handle it as it was possible to make myself. A very considerable literature existed about the actual struggle, which was the Revolutionary battle of Oriskany,[2] fought only a few miles from where I was born. This literature was in part the narratives of survivors of the fight, in part imaginative accounts based on these by later writers. I found to my surprise that the people who were really in the fight gave one much less of an idea of a desperate forest combat than did those who pictured it in fancy. Of course, here it might be that the veterans were inferior in powers of narration to the professional writer. Then I extended the test to writers themselves. I compared the best accounts of Franco-German battles, written for the London newspapers by trained correspondents of distinction who

---

1 Literally, "escape [he] who can" (French). Every man for himself.
2 The Battle of Oriskany for control of Fort Stanwix on 6 August 1777 was considered to be one the bloodiest conflicts in the Revolutionary War. At stake was control of the Hudson Valley in northern New York.

were on the spot, with the choicest imaginative work of novelists, some of them mentioned above, who had never seen a gun fired in anger. [There was literally no comparison between the two. The line between journalism and literature obtruded itself steadily.] Nor were cases lacking in which some of these war correspondents had in other departments of work showed themselves capable of true literature. I have the instance of David Christie Murray[1] in mind. He saw some of the stiffest fighting that was done in his time, and that, too, at an early stage of his career, but he never tried to put a great battle chapter into one of his subsequent novels, and if he had I don't believe it would have been great.

Our own writers of the elder generation illustrate this same truth. Gen. Lew Wallace, Judge Tourgée, Dr. Weir Mitchell,[2] and numbers of others saw tremendous struggles on the battlefield, but to put the reality into type baffles them. The four huge volumes of *The Century's Battles and Leaders of the Civil War* are written almost exclusively by men who took an active part in the war, and many of them were in addition men of high education and considerable literary talent, but there is not a really moving story of a fight in the whole work. When Warren Lee Goss began his *Personal Recollections of a Private*,[3] his study of the enlistment, the early marching and drilling, and the new experiences of camp life was so piquant and fresh that I grew quite excited in anticipation. But when he came to the fighting, he fell flat. The same may be said, with more reservations, about the first parts of Judge Tourgée's more recent *Story of a Thousand* (1896). It seems as if the actual sight of a battle has some dynamic quality in it which overwhelms and crushes the literary faculty in the observer. At best, he gives us a conventional account of what happened; but on analysis you

---

1 David Christie Murray (1847-1907) was an English author and journalist who was noted for his acute portrayal of combat, starting with his coverage of the Russo-Turkish War of 1877-78.

2 Lew Wallace (1827-1905) was a lawyer who became a general in the union army, fighting at the battle of Shiloh. He was later the governor of New Mexico Territory. Of his novels, *Ben Hur: A Tale of the Christ* (1880) has remained popular, inspiring a celebrated motion picture. Albion Tourgée (1838-1905) was also a soldier and a lawyer who wrote novels, among them *A Fool's Errand* (1879) and *Bricks Without Straw* (1880), both depicting Reconstruction in the South. Silas Weir Mitchell (1829-1914) was a physician who wrote historical novels. He treated Charlotte Perkins Gilman, who made reference to him in her celebrated story "The Yellow Wallpaper" (1892).

3 Highly popular, Goss published his war memoir in *The Century Illustrated Monthly Magazine* 29 (1884-85): 107-13. It may have influenced some aspects of Crane's realistic portrait of battle in *The Red Badge* a decade later.

find that this is not what he really saw, but what all his reading has taught him that he must have seen. In the same way battle painters depict horses in motion, not as they actually move, but as it has been agreed by numberless generations of draughtsmen to say that they move. At last, along comes a Muybridge,[1] with his instantaneous camera, and shows that the real motion is entirely different.

It is this effect of a photographic revelation which startles and fascinates one in *The Red Badge of Courage*. The product is breathlessly interesting, but still more so is the suggestion behind it that a novel force has been disclosed, which may do all sorts of other remarkable things. Prophecy is known of old as a tricky and thankless hag, but all the same I cannot close my ears to her hint that a young man who can write such a first book as that will make us all sit up in good time.

4. Arthur G. Sedgwick, *The Nation* (2 July 1896): 15

[Arthur George Sedgwick (1844-1915) was born in 1844 in New York City, graduated from Harvard in 1864, and enlisted in the 20th Massachusetts Volunteer Infantry, where he became a First Lieutenant. He was captured and endured life in a Confederate prison camp. Following his service, he graduated from Harvard Law School and became the editor of the *American Law Review* before joining the editorial staff of the *New York Evening Post* and *The Nation*.]

Mr. Stephen Crane is said never to have seen a battle; but his first book, *The Red Badge of Courage*, is made up of the account of one. The success of the story, however, is due, not merely to what Mr. Crane knows of battlefields, but to what he knows of the human heart. He describes the adventures of a private—a raw recruit—in one of those long engagements, so common in our civil war, and indeed in all modern wars, in which the field of battle is too extensive for those in one part of it to know what is going on elsewhere, and where often a regiment remains in ignorance for some time whether it is victorious or defeated, where the nature of the country prevents hand-to-hand fighting, and a *coup d'œil*[2] of the whole scene is out of the question. In such an action Mr. Crane's hero plays an active part. It is what goes on in his mind that we hear of, and his experience is in part so exactly what old soldiers tell young soldiers to expect that Mr. Crane might easily have got it at second-hand. The hero is at first mortally afraid

---

1 Eadweard James Muybridge (1830-1904) was a British photographer who experimented in capturing motion. His pictures demonstrated that at times all four hooves of a horse are off the ground.
2 Glance (French).

that he is going to be afraid, he then does his duty well enough, but later is seized with a panic and runs away, only to come out a hero again in the end. His panic and flight are managed well; the accidental wound which he luckily gets in running, helps him to a reputation for bravery before he has earned it. When he fights in the end, he fights like a devil, he saves the regimental flag, he is insane with the passion of battle; he is baptized into the brotherhood of those who have been to hell and returned alive. The book is undeniably clever; its vice is over-emphasis. Mr. Crane has not learnt the secret that carnage is itself eloquent, and does not need epithets to make it so. What is a "crimson roar"? Do soldiers hear crimson roars, or do they hear simply roars? If this way of getting expression out of language is allowable, why not extend it to the other senses, and have not only crimson sounds, but purple smells, prehensile views, adhesive music? Color in language is just now a fashionable affectation;[1] Mr. Crane's originality does not lie in falling into it. *George's Mother* is the story of a degenerate drunkard who breaks his mother's heart; *Maggie* is a story of the Bowery, in the "dialect" of "Chimmie Fadden."[2]

Taking all three stories together, we should classify Mr. Crane as a rather promising writer of the animalistic school. His types are mainly human beings of the order which makes us regret the power of literature to portray them. Not merely are they low, but there is little that is interesting in them. We resent the sense that we must at certain points resemble them. Even the old mother is not made pathetic in a human way; her son disgusts us so that we have small power of sympathy with her left. Maggie it is impossible to weep over. We can feel only that it is a pity that the gutter is so dirty, and turn in another direction. In short, Mr. Crane's art is to us very depressing. Of course, there is always the crushing reply that one who does not love art for the sake of art is a poor devil, not worth writing for. But we do not; we do not even love literature for its own sake.

It is only fair to say that what we have called animalism others pronounce wonderful realism. We use the word animalism for the sake of clearness, to denote a species of realism which deals with man considered as an animal, capable of hunger, thirst, lust, cruelty, vanity, fear, sloth, predacity, greed, and other passions and appetites that make him kin to the brutes, but which neglects, so far as possible, any

---

1 Influenced by Impressionism in painting, many writers in the late nineteenth century infused their prose with color imagery, attempting to capture the experience of perceiving reality.

2 Edward Waterman Townsend was famous for his stories of the Bowery featuring a protagonist named Chimmie Fadden. "Love and War" was one of his well-known stories.

higher qualities which distinguish him from his four-footed relatives, such as humor, thought, reason, aspiration, affection, morality, and religion. Real life is full of the contrasts between these conflicting tendencies, but the object of the animalistic school seems always to make a study of the *genus homo* which shall recall the menagerie at feeding-time rather than human society.

5. Thomas Wentworth Higginson, "A Bit of War Photography," *The Philistine* 3 (July 1896): 33-38

[Thomas Wentworth Higginson (1823-1911) enrolled at Harvard at age thirteen and graduated Phi Beta Kappa in 1841. He worked on behalf of abolition and the rights of women, and in the Civil War he was a colonel in charge of a regiment composed of freed slaves, the First South Carolina Volunteers. After the war he devoted the rest of his life to literature. Here he joins the debate about the quality of *The Red Badge of Courage* by arguing in defense of Crane's prose style.]

After the applause won by Mr. Stephen Crane's *Red Badge of Courage*, a little reaction is not strange; and this has already taken, in some quarters, a form quite unjust and unfair. Certainly any one who spent so much as a week or two in camp, thirty years ago, must be struck with the extraordinary freshness and vigor of the book. No one except Tolstoi, within my knowledge, has brought out the daily life of war so well; it may be said of these sentences, in Emerson's phrase, "Cut these and they bleed."[1] The breathlessness, the hurry, the confusion, the seeming aimlessness, as of a whole family of disturbed ants, running to and fro, yet somehow accomplishing something at last; all these aspects, which might seem the most elementary and the easiest to depict, are yet those surest to be omitted, not merely by the novelists, but by the regimental histories themselves.

I know that when I first read Tolstoi's *War and Peace*, *The Cossacks* and *Sevastopol*, it seemed as if all other so called military novels must become at once superannuated and go out of print. All others assumed, in comparison, that bandbox aspect which may be seen in most military or naval pictures; as in the well known engraving of the death of Nelson,[2] where the hero is sinking on the deck in perfect toi-

---

1 Ralph Waldo Emerson was quoted as having said "cut these words and they would bleed; they are vascular and alive." Emerson was praising Michel de Montaigne, who essentially invented the formal essay in the sixteenth century and became a master of the form.

2 Lord Horatio Nelson died heroically in a naval victory at the Battle of Trafalgar in 1805. A monument to the event was erected at what is   *(continued)*

lette, at the height of a bloody conflict, while every soldier or sailor is grouped around him, each in spotless garments and heroic attitude. It is this Tolstoi quality—the real tumult and tatters of the thing itself—which amazes the reader of Crane's novel. Moreover, Tolstoi had been through it all in person; whereas this author is a youth of twenty-four, it seems, born since the very last shot fired in the Civil War. How did he hit upon his point of view?

Yet this very point of view, strange to say, has been called a defect. Remember that he is telling the tale, not of a commanding general, but of a common soldier—a pawn in the game; a man who sees only what is going on immediately around him, and, for the most part, has the key to nothing beyond. This he himself knows well at the time. Afterward, perhaps, when the affair is discussed at the campfire, and his view compared with what others say, it begins to take shape, often mixed with all sorts of errors; and when it has reached the Grand Army Post and been talked over afterward for thirty years, the narrator has not a doubt of it all. It is now a perfectly ordered affair, a neat and well arranged game of chess, often with himself as a leading figure. That is the result of too much perspective. The wonder is that this young writer, who had no way of getting at it all except the gossip—printed or written—of these very old soldiers, should be able to go behind them all, and give an account of their life, not only more vivid than they themselves have ever given, but more accurate. It really seems a touch of that marvelous intuitive quality which for want of a better name we call genius.

Now is it a correct criticism of the book to complain, as one writer has done, that it does not dwell studiously on the higher aspects of the war? Let the picture only be well drawn, and the moral will take care of itself; never fear. The book is not a patriotic tract, but a delineation; a cross section of the daily existence of the raw enlisted-man. In other respects it is reticent, because it is truthful. Does any one suppose that in the daily routine of the camp there was room for much fine talk about motives and results—that men were constantly appealing, like Carlyle's Frenchman, "to posterity and the immortal Gods?"[1] Fortunately or unfortunately, the Anglo Saxon is not built that way; he errs on the other side; habitually understates instead of overstating his

---

now called Trafalgar Square in London. Daniel Maclise did a painting of the death scene that was hung in the Royal Gallery of the Palace of Westminster. In 1876 Charles W. Sharpe created an engraving of the scene that sold widely.

1 Actually, it was Francis Bacon (1561-1626) who was quoted as having said in 1623 "it is enough for me that I have sown unto posterity and the Immortal God."

emotions; and while he is making the most heroic sacrifices of his life, usually prefers to scold about rations or grumble at orders. He is to be judged by results; not by what he says, which is often ungracious and unornamental, but by what he does.

The very merit of this book is that in dealing with his men the author offers, within this general range, all the essential types of character—the man who boasts and the man who is humble—the man who thinks he may be frightened and is not, and the man who does not expect to be, but is. For his main character he selects a type to be found in every regiment—the young man who does not know himself, who first stumbles into cowardice, to his own amazement, and then is equally amazed at stumbling into courage; who begins with skulking, and ends by taking a flag. In Doyle's *Micah Clarke*[1] the old Roundhead soldier tells his grandchildren how he felt inclined to bob his head when he first heard bullets whistle, and adds "If any soldier ever told you that he did not, the first time that he was under fire, then that soldier is not a man to trust." This is putting it too strongly, for some men are born more stolid, other more nervous; but the nervous man is quite as likely to have the firmer grain, and to come out the more heroic in the end. In my own limited experience, the only young officer whom I ever saw thoroughly and confessedly frightened, when first under fire, was the only one of his regiment who afterwards chose the regular army for his profession, and fought Indians for the rest of his life.

As for *The Red Badge of Courage*, the test of the book is in the way it holds you. I only know that whenever I take it up I find myself reading it over and over, as I do Tolstoi's *Cossacks*,[2] and find it as hard to put down. None of Doyle's or Weyman's books[3] bear rereading, in the same way; you must wait till you have forgotten their plots. Even the slipshod grammar seems a part of the breathless life and action. How much promise it gives, it is hard to say. Goethe[4] says that as soon as a man has done one good thing, the world conspires against him to keep him from doing another. Mr. Crane has done one good thing, not

---

1 Arthur Conan Doyle's (1859-1930) *Micah Clarke* (1889) is a historical novel set during the Monmouth Rebellion in England in 1685.

2 Leo Tolstoy's (1828-1910) novel *The Cossacks* (1863) is set in 1863 in the Caucasian War. An aristocratic officer becomes more fully human by associating with the common folk.

3 Stanley J. Weyman (1855-1928) was a British author and historian whose most famous works had appeared in the 1890s just before Crane's *The Red Badge of Courage*. Although he tended toward the romantic, his portraits of war were notable for their historical authenticity.

4 Johann Wolfgang von Goethe (1749-1832) was a famous German statesman and writer whose work was much admired in nineteenth-century America.

to say two; but the conspiracy of admiration may yet be too much for him. It is earnestly to be hoped, at least, that he may have the wisdom to stay in his own country and resist the temptation to test his newly-found English reputation by migrating—an experiment by which Bret Harte has been visibly dwarfed and Henry James hopelessly diluted.[1]

6. William Morton Payne, *The Dial* 20 (1 February 1896): 80

[William Morton Payne (1858-1919) was the Associate Editor of *The Dial* in Chicago and a frequent reviewer whose judgment came to represent the position of the magazine. This brief assessment of the novel was later significantly expanded by the owner of the publication, Alexander McClurg.]

The Red Badge of Courage is a book that has been getting a good deal of belated praise within the past few weeks, but we cannot admit that much of it is deserved. There is almost no story to Mr. Crane's production, but merely an account, in rough-shod descriptive style, of the thoughts and feelings of a young soldier during his first days of active fighting. The author constructs for his central character a psychological history that is plausible, but hardly convincing. We do not know, nor does the writer, what it is that actually does go on in the mind of a man who is passing through his baptism of fire. It may be retorted that we do not know any the more that Count Tolstoi is giving us the real thing in his war-stories, or 'Stendhal' in the *Chartreuse de Parme*,[2] but the descriptions in these books at least seem inevitable while we are reading them, and Mr. Crane's descriptions do not.

---

1 Both Bret Harte (1836-1902), perhaps the most famous writer of short stories in America, and Henry James (1843-1916), a great novelist on the international theme, had left the United States for life in Europe. The general estimate at the time was that their work had suffered from the journey.

2 Marie-Henri Beyle (1783-1842), a French writer who wrote under the name Stendhal, published a novel about the Napoleonic wars in 1839 entitled in English *The Charterhouse of Parma*. It was notable for its graphic descriptions of war scenes.

Appendix C: A Debate about Crane's Novel

[As reviews of *The Red Badge* continued to appear in the United States and England, a debate among commentators developed about not only the general quality of the novel but also about its style, especially its similes and metaphors. Crane's prose was distinctive for its color images and for its comparisons of actions and situations as being "like" historic events, and a spirited disagreement errupted among General Alexander C. McClurg, Ripley Hitchcock, and Sydney Brooks about the issue. The page references in these comments have been changed to refer to this Broadview edition.]

1. General Alexander C. McClurg, *The Dial* 20 (16 April 1896): 227-28

[General Alexander C. McClurg (1832-1901) owned the publishing house that issued *The Dial*, so he had easy access to its pages. His spirited attack on Crane's novel was inspired in part by the brief negative review by William Morton Payne in that magazine on 1 February 1896, and in some measure by the favorable notices appearing elsewhere in England. His comments contain at least two notable errors: one is that *The Red Badge* came out first in the United States, not in England, as McClurg assumes; the second is that it is in no sense a "vicious satire" on American soldiers.]

Must we come to judge of books only by what the newspapers have said of them, and must we abandon all the old standards of criticism? Can a book and an author, utterly without merit, be puffed into success by entirely undeserved praise, even if that praise come from English periodicals?

One must ask these questions after he has been seduced into reading a book recently reprinted in this country entitled *The Red Badge of Courage, an Episode of the American Civil War*. The chorus of praise in the English papers has been very extravagant, but it is noticeable that so far, at least, the American papers have said very little about the merits or demerits of the book itself. They simply allude to the noise made over it abroad, and therefore treat its author as a coming factor in our literature. Even *The Dial's* very acute and usually very discerning critic of contemporary fiction (Mr. Payne) treats the book and the author (in your issue of Feb. 1)[1] in very much this way—

---

1 See Payne's comments in Appendix B6.

that is, as a book and an author to be reckoned with, not because of any good which he himself finds in them, but because they have been so much talked about.

The book has very recently been reprinted in America, and would seem to be an American book, on an American theme, and by an American author, yet originally issued in England. If it is really an American production one must suppose it to have been promptly and properly rejected by any American publishers to whom it may have been submitted, and afterward more naturally taken up by an English publisher.

It is only too well known that English writers have had a very low opinion of American soldiers, and have always, as a rule, assumed to ridicule them. *Blackwood's Magazine* is quoted by a recent writer as saying during the War: "We cannot even pretend to keep our countenance when the exploits of the Grand Army of the Potomac are filling all Europe with inextinguishable laughter," and adds "we know not whether to pity most the officers who lead such men, or the men who are led by such officers" (Vol. 90, pp. 395–96). And again, in January, 1862: "Englishmen are unable to see anything peculiarly tragical in the fact that half a million of men have been brought together in arms to hurl big words at each other across a river" (Vol. 91, p. 118). Again, in April, 1862, "Blackwood" tells us that Americans "do not demand our respect because of their achievements in art, or in literature, or in science, or philosophy. They can make no pretence to the no less real, though less beneficent, reputation of having proved themselves a great military power" (Vol. 91, p. 534). And in October, 1861, "Blackwood" said exultantly: "The venerable Lincoln, the respectable Seward, the raving editors, the gibbering mob, and the swift-footed warriors of Bull's Run,[1] are no malicious tricks of fortune, played off on an unwary nation, but are all of them the legitimate offspring of the Great Republic," and is "glad that the end of the Union seems more likely to be ridiculous than terrible" (Vol. 90, p. 396).

We all know with what bitterness and spitefulness the *Saturday Review* always treats Americans; and with what special vindictiveness it reviews any book upon our late struggle written from the Northern standpoint. And so it is with all British periodicals and all British writers. They are so puffed up with vain-glory over their own soldiers who seldom meet men of their own strength, but are used in every part

---

1   Abraham Lincoln was President of the United States during the Civil War; William H. Seward was Secretary of State; the Battle of Bull Run (not bull's run) was the first major engagement of the war. It was fought on 21 July 1861 in Virginia and proved to be a Southern victory. The South called the engagement the First Manassas.

of the world for attacking and butchering defenseless savages, who happen to possess some property that Englishmen covet, that they cannot believe that there can be among any peoples well-disciplined soldiers as gallant and courageous as their own.

Under such circumstances we cannot doubt that *The Red Badge of Courage* would be just such a book as the English would grow enthusiastic over, and we cannot wonder that the redoubtable *Saturday Review* greeted it with the highest encomiums, and declared it the actual experiences of a veteran of our War, when it was really the vain imaginings of a young man born long since that satire upon American soldiers and American armies. The hero of the book (if such he can be called—"the youth" the author styles him) is an ignorant and stupid country lad, who, without a spark of patriotic feeling, or even of soldierly ambition, has enlisted in the army from no definite motive that the reader can discover, unless it be because other boys are doing so; and the whole book, in which there is absolutely no story, is occupied with giving what are supposed to be his emotions and his actions in the first two days of battle. His poor weak intellect, if indeed he has any, seems to be at once and entirely overthrown by the din and movement of the field, and he acts throughout like a madman. Under the influence of mere excitement, for he does not even appear to be frightened, he first rushes madly to the rear in a crazy panic, and afterwards plunges forward to the rescue of the colors under exactly the same influences. In neither case has reason or any intelligent motive any influence on his action. He is throughout an idiot or a maniac, and betrays no trace of the reasoning being. No thrill of patriotic devotion to cause or country ever moves his breast, and not even an emotion of manly courage. Even a wound which he finally gets comes from a comrade who strikes him on the head with his musket to get rid of him; and this is the only "Red Badge of Courage" (!) which we discover in the book. A number of other characters come in to fill out the two hundred and thirty-three pages of the book,—such as "the loud soldier," "the tall soldier," "the tattered soldier," etc., but not one of them betrays any more sense, self-possession, or courage than does "the youth." On the field all is chaos and confusion. "The young lieutenant," "the mounted officer," even "the general," are all utterly demented beings, raving and talking alike in an unintelligible and hitherto unheard-of jargon, rushing about in a very delirium of madness. No intelligent orders are given; no intelligent movements are made. There is no evidence of drill, none of discipline. There is a constant, senseless, and profane babbling going on, such as one could hear nowhere but in a madhouse. Nowhere are seen the quiet, manly, self-respecting, and patriotic men, influenced by the highest sense of duty, who in reality fought our battles.

It can be said most confidently that no soldier who fought in our recent War ever saw any approach to the battle scenes in this book— but what wonder? We are told that it is the work of a young man of twenty-three or twenty-four years of age, and so of course must be a mere work of diseased imagination. And yet it constantly strains after so-called realism. The result is a mere riot of words.

Although its burlesques and caricatures are quite enough to dismiss it from attention, it is worth while to give some samples of its diction to show that there is in it an entire lack of any literary quality. Notice the violent straining after effect in the mere unusual association of words, in the forced and distorted use of adjectives. Notice, too, the absurd similes, and even the bad grammar. Startling sentences are so frequent they might be quoted indefinitely; but here are a few:

"A brigade ahead of them and on the right went into action *with a rending roar. It was as if it had exploded*" (p. 59).

"The lieutenant of the youth's company was shot in the hand. He began to swear so wondrously that a nervous laugh went along the regimental line. The officer's profanity sounded conventional. It relieved the tightened senses of the new men. *It was as if he had hit his fingers with a tack hammer at home*" (p. 61).

"Another [mounted officer] was galloping about *bawling*. His hat was gone, and his clothes were awry. *He resembled a man who has come from bed to go to a fire.* The hoofs of his horse often threatened the heads of the running men, but they scampered with singular fortune. In this rush they were apparently all deaf and blind. They heeded not the largest and longest of oaths which were thrown at them from all directions" (p. 62).

"The battle reflection that shone for an instant in the faces on the mad current made the youth feel that forceful hands from heaven would not have been able to have held him in place if he could have got intelligent control of his legs" (p. 62).

"*A small thrillful boy*" (p. 63).

"The cartridge-boxes were pulled around into various positions, and adjusted with great care. *It was as if seven hundred new bonnets were being tried on*" (p. 63).

"Buried in the smoke of many rifles, his anger was directed not so much against the men *whom he knew were rushing* toward him as against the swishing battle phantoms which were choking him, stuffing their smoke robes down his parched throat" (p. 65).

"There was a *blare of heated rage*" (p. 65).

"The officers at their intervals rearward ... were bobbing to and fro roaring directions. *The dimensions of their howls were extraordinary*" (p. 66).

"To the youth it was like an onslaught of redoubtable dragons. He became like the man who lost his legs at the approach of the red and green monster. He waited in a sort of horrified, listening attitude. He seemed to shut his eyes, and wait to be gobbled" (p. 71).

"*A crimson roar* came from a distance" (p. 78).

"With the courageous words of the artillery and the spiteful sentences of the musketry mingled *red cheers*" (p. 79).

"The youth had reached an anguish when *the sobs scorched him*" (p. 84).

"*They were ever up-raising the ghost of shame on the stick of their curiosity*" (p. 90).

"The *new silence of his wound* made much worryment" (p. 99).

"The distance *was splintering* and blaring with the noise of fighting" (p. 107).

" ... began *to mutter softly in black curses*" (p. 138).

"His corpse would be for those eyes *a great and salt reproach*" (p. 145).

It is extraordinary that even a prejudiced animus could have led English writers to lavish extravagant praise on such a book; it is still more extraordinary that an attempt should be made to foist it upon the long-suffering American public, and to push it into popularity here. Respect for our own people should have prevented its issue in this country.

There may have been a moderate number of men in our service who felt and acted in battle like those in this book; but of such deserters were made. They did not stay when they could get away: why should they? The army was no healthy place for them, and they had no reason to stay; there was no moral motive. After they had deserted, however, they remained "loud soldiers," energetic and blatant,—and they are possibly now enjoying good pensions. It must have been some of these fellows who got the ear of Mr. Crane and told him how they felt and acted in battle.

2. Ripley Hitchcock, *The Dial* (1 May 1896): 263

[Ripley Hitchcock (1857-1918) was Stephen Crane's editor at Appleton & Co., the publisher of *The Red Badge of Courage*. He graduated from Harvard in 1877 and worked as a reporter for *The New York Tribune* before becoming a literary consultant and editor at Appleton, where he handled Rudyard Kipling and Theodore Dreiser as well as the aspiring young writer of *Maggie* and *The Red Badge*. Here he defends the reputation of the novel and responds to those critics who have attacked it.]

It is with a certain hesitation that we write you to correct the author of a somewhat bitter letter published in your journal for April 16, for we recognize the signature as that of a gallant soldier, as well as a student of literature. But as the author of that letter labors under several misapprehensions, we think that he will be glad to learn the facts.

The Red Badge of Courage was read and accepted by us in December, 1894, and, in book form, it was first published in this country in October, 1895. Although the book was copyrighted in England at the same time, it was not formally published there for two months. Meantime the American journals had reviewed it and had begun an almost universal chorus of eulogy. October 19, 1895, the New York Times devoted a column and a half to a strong review of "this remarkable book." On October 13, the Philadelphia Press compared Mr. Crane and Bret Harte, not to the disadvantage of the former. On October 26, the New York Mail and Express, in one of several notices, said, "The author has more than talent—there is genius in the book." On October 26, the Boston Transcript, in speaking of "this tremendous grasping of the glory and carnage of war," added at the close of a long and enthusiastic review, "The book forces upon the reader the conviction of what fighting really means." Other favorable reviews appeared in October issues of the following American newspapers: New York Herald, Brooklyn Eagle, Cleveland World, St. Paul Pioneer Press, Boston Daily Advertiser, New York World, St. Paul Globe, New York Commercial Advertiser, Kansas City Journal, Chicago Evening Post, Boston Courier, Cleveland Plain Dealer, Boston Beacon, Hartford Times, Sioux City Times, New Haven Leader, and Minneapolis Journal, and to these names, taken almost at random, we might add many others. These journals reviewed The Red Badge favorably in October, and others, including weeklies like The Critic and The Outlook, followed in November with emphatic recognition of the strength and high talent shown in the book.

It was not until the end of November, two months after publication here, that the first reviews appeared in England. By that time American reviewers from Maine to California had "greeted" the book with the highest "encomiums." The English "encomiums" became specially marked in late December, January and February.

We state these facts in view of your correspondent's remarks that "So far, at least, the American papers have said very little about the merits or demerits of the book," and, "The book has very recently been reprinted in Amcrica," and, "Respect for our own people should have prevented its issue in this country." "Our country" was the first to recognize Mr. Crane's genius, and our people have read his book so eagerly that it continues to be the most popular work of fiction in the market, and it has been the one most talked of and written about since October last.

A glance at the back of the *Red Badge* title-page would have shown that the book could not have been "first published" in England and "reprinted" here, while the literary departments of journals throughout our country, and the opinions of American men of letters like Mr. Howells and Mr. Hamlin Garland, have proved, happily, that Americans are ready to recognize American talent, and that, *pace* your correspondent, a prophet is not without honor even in his own country.

As to other points, against the opinion of the gallant veteran who criticizes the book might be put the opinions of other veterans who have found only words of praise.

3. Sydney Brooks, *The Dial* 20 (16 May 1896): 297-98

[Sydney Brooks (1872-1937) was a British writer who frequently contributed to *The Saturday Review*, *Harper's Magazine*, and other American periodicals. At the time he wrote this essay he was in Chicago. He died in 1937.]

It really requires some courage to confess it, but I was one of the first English reviewers to whose lot fell the reviewing of Mr. Stephen Crane's book, *The Red Badge of Courage*. Worse still—a quite damning fact, I fear—I even ventured to praise it. Mr. Crane I had never heard of when his book came to me in the ordinary course of business, but I read the volume with the greatest interest; I thought it in many ways a remarkable performance, and I did my best to give reasons for the faith that was in me. But apparently it is a subtle insult for an Englishman to praise an American book. I used to think that a good book was a good book the whole world over. It is only since landing in this country and picking up *The Dial* of April 16 that I have learned better. Your correspondent, "A.C. McC.,"[1] is my authority. Now, I am truly sorry that any criticisms of mine or of my brother reviewers in London should have so annoyed your correspondent, for he evidently was very much annoyed. He came out on the warpath, arrested Mr. Crane as a literary spy, court-martialled him, and shot the poor fellow off-hand.

This book, says "A.C. McC." in effect, cannot be a good one for Americans to read because the English have praised it. He puts the whole thing in a nutshell, you see. This English praise, he is convinced, is a Grecian gift. I personally thought I was merely pointing out the merits of what seemed to me a book that deserved some notice. But he saw the ambush we English reviewers were laying. Deep under our affected enthusiasm for this young writer was an intense desire to

---

1   General Alexander C. McClurg.

insult America. It sounds oddly, does n't it? But he has chapter and verse to prove it. He comes across some cruel, senseless gibes at the Union soldiers in *Blackwood's Magazine*. They are over thirty years old, and to-day, from one end of England to the other, you could not find a man to express anything but the bitterest shame of them. But what of that? "There," exclaims "A.C. McC." exultantly, "that is why these English are praising Stephen Crane. The hero of his book is a coward. Thirty years ago an ignorant British magazine talked of 'the swift-footed warriors of Bull's Run.' Don't you see the connection? It is all a deep-laid plot to throw mud at American soldiers." To be sure! And so when I sat, pipe in mouth, a peaceable, jaded reviewer, happy to have come across a book above the dull dead level, my mind was really full of schemes for avenging Bunker's Hill![1]

Your correspondent's letter is a compound of misjudged patriotism and bad criticism. Take only these two sentences. "The book," he says, "is a vicious satire upon American soldiers and American armies." "Respect for our own people should have prevented its issue in this country." A curious attitude to take up towards a book, unworthy of an American, as it seems to me, and peculiarly unworthy of an American who, as I hear, fought through the war with distinction. I will say at once that no such idea ever presented itself to a single Englishman into whose hands the book fell. The most insignificant thing about the book, the one point which every sensible reviewer would at once dismiss from his mind as quite immaterial, is the fact that the hero fought for the North. If he had been an Englishman in the ditches before Sebastopol, or a Frenchman at Sedan,[2] the book would have been just as remarkable, and the praise of the English journals no less warm. But to "A.C. McC." Mr. Crane's one unforgivable crime lies in portraying a Northerner who fled from the field.

Scarcely less wrong-headed is your correspondent's criticism of the book as a piece of literature. He has missed the whole point of the tale. Part of Mr. Crane's plan, I take it, was to give an idea of the impressions made on a raw recruit by the movements of a regiment in battle. Who can doubt that to a man who but yesterday was working at the plough the whole thing appears one intolerable confusion? As for the style in which the book is written, "A.C. McC." finds in it "an entire

---

1 The Battle of Bunker Hill (not Bunker's Hill) was fought near Boston in the Revoutionary War.
2 The references are to the Siege of Sevastopol (1854-55) in Russia, in which British and French forces defeated the Russians during the Crimean War, and to the Battle of Sedan (1870), in which the Prussians captured Emperor Napoleon III.

lack of any literary quality." Mr. Crane, once more, is an author "utterly without merit." No half-measures with "A.C. McC." Again quotations are at hand. Detached sentences are given, and anything disapproved of is italicised. The odd part about it is that most of the expressions thus crucified seem to me admirable and picturesque. That there is a youthful and occasionally reckless daring about some, is true enough. But on the whole I am prepared to back Mr. Crane's sense of language against "A.C. McC.'s."

⌈However, I am concerned little here with the merits of Mr. Crane's work. The book can take care of itself quite well.⌉ I was surprised at "A.C. McC.'s" singular criticisms, and thought that a few words from "the other side" might be fairly called for.

Appendix D: The Deleted Chapter 12 of The Red Badge of Courage

[As Stephen Crane worked on The Red Badge of Courage in 1894, he originally wrote a partial draft of Chapter 12 in which Henry Fleming considers the responsibility for his desertion. As the novel was prepared for book publication the following year, however, Crane deleted that manuscript draft, possibly at the recommendation of his editor, Ripley Hitchcock, at Appleton & Company. In any event, the original chapter was never completed and was not included in the publication of the novel in 1895. Nor did Crane attempt to have it placed into the English edition of the novel that came out in 1896. Nevertheless, one group of scholars has argued that the partial draft should be incorporated into the novel to make it consistent with Crane's original design for the book. It is included here so that readers can make up their own minds about the wisdom of incorporating it into the published novel. The deleted chapter is also discussed in the Introduction to this volume. The asterisks in the text indicate places where Crane left the passages incomplete.]

It was always clear to the youth that he was entirely different from other men, that his mind had been cast in a unique mold. Hence laws that might be just to the ordinary man were, when applied to him, peculiar and galling outrages. Minds, he said, were not made all with one stamp and colored green. He was of no general pattern. It was not right to measure his acts by a worldwide standard. The laws of the world were wrong because through the vain spectacles of their makers, he appeared, with all men, as of a common size and of a green color. There was no justice on the earth when justice was meant. Men were too puny and prattling to know anything of it. If there was a justice, it must be in the hands of a God.

He regarded his sufferings as unprecedented. No man had ever achieved such misery. There was a melancholy grandeur in the isolation of his experiences. He saw that he was a speck raising his minute arms against all possible forces and fates which were swelling down upon him in black tempests. He could derive some consolation from viewing the sublimity of the odds.

As he went on, he began to feel that nature, for her part, would not blame him for his rebellion. He still distinctly felt that he was arrayed against the universe but he believed now that there was no malice in the vast breasts of his space-filling foes. It was merely law, not merciful to the individual; but just, to a system. Nature had provided the

creations with various defenses and ways of escape that they might
fight or flee, and she had limited dangers in powers of attack and
pursuit that the things might resist or hide with a security proportion-
ate to their strength and wisdom. It was cruel but it was war. Nature
fought for her system; individuals fought for liberty to breathe. The
animals had the privilege of using their legs and their brains. It was all
the same old philosophy. He could not omit a small grunt of satisfaction as he saw with what brilliancy he had reasoned it out.

He now said that, if, as he supposed, his life was being relentlessly
pursued, it was not his duty to bow to the approaching death. Nature
did not expect submission. On the contrary, it was his business to kick
and bite and give blows as a stripling in the hands of a murderer. The
law was that he should fight. He would be saved according to the
importance of his strength.

His egotism made him feel safe, for a time, from the iron hands.

It being in his mind that he had solved these matters, he eagerly
applied his findings to the incident of his flight from the battle. It was
not a fault, a shameful thing; it was an act obedient to a law. It was—

But he was aware that when he had erected a vindicating structure
of great principles, it was the calm toes of tradition that kicked it all
down about his ears. He immediately antagonized then this devotion
to the bygone, this universal adoration of the past. From the bitter pin-
nacle of his wisdom he saw that mankind not only worshipped the
gods of the ashes but that the gods of the ashes were worshipped
because they were the gods of the ashes. He perceived with anger the
present state of affairs in its bearing upon his case. And he resolved to
reform it all.

He had, presently, a feeling that he was the growing prophet of a
world-reconstruction. Far down in the untouched depths of his being,
among the hidden currents of his soul, he saw born a voice. He conceived a new world modeled by the pain of his life, and in which no
old shadows fell blighting upon the temple of thought. And there were
many personal advantages in it.

★ ★ ★ ★ ★

He thought for a time of piercing orations starting multitudes and of
books wrung from his heart. In the gloom of his misery, his eyesight
proclaimed that mankind were bowing to wrong and ridiculous idols.
He said that if some all-powerful joker should take them away in the
night, and leave only manufactured shadows falling upon the bended
heads, mankind would go on counting the hollow beads of their
progress until the shriveling of the fingers. He was ablaze with desire
to change. He saw himself, a sunlit figure upon a peak, pointing with

true and unchangeable gesture. "There!" And all men could see and no man would falter.

Gradually the idea grew upon him that the cattle which cluttered the earth would, in their ignorance and calm faith in the next day, blunder stolidly on and he would be beating his fists against the brass of accepted things. A remarkable facility for abuse came to him then and in supreme disgust and rage, he railed. To him there was something terrible and awesome in these words spoken from his heart to his heart. He was very tragic.

★ ★ ★ ★ ★

He saw himself chasing a thought-phantom across the sky before the assembled eyes of mankind. He could say to them that it was an angel whose possession was existence perfected; they would declare it to be a greased pig. He had no desire to devote his life to proclaiming the angel, when he could plainly perceive that mankind would hold, from generation to generation, to the theory of the greased pig.

It would be pleasure to reform a docile race. But he saw that there were none and he did not intend to raise his voice against the hooting of continents.

Thus he abandoned the world to its devices. He felt that many men must have so abandoned it, but he saw how they could be reconciled to it and agree to accept the stone idols and the greased pigs, when they contemplated the opportunities for plunder.

For himself, however, he saw no salve, no reconciling opportunities. He was entangled in the errors. He began to rage anew against circumstances which he did not name and against processes of which he knew only the name. He felt that he was being grinded beneath stone feet which he despised. The detached bits of truth which formed the knowledge of the world could not save him. There was a dreadful, unwritten martyrdom in his state.

He made a little search for some thing upon which to concentrate the hate of his despair; he fumbled in his mangled intellect to find the Great Responsibility.

He again hit upon nature. He again saw her grim dogs upon his trail. They were unswerving, merciless and would overtake him at the appointed time. His mind pictured the death of Jim Conklin and in the scene, he saw the shadows of his fate. Dread words had been said from star to star. An event had been penned by the implacable forces.

He was of the unfit, then. He did not come into the scheme of further life. His tiny part had been done and he must go. There was no room for him. On all the vast lands there was not a foothold. He must be thrust out to make room for the more important.

Regarding himself as one of the unfit, he believed that nothing could exceed for misery, a perception of this fact. He thought that he measured with his falling heart, tossed in like a pebble by his supreme and awful foe, the most profound depths of pain. It was a barbarous process with affection for the man and the oak, and no sympathy for the rabbit and the weed. He thought of his own capacity for pity and there was an infinite irony in it.

He desired to revenge himself upon the universe. Feeling in his body all spears of pain, he would have capsized, if possible, the world and made chaos. Much cruelty lay in the fact that he was a babe.

Admitting that he was powerless and at the will of law, he yet planned to escape; menaced by fatality he schemed to avoid it. He thought of various places in the world where he imagined that he would be safe. He remembered hiding once in an empty flour-barrel that sat in his mother's pantry. His playmates, hunting the bandit-chief, had thundered on the barrel with their fierce sticks but he had lain snug and undetected. They had searched the house. He now created in thought a secure spot where an all-powerful eye would fail to perceive him, where an all-powerful stick would fail to bruise his life.

There was in him a creed of freedom which no contemplation of inexorable law could destroy. He saw himself living in watchfulness, frustrating the plans of the unchangeable, making of fate a fool. He had ways, he thought, of working out his

Appendix E: Stephen Crane, "The Veteran"

["The Veteran" was included in Crane's volume of Civil War stories, *The Little Regiment and Other Episodes of the American Civil War* (1896), even though it takes place many years after the conclusion of that conflict. The justification must have been that Henry Fleming, from *The Red Badge of Courage*, is Crane's most celebrated character, and this story covers the end of his life. It is also important because it specifies that Henry deserted his post at the Battle of Chancellorsville, a point not made clear in the novel.]

THE VETERAN

Out of the low window could be seen three hickory trees placed irregularly in a meadow that was resplendent in springtime green. Farther away, the old, dismal belfry of the village church loomed over the pines. A horse meditating in the shade of one of the hickories lazily swished his tail. The warm sunshine made an oblong of vivid yellow on the floor of the grocery. "Could you see the whites of their eyes?" said the man who was seated on a soap box.

"Nothing of the kind," replied old Henry warmly. "Just a lot of flitting figures, and I let go at where they 'peared to be the thickest. Bang!"

"Mr. Fleming," said the grocer—his deferential voice expressed somehow the old man's exact social weight—"Mr. Fleming, you never was frightened much in them battles, was you?"

The veteran looked down and grinned. Observing his manner, the entire group tittered. "Well, I guess I was," he answered finally. "Pretty well scared, sometimes. Why, in my first battle I thought the sky was falling down. I thought the world was coming to an end. You bet I was scared."

Every one laughed. Perhaps it seemed strange and rather wonderful to them that a man should admit the thing, and in the tone of their laughter there was probably more admiration than if old Fleming had declared that he had always been a lion. Moreover, they knew that he had ranked as an orderly sergeant, and so their opinion of his heroism was fixed. None, to be sure, knew how an orderly sergeant[1] ranked,

---

1 A First-Sergeant, normally the senior non-commissioned officer of a company. After his ignominious beginning, Henry Fleming apparently performed well in the Civil War.

but then it was understood to be somewhere just shy of a major general's stars. So, when old Henry admitted that he had been frightened, there was a laugh.

"The trouble was," said the old man, "I thought they were all shooting at me. Yes, sir, I thought every man in the other army was aiming at me in particular, and only me. And it seemed so darned unreasonable, you know. I wanted to explain to 'em what an almighty good fellow I was, because I thought then they might quit all trying to hit me. But I couldn't explain, and they kept on being unreasonable— blim!—blam!—bang! So I run!"

Two little triangles of wrinkles appeared at the corners of his eyes. Evidently he appreciated some comedy in this recital. Down near his feet, however, little Jim, his grandson, was visibly horror-stricken. His hands were clasped nervously, and his eyes were wide with astonishment at this terrible scandal, his most magnificent grandfather telling such a thing.

"That was at Chancellorsville.[1] Of course, afterward I got kind of used to it. A man does. Lots of men, though, seem to feel all right from the start. I did, as soon as I 'got on to it,' as they say now; but at first I was pretty well flustered. Now, there was young Jim Conklin, old Si Conklin's son—that used to keep the tannery—you none of you recollect him—well, he went into it from the start just as if he was born to it. But with me it was different. I had to get used to it."

When little Jim walked with his grandfather he was in the habit of skipping along on the stone pavement in front of the three stores and the hotel of the town and betting that he could avoid the cracks. But upon this day he walked soberly, with his hand gripping two of his grandfather's fingers. Sometimes he kicked abstractedly at dandelions that curved over the walk. Any one could see that he was much troubled.

"There's Sickles's colt over in the medder, Jimmie," said the old man. "Don't you wish you owned one like him?"

"Um," said the boy, with a strange lack of interest. He continued his reflections. Then finally he ventured, "Grandpa—now—was that true what you was telling those men?"

"What?" asked the grandfather. "What was I telling them?"

"Oh, about your running."

"Why, yes, that was true enough, Jimmie. It was my first fight, and there was an awful lot of noise, you know."

---

1 This assertion by Henry Fleming is the best evidence that *The Red Badge of Courage* takes place at the Battle of Chancellorsville. The internal evidence in the reference to rivers and other topographical details make it possible, but it is not certain in the novel itself.

Jimmie seemed dazed that this idol, of its own will, should so totter. His stout boyish idealism was injured.

Presently the grandfather said: "Sickles's colt is going for a drink. Don't you wish you owned Sickles's colt, Jimmie?"

The boy merely answered, "He ain't as nice as our'n." He lapsed then into another moody silence.

One of the hired men, a Swede, desired to drive to the county seat for purposes of his own. The old man loaned a horse and an unwashed buggy. It appeared later that one of the purposes of the Swede was to get drunk.

After quelling some boisterous frolic of the farm hands and boys in the garret, the old man had that night gone peacefully to sleep, when he was aroused by clamouring at the kitchen door. He grabbed his trousers, and they waved out behind as he dashed forward. He could hear the voice of the Swede, screaming and blubbering. He pushed the wooden button, and, as the door flew open, the Swede, a maniac, stumbled inward, chattering, weeping, still screaming: "De barn fire! Fire! Fire! De barn fire! Fire! Fire! Fire!"

There was a swift and indescribable change in the old man. His face ceased instantly to be a face; it became a mask, a gray thing, with horror written about the mouth and eyes. He hoarsely shouted at the foot of the little rickety stairs, and immediately, it seemed, there came down an avalanche of men. No one knew that during this time the old lady had been standing in her night clothes at the bedroom door, yelling: "What's th' matter? What's th' matter? What's th' matter?"

When they dashed toward the barn it presented to their eyes its usual appearance, solemn, rather mystic in the black night. The Swede's lantern was overturned at a point some yards in front of the barn doors. It contained a wild little conflagration of its own, and even in their excitement some of those who ran felt a gentle secondary vibration of the thrifty part of their minds at sight of this overturned lantern. Under ordinary circumstances it would have been a calamity.

But the cattle in the barn were trampling, trampling, trampling, and above this noise could be heard a humming like the song of innumerable bees. The old man hurled aside the great doors, and a yellow flame leaped out at one corner and sped and wavered frantically up the old gray wall. It was glad, terrible, this single flame, like the wild banner of deadly and triumphant foes.

The motley crowd from the garret had come with all the pails of the farm. They flung themselves upon the well. It was a leisurely old machine, long dwelling in indolence. It was in the habit of giving out water with a sort of reluctance. The men stormed at it, cursed it; but it continued to allow the buckets to be filled only after the wheezy windlass had howled many protests at the mad-handed men.

With his opened knife in his hand old Fleming himself had gone headlong into the barn, where the stifling smoke swirled with the air currents, and where could be heard in its fulness the terrible chorus of the flames, laden with tones of hate and death, a hymn of wonderful ferocity.

He flung a blanket over an old mare's head, cut the halter close to the manger, led the mare to the door, and fairly kicked her out to safety. He returned with the same blanket, and rescued one of the work horses. He took five horses out, and then came out himself, with his clothes bravely on fire. He had no whiskers, and very little hair on his head. They soused five pailfuls of water on him. His eldest son made a clean miss with the sixth pailful, because the old man had turned and was running down the decline and around to the basement of the barn, where were the stanchions of the cows. Some one noticed at the time that he ran very lamely, as if one of the frenzied horses had smashed his hip.

The cows, with their heads held in the heavy stanchions, had thrown themselves, strangled themselves, tangled themselves: done everything which the ingenuity of their exuberant fear could suggest to them.

Here, as at the well, the same thing happened to every man save one. Their hands went mad. They became incapable of everything save the power to rush into dangerous situations.

The old man released the cow nearest the door, and she, blind drunk with terror, crashed into the Swede. The Swede had been running to and fro babbling. He carried an empty milk pail, to which he clung with an unconscious, fierce enthusiasm. He shrieked like one lost as he went under the cow's hoofs, and the milk pail, rolling across the floor, made a flash of silver in the gloom.

Old Fleming took a fork, beat off the cow, and dragged the paralyzed Swede to the open air. When they had rescued all the cows save one, which had so fastened herself that she could not be moved an inch, they returned to the front of the barn and stood sadly, breathing like men who had reached the final point of human effort.

Many people had come running. Some one had even gone to the church, and now, from the distance, rang the tocsin note[1] of the old bell. There was a long flare of crimson on the sky, which made remote people speculate as to the whereabouts of the fire.

The long flames sang their drumming chorus in voices of the heaviest bass. The wind whirled clouds of smoke and cinders into the faces of the spectators. The form of the old barn was outlined in black amid these masses of orange-hued flames.

---

1 An alarm bell.

And then came this Swede again, crying as one who is the weapon of the sinister fates. "De colts! De colts! You have forgot de colts!"

Old Fleming staggered. It was true; they had forgotten the two colts in the box stalls at the back of the barn. "Boys," he said, "I must try to get 'em out." They clamoured about him then, afraid for him, afraid of what they should see. Then they talked wildly each to each. "Why, it's sure death!" "He would never get out!" "Why, it's suicide for a man to go in there!" Old Fleming stared absent-mindedly at the open doors. "The poor little things!" he said. He rushed into the barn.

When the roof fell in, a great funnel of smoke swarmed toward the sky, as if the old man's mighty spirit, released from its body—a little bottle—had swelled like the genie of fable. The smoke was tinted rose-hue from the flames, and perhaps the unutterable midnights of the universe will have no power to daunt the colour of this soul.

Select Bibliography

Books by Stephen Crane

Maggie: A Girl of the Streets. New York: Appleton, 1896. Privately printed in 1893 with Johnston Smith listed as author.

The Black Riders and Other Lines. Boston: Copeland & Day, 1895.

The Red Badge of Courage: An Episode of the Civil War. New York: Appleton, 1895.

George's Mother. New York: Edward Arnold, 1896.

The Little Regiment and Other Episodes of the American Civil War. New York: Appleton, 1896.

The Third Violet. New York: Appleton, 1897.

The Open Boat and Other Stories. London: Heinemann, 1898.

War is Kind. New York: Stokes, 1899.

Active Service. New York: Stokes, 1899.

The Monster and Other Stories. New York: Harper, 1899.

Whilomville Stories. New York: Harper, 1900.

Great Battles of the World. Philadelphia: Lippincott, 1901.

The O'Ruddy: A Romance. New York: Stokes, 1903. Novel completed by Robert Barr.

The Sullivan County Sketches of Stephen Crane. Ed. Melvin Schoberlin. Syracuse: Syracuse UP, 1949.

The War Dispatches of Stephen Crane. Ed. R.W. Stallman and E.R. Hagemann. New York: New York UP, 1964.

Stephen Crane in the West and Mexico. Ed. Joseph Katz. Kent: Kent State UP, 1970.

The Red Badge of Courage: A Facsimile Edition of the Manuscripts. 2 vols. Ed. Fredson Bowers. Washington, DC: NCR Microcard Edition, 1973.

The Works of Stephen Crane. 10 vols. Ed. Fredson Bowers. Charlottesville: UP of Virginia, 1969-76.

Biographies

Colvert, James B. *Stephen Crane.* New York: Harcourt Brace, 1984.

Linson, Corwin Knapp. *My Stephen Crane.* Ed. Edwin H. Cady. Syracuse: Syracuse UP, 1958.

Sorrentino, Paul. *Stephen Crane: A Life of Fire.* Cambridge: Harvard UP, 2014.

Stallman, R.W. *Stephen Crane: A Biography.* New York: Braziller, 1968.

Wertheim, Stanley, and Paul Sorrentino. *The Crane Log: A Documentary Life of Stephen Crane, 1871-1900*. New York: G.K. Hall, 1994.

Letters

The Correspondence of Stephen Crane. Ed. Stanley Wertheim and Paul Sorrentino. 2 vols. New York: Columbia UP, 1988.
Stephen Crane: Letters. Ed. R.W. Stallman and Lillian Gilkes. New York: New York UP, 1960.
Stephen Crane's Love Letters to Nellie Crouse. Ed. Edwin H. Cady and Lester G. Wells. Syracuse: Syracuse UP, 1954.

Bibliographies

Dooley, Patrick. *Stephen Crane: An Annotated Bibliography of Secondary Scholarship*. New York: G.K. Hall, 1992.
Stallman, R.W. *Stephen Crane: A Critical Bibliography*. Ames: Iowa State UP, 1972.
Williams, Ames, and Vincent Starrett. *Stephen Crane: A Bibliography*. Glendale: John Valentine, 1948.

Critical Studies: Books

Ahnebrink, Lars. *The Beginnings of Naturalism in American Fiction*. Uppsala: Sweden, 1950.
Bergon, Frank. *Stephen Crane's Artistry*. New York: Columbia, 1975.
Berryman, John. *Stephen Crane*. New York: William Sloane Associates, 1950.
Brown, Bill. *The Material Unconscious: American Amusements, Stephen Crane, and the Economics of Play*. Cambridge: Harvard UP, 1996.
Cady, Edwin. *Stephen Crane*. New York: Twayne, 1962.
Dooley, Patrick K. *The Pluralistic Philosophy of Stephen Crane*. Urbana: U of Illinois P, 1992.
Fagg, John. *On the Cusp: Stephen Crane, George Bellows, and Modernism*. Tuscaloosa: U of Alabama P, 2009.
Gibson, Donald B. *The Fiction of Stephen Crane*. Carbondale: Southern Illinois UP, 1968.
Gullason, Thomas A. *Stephen Crane's Career: Perspectives and Evaluations*. New York: New York UP, 1972.
Halliburton, David. *The Color of the Sky: A Study of Stephen Crane*. Cambridge: Cambridge UP, 1989.
Holton, Milne. *Cylinder of Vision: The Fiction and Journalistic Writing of Stephen Crane*. Baton Rouge: Louisiana State UP, 1972.

LaFrance, Marston. *A Reading of Stephen Crane*. New York: Oxford UP, 1971.

Milne, Gordon. *Stephen Crane at Brede: An Anglo-American Literary Circle of the 1890s*. Washington, DC: UP of America, 1980.

Mitchell, Lee Clark, ed. *New Essays on* The Red Badge of Courage. New York: Cambridge UP, 1986.

Monteiro, George. *Stephen Crane's Blue Badge of Courage*. Baton Rouge: Louisiana State UP, 2000.

Nagel, James. *Stephen Crane and Literary Impressionism*. University Park: Pennsylvania State UP, 1980.

Pizer, Donald, ed. *Critical Essays on Stephen Crane's* The Red Badge of Courage. Boston: G.K. Hall, 1990.

Robertson, Michael. *Stephen Crane, Journalism, and the Making of Modern American Literature*. New York: Columbia UP, 1997.

Sorrentino, Paul M. *Student Companion to Stephen Crane*. Westport: Greenwood, 2006.

——, ed. *Stephen Crane Remembered*. Tuscaloosa: U of Alabama P, 2006.

Weatherford, Richard M. *Stephen Crane: The Critical Heritage*. London: Routledge & Kegan Paul, 1973.

Wertheim, Stanley. *A Stephen Crane Encyclopedia*. Westport: Greenwood, 1997.

Wolford, Chester L. *The Anger of Stephen Crane: Fiction and the Epic Tradition*. Lincoln: U of Nebraska P, 1983.

Articles on *The Red Badge of Courage*

Albrecht, Robert C. "Content and Style in *The Red Badge of Courage*." *College English* 28 (1966): 487-92.

Binder, Henry. "*The Red Badge of Courage* Nobody Knows." *Studies in the Novel* 10 (1978): 9-47.

Breslin, Paul. "Courage and Convention: *The Red Badge of Courage*." *Yale Review* 66 (1976): 209-22.

Casey, John Anthony. "Searching for a War of One's Own: Stephen Crane, *The Red Badge of Courage*, and the Glorious Burden of the Civil War Veteran." *American Literary Realism* 44 (2011): 1-22.

Cox, James Trammel. "The Imagery of *The Red Badge of Courage*." *Modern Fiction Studies* 5 (1959): 209-19.

Fraser, John. "Crime and Forgiveness: *The Red Badge of Courage* in Times of War." *Criticism* 9 (1967): 243-56.

Fryckstedt, Olov. "Cosmic Pessimism in Stephen Crane's *Red Badge of Courage*." *Studia Neophilologica* 32 (1961): 265-81.

Hart, John F. "*The Red Badge of Courage* as Myth and Symbol." *University of Kansas City Review* 19 (1953): 249-56.

Hungerford, Harold R. "'That Was Chancellorsville': The Factual Framework of *The Red Badge of Courage*." *American Literature* 34 (1963): 520-31.

Johanningsmeier, Charles. "The 1894 Syndicated Newspaper Appearances of *The Red Badge of Courage*." *American Literary Realism* 40 (2008): 226-47.

Lawson, Andrew. "The Red Badge of Class: Stephen Crane and the Industrial Army." *Literature and History* 14, No. 2 (2005): 53-68.

Mailloux, Stephen. "*The Red Badge of Courage* and Interpretive Conventions: Critical Response to a Text." *Studies in the Novel* 10 (1978): 48-63.

McDermott, John J. "Symbolism and Psychological Realism in *The Red Badge of Courage*." *Nineteenth Century Fiction* 23 (1968): 324-31.

Nagel, James. "Limitations of Perspective in the Fiction of Stephen Crane." *Stephen Crane Studies* 15 (2006): 9-12.

——. "Stephen Crane and the Narrative Methods of Impressionism." *Studies in the Novel* 10 (1978): 76-85.

Pease, Donald. "Fear, Rage, and the Mistrials of Representation in *The Red Badge of Courage*." In *American Realism: New Essays*, ed. Eric Sundquist, 155-75. Baltimore: Johns Hopkins UP, 1982.

Pizer, Donald. "*The Red Badge of Courage* Nobody Knows: A Brief Rejoinder." *Studies in the Novel* 11 (1979): 77-81.

——. "What Unit Did Henry Belong to at Chancellorsville, and Does It Matter?" *Stephen Crane Studies* 16 (2007): 2-13.

Pratt, Lyndon Upson. "A Possible Source of *The Red Badge of Courage*." *American Literature* 11 (1939): 1-10.

Rathbun, John W. "Structure and Meaning in *The Red Badge of Courage*." *Ball State University Forum* 10 (1969): 8-16.

Rechnitz, Robert M. "Depersonalization and the Dream in *The Red Badge of Courage*." *Studies in the Novel* 6 (1974): 76-87.

Reckson, Lindsay Vail. "A 'Reg'lar Jim Dandy': Archiving Ecstatic Performance in Stephen Crane." *Arizona Quarterly* 68 (2012): 55-86.

Reynolds, Kirk M. "*The Red Badge of Courage*: Private Henry's Mind as Sole Point of View." *South Atlantic Quarterly* 52 (1987): 59-69.

Sanner, Kristin N. "Searching for Identity in *The Red Badge of Courage*: Henry Fleming's Battle with Gender." *Stephen Crane Studies* 18 (2009): 2-16.

Schneider, Michael. "Monomyth Structure in *The Red Badge of Courage*." *American Literary Realism* 20 (1987): 45-55.

Shanahan, Daniel. "The Army Motif in *The Red Badge of Courage* as a Response to Industrial Capitalism." *Papers on Language and Literature* 32 (1996): 399-409.

Shaw, Mary Neff. "Henry Fleming's Heroics in *The Red Badge of Courage*: A Satiric Search for a 'Kinder, Gentler' Heroism." *Studies in the Novel* 22 (1990): 418-28.

Shulman, Robert. "*The Red Badge of Courage* and Social Values: Crane's Myth of His America." *Canadian Review of American Studies* 12 (1981): 1-19.

Solomon, Eric. "The Structure of *The Red Badge of Courage*." *Modern Fiction Studies* 5 (1959): 220-34.

Vanderbilt, Kermit, and Daniel Weiss. "From Rifleman to Flag-bearer: Henry Fleming's Separate Peace in *The Red Badge of Courage*." *Modern Fiction Studies* 11 (1966): 371-80.

Van Meter, Jan. "Sex and War in *The Red Badge of Courage*: Cultural Themes and Literary Criticism." *Genre* 7 (1974): 71-90.

Weiss, Daniel. "*The Red Badge of Courage*." *Psychoanalytic Review* 52 (1965): 176-96, 460-84.

Wood, Adam H. "'Crimson Blotches on the Pages of the Past': Histories of Violence in Stephen Crane's *The Red Badge of Courage*." *War, Literature, and the Arts* 21 (2009): 38-57.

Manuscripts

The major collection of Stephen Crane manuscripts is at the Clifton Waller Barrett Library at the University of Virginia. Other important holdings are at Syracuse University Library and the Columbia University Library.

from the publisher

A name never says it all, but the word "broadview" expresses a good deal of the philosophy behind our company. We are open to a broad range of academic approaches and political viewpoints. We pay attention to the broad impact book publishing and book printing has in the wider world; we began using recycled stock more than a decade ago, and for some years now we have used 100% recycled paper for most titles. As a Canadian-based company we naturally publish a number of titles with a Canadian emphasis, but our publishing program overall is internationally oriented and broad-ranging. Our individual titles often appeal to a broad readership too; many are of interest as much to general readers as to academics and students.

Founded in 1985, Broadview remains a fully independent company owned by its shareholders—not an imprint or subsidiary of a larger multinational.

If you would like to find out more about Broadview and about the books we publish, please visit us at **www.broadviewpress.com**. And if you'd like to place an order through the site, we'd like to show our appreciation by extending a special discount to you: by entering the code below you will receive a 20% discount on purchases made through the Broadview website.

Discount code: **broadview20%**

Thank you for choosing Broadview.

Please note: this offer applies only to sales of bound books within the United States or Canada.

The interior of this book is printed on 100% recycled paper.